Discovery at Dogwood Cottage

Beau Monde Secrets, Book 2

Anne Rollins

Dearest Reader;

Thank you for your support of a small press. At Dragonblade Publishing, we strive to bring you the highest quality Historical Romance from some of the best authors in the business. Without your support, there is no 'us', so we sincerely hope you adore these stories and find some new favorite authors along the way.

Happy Reading!

CEO, Dragonblade Publishing

Additional Dragonblade books by
Author Anne Rollins

Beau Monde Secrets Series
Secrets at Selwyn Castle (Book 1)
Discovery at Dogwood Cottage (Book 2)

Author's Note

The modern concept of neurodivergence did not exist in nineteenth-century England. In 1817, Arabella Canning would probably be labelled "shy" or be said to have a "nervous temperament," while George Kirkland might be called "careless," "impulsive," or "slovenly." But if they were alive today, Arabella would be considered autistic, and George would be diagnosed with ADHD.

In creating these characters, I drew from my own experience as an autistic woman with ADHD. But no two neurodivergent people are alike, and my experiences may not match the experiences of other people with the same diagnoses. Neither George nor Arabella should be taken as definitive representations of neurodivergence.

Chapter One

England, Friday June 6, 1817

"WELL, GENTLEMEN, I believe I shall leave you to your wine." Betsy Kirkland stood up from the table, looking relieved. The lines on her face had grown deeper over the course of the two-hour meal.

Probably exhausted, George Kirkland thought. "You ought to get a nice rest," he advised his aunt. "You must have worked very hard today." Uncle William employed a good cook, but Aunt Betsy served as the housekeeper at Kirkland House. Any entertainment her brother hosted involved a good deal of work on her part.

"Thank you for an excellent meal, Aunt Betsy," Vincent Kirkland chimed in. "And please thank the cook for us, as well."

A smile broke across Aunt Betsy's face, transforming wrinkles of exhaustion into lines of good humor. "I will pass on your praise," she promised.

Once the door closed behind her, all the guests turned their eyes towards Uncle William. A rather strange assortment of guests gathered around the table. Having been to dinner at Kirkland House many times, George knew how much this dinner differed from the norm. Normally there would have been a roughly equal number of men and women, Aunt Betsy had a reputation as a matchmaker. More than one happy marriage had been made at her dinner table. At George's last visit two years ago, in fact, his aunt had shown alarming signs of wanting to pair him off with a young heiress. That had scared him into avoiding further invitations to visit Kirkland House, right up until Uncle Willian had directly summoned him.

Tonight, there were no heiresses dining at Uncle William's heavily laden table. In fact, there were no women at all apart from Aunt Betsy, who played her usual role as gracious hostess. All of the guests were Kirkland men. Next to George sat his cousin Vincent. There was nothing odd about the two of *them* having been invited to dine. George and Vincent were the offspring of William's two older brothers, and Uncle William had always remained on good terms with those families.

No, the strange thing was that Augustus and Benedict Kirkland had also been invited to dinner tonight. Their father, Grandfather Kirkland's youngest son, had quarreled violently with the rest of the family decades ago. Like Uncle William, Uncle Ambrose had eschewed the genteel professions in order to pursue more lucrative work in trade. Unlike Uncle William, he had neither amassed an impressive fortune nor taken any effort to keep on good terms with the rest of the family. When Ambrose married the daughter of a linen draper and failed to inform his parents of the fact until after the wedding, Grandfather Kirkland had washed his hands of him. Ambrose died without ever having been reconciled with the family.

So far as George knew, Uncle William still did not care much for that side of the family, and he rarely invited those two nephews to his house. He did not look down on them for being engaged in trade, since he had made his fortune by investing in a cotton mill, but he always claimed that "the Manchester Kirklands" were ill-mannered.

So what were Benedict and Augustus doing here now? George pondered the question while the claret traveled around the table.

All the men took a glass of wine, except for Uncle William, who stuck to water.

"Can't have wine after dinner. Betsy's orders." The sour look on Uncle William's face showed how little he liked these orders. He took a sip of water, then cleared his throat.

"We may as well get down to business. I hope you realize that I've called you all here for a reason. I don't take pleasure in having a pack of young wolves eating at my expense." Uncle William's keen blue eyes glared out from underneath bushy white eyebrows. What he lacked in hair on the top of his head, he made up for with his eyebrows and side whiskers.

"Of course not," Vincent said soothingly. He caught George's eye and grinned. They both knew that Uncle William, cranky though he might be, genuinely enjoyed having his nieces and nephews about. When Vincent, George and their sisters were children, Uncle William had invited them to his summer house for long holidays, bestowing sweets and unearned guineas upon them at every encounter. As they grew up, the sweets and guineas were replaced by unsolicited advice and expensive birthday presents.

This year, Uncle William had sent George an ornate inkstand for his twenty-fifth birthday. George initially considered selling it, since it looked entirely out of place in his shabby, cluttered chambers, but he could not bring himself to do so. He had the superstitious feeling that its elegance might inspire him to even better writing.

"So why *did* you summon us, Uncle William?" George had wondered that ever since he got the unexpected invitation. He'd accepted, despite the expense of traveling from London to Bath, on the grounds that the food here would be far better than what he would eat at home. He also hoped a few days away from his familiar haunts might help rekindle his literary muse, who seemed to have gone silent lately. It had been weeks since he'd made any real progress on his latest manuscript.

Uncle William sat up straighter and put down his glass of

water. "I called you all here because I wanted to talk to you about Dogwood Cottage."

"What's Dogwood Cottage? You haven't any estate, Mr. Kirkland." Augustus blinked owlishly. "Do you?" He was already on his second glass of claret. Perhaps that was why he sounded so befuddled.

"Hmph!" Uncle William's scowl deepened. A wise man would have apologized, or at least backtracked. Augustus just stared insouciantly back.

George hurried to intervene before Uncle William had one of his famous explosions of temper. "Dogwood Cottage is Uncle William's holiday place up in Lancashire. It overlooks Pendle Water. It is a pleasant, cozy house. Lovely gardens, too."

When William's wife had been alive, she spent her summers there, escaping the smoke of Preston's mills. Most years, George and his sister had joined Aunt Helena for a month or more, playing in the garden or hunting for hidden treasure by day and trying to catch the resident ghost by night. They'd succeeded only in covering the kitchen floor with flour, to the great dismay of both Aunt Helena and the cook. In hindsight, it was rather surprising that they kept being invited back year after year, given how much trouble they caused.

Uncle William did not quite smile, but his scowl relaxed. "Yes, exactly," he agreed. "It's no mansion, but it's a fine building suitable for a gentleman of modest means. I'd be living there still if it weren't for my health. Since I cannot use it, I think it's time to pass Dogwood Cottage on to someone who *can*. A house ought to be lived in."

"Very proper," Vincent put in. "And very generous of you."

Augustus gulped down his wine so hastily that some of it spilled out of the corner of his mouth. To George's dismay, he wiped his face with his coat sleeve rather than his napkin. George turned his face away to hide his revulsion.

"Is there an estate to go with the house?" Augustus licked his lips to catch the last drop of wine, looking greedier than ever.

Uncle William shook his head. "It used to be a good-sized farm, but most of the fields were sold long ago. There's just an orchard, some gardens, and a stable left. Maybe room for a chicken coop or such, but no estate or farmland."

George nodded, though he thought Uncle William understated the extent of the property. He remembered not only chickens but also a duckpond and a small pasture with room for a milk cow. The orchard was extensive, too. The cherries had been fabulous, though he remembered the apples being sour. There was enough land for a gentleman to play farmer, if not enough to financially support him.

Uncle William noisily cleared his throat, then took another sip of water. "The house does require a gardener and maidservants and whatnot to keep it in order. I know none of you lads are precisely flush in the pocket, but you needn't worry. The house will come with money for its maintenance, settled on the new owner—*provided* my conditions are met."

Augustus put down his wine glass with unseemly haste. "Money?" His eyes widened. "How much money are we talking about?"

Once again, Vincent and George exchanged rueful glances. Vincent's wrinkled nose suggested that he shared George's disgust. None of the four cousins were particularly well-to-do, but that was no excuse for so openly displaying such avarice.

That said, George could not help wondering about the money, too. He could certainly use a steady income. Last year, he'd impulsively quit his job as a solicitor's clerk so he could devote more of his time to his literary career. He did not exactly regret the decision, but he had grown tired of cranking out essays on subjects that did not interest him just to keep himself fed. The income from twenty thousand pounds would free him up to focus on his preferred writing projects—the ones he kept secret.

"Bunch of vultures," Uncle William grumbled. "The money's more important to you than the house, I'd wager." He shook his head, looking dour. "Well, that's foolishness. A fine old house that's stood for centuries is of far greater value than a few thousand pounds in the Funds."

Vincent nodded and thoughtfully stroked his chin. George fought to hide a smile. Even Uncle William did not believe what he just said. Uncle William had been a shrewd businessman in his day and he knew the value of a pound more than anyone. Besides, he undoubtedly had more than a *few* thousand pounds in the Funds.

"But how much money?" Augustus asked. "Will it really be adequate for the upkeep of the house?"

Uncle William snorted and deepened his scowl. Then he reluctantly answered the question. "Since you have asked so bluntly, I may as well tell you that a settlement of twenty thousand pounds will accompany the house."

Augustus's eyes widened, but he did not otherwise betray his reaction to this news. The others did not remain so impassive. In his shock, Benedict dropped his napkin. Vincent pursed his lips thoughtfully. George had to close his jaw quickly, lest he be caught gaping. To someone like him, twenty thousand pounds was an entire fortune!

"So, you're trying to decide how to make out your will, is that it?" Vincent furrowed his brow, the corners of his mouth turning down slightly. "Surely there is no haste. You seem in good health."

Apart from his bad temper, George silently modified. Aunt Betsy's restrictions on her brother's eating and drinking had made his gout attacks much rarer, so he was in better health now than he had been when he moved to Bath. (Uncle William might insist that drinking the famous water from the Pump Room had vanquished his gout, but George privately gave all the credit to Aunt Betsy.)

"This isn't about my will," Uncle William said sharply. "That's none of your business. I shall leave the bulk of my fortune to whomever I please, and I can tell you right now that none of you lot ought to count on being my heir!"

"Of course not," Vincent said quickly. "We all know that your fortune is yours to do what you like with. But I thought you called us here to talk about who would inherit Dogwood Cottage?"

George didn't think his cousin deserved the scowl Uncle William directed at him. Vincent had asked a very reasonable question—one he'd been wondering about, too.

"As I was saying," Uncle William grumbled, "the cottage ought not be left empty. I don't intend to wait until my demise to see someone enjoy it. I plan to give it away now, while I'm still alive. The house needs a proper caretaker, anyway. Someone who will keep an eye on things. We don't want burglars breaking in again."

George lowered his wine glass so abruptly, some of his claret splashed out. He mopped it up hastily with his napkin. "Burglars have broken into the house? I hope they didn't take Aunt Helena's favorite tea set. You know, the blue willow one?" He had always liked that pattern.

"Didn't take anything as far I know," Uncle William explained, "but they certainly made a mess. Tore up half-a-dozen paving stones in the kitchen!"

"Ah! Looking for the hidden treasure!" Vincent suggested. "I don't suppose they found anything." He and George shared a grin, remembering the time they had taken a chisel to the bricks around the kitchen fireplace in an attempt to find the treasure that the house's original owner had supposedly hidden in the kitchen walls.

"There's nothing to find! Pack of nonsense!" Scowling, Uncle William reached for his glass. The face he made after tasting it suggested he wished it were something stronger than water. "The house itself is treasure enough. I don't know why anyone would damage the place on account of some superstition! The people who owned the cottage before me were respectable farmers, not pirates or highwaymen. They wouldn't even have had a treasure worth hiding!"

"But who will you give the house to, Uncle William?" Augustus asked.

George glanced nervously at Augustus and Benedict. Benedict stared at Uncle William, his mouth agape. Augustus leaned forward in his chair, patently eager to hear the answer to his question. George knew he was being profoundly unfair to the two brothers, but he could not stomach the idea of one of *them* living in Dogwood Cottage. Would they even appreciate the charm of the house or the beauty of its gardens?

George knew better than to consider himself a likely prospect, given how often Uncle William had labelled him "shiftless" or "irresponsible." But Vincent would be a far worthier heir than either of his other cousins.

"Well now, it's not entirely up to *me* who will win the cottage." Uncle William smiled slyly.

Win? That was a rather odd choice of words. George narrowed his eyes. "Is this some kind of contest, Uncle William? How fun that would be!" Or, rather, how strange. But Uncle William did sometimes take odd crotchets.

Uncle William leaned back in his chair and rested his hands on his comfortably round belly. All of his grumpiness disappeared, replaced by a mischievous twinkle in his eyes. "I suppose it is a contest, in a manner of speaking. One might even call it a race."

George waited for his uncle to explain himself, but Uncle William seemed determined to milk all the suspense possible out of the situation. He beamed at his four nephews, waiting for them to beg for more information. He was plainly enjoying himself.

Benedict finally asked the question they were all wondering. "What kind of race? A footrace? A horse race?"

Uncle William chuckled. "Not exactly. You see, the fact of the matter is, I plan to leave the cottage to whichever one of you boys is the first to marry."

The four cousins exchanged puzzled glances. Was Uncle William serious? George couldn't tell, and judging from the confusion on the other young men's faces, neither could they.

Vincent broke the shocked silence. "The first to *marry*? But Uncle . . . you can't encourage people to enter rashly into the state of matrimony. The choice of wife is one of the most important decisions in a man's life." He shook his head solemnly, looking every inch the righteous clergyman. "Giving the cottage to the first of us to marry—assuming none of us are already betrothed—"

Vincent paused to look around the room, but the other Kirland bachelors all shook their heads. George had absolutely no marital prospects at all, and it seemed that neither Augustus nor Benedict had a fiancée, either. Benedict's mouth still hung ajar. Augustus rested his chin on his hand, looking thoughtful.

Vincent had not finished delivering his sermon. "In short, Uncle William, I very much fear that this 'race' of yours will encourage imprudence, irreverence, and licentiousness." He crossed his arms in front of his chest and lifted his chin. His classical features made the pose look particularly noble. "I shall have nothing to do with this profoundly immoral contest."

Licentiousness? George raised his brows at that. Imprudent, yes—a man who rushed into marriage might very well come to regret it. But how could it be licentious for a man to marry?

Uncle William apparently shared his opinion. "You're a curate, not a monk," he reminded Vincent. "But if you're too high-minded to take part in the challenge, that will only narrow down the competition." He shifted his eyes back and forth between George, Benedict, and Augustus. It might have been George's imagination, but he thought Uncle William's eyes lingered on him longer than on his other two nephews.

George returned his uncle's keen gaze with a rueful smile and a shrug of his shoulders. "It's a pity I don't have a sweetheart. Dogwood Cottage is a charming house and it would be a lovely place to raise a family." He spoke mostly out of politeness, but it was true. With trees for climbing, a duckpond for swimming, and a river for fishing, the house would be perfect for children.

For the first time since dinner ended, Benedict spoke. "I don't mind getting married, but who am I supposed to marry?"

George quickly turned his snicker into a cough to hide his amusement. A twitch of Vincent's lips showed that the question amused even the upright young cleric.

Uncle William, lacking their tact, simply laughed outright. "That, my boys, is up to you to decide, not me. You shall have to find your own brides."

Vincent made a scoffing sound and shook his head. George caught his cousin's eye and shrugged his shoulders again. Then he lifted his wine glass and drained the last of his claret. It really was a pity that he had no special young lady in his life. He would hate to see a house where he'd spent so many pleasant hours given away to someone who would not appreciate it. For a prize like that, he would not mind the shackles of matrimony.

But in order to marry, a man needed a bride.

Chapter Two

"SEVEN, EIGHT, NINE, ten—ready or not, here I come!" Arabella Canning pulled her hands away from her eyes and looked about the room. It only took her a moment to find Charlie. He had hidden by the window, making an enormous lump in the curtain. Though most of his body was covered, the toe of one small shoe poked out.

But Arabella knew better than to let on that she knew where her godson had hidden himself. "Where's Charlie? I don't see him anywhere!" The shape behind the curtain giggled.

Arabella rose to her feet and tiptoed with exaggerated care across the floor to the sofa. "Is he under the sofa?" The sofa was so low to the ground that Charlie would have to be flattened like a pancake to fit beneath it, but she squatted down and peered beneath the furniture, as if it were a likely hiding place. "No Charlie! Where could he be?"

The giggling grew louder, and Charlie peeked out from behind the curtain. But Arabella pretended not to see him. Instead, she shaded her eyes with one hand and peered around the room. "He must be *very* good at hiding," she declared. "*Much* better than his godmother."

Two momentous things happened almost simultaneously. First, Charlie flung the curtain aside and crowed with delight. "I'm right here, Aunt Arabella! And I win *again*!"

Only a moment later, the butler opened the morning room door and announced, "Mr. Kirkland."

Arabella whirled around, her brows arched in surprise. Caroline had said nothing about her father coming to visit. In fact, Mr. Kirkland had been very ill just two weeks ago. When Arabella left for her visit, the curate was still handling all the services at St. Mark's. She could not imagine what exigency could have driven Mr. Kirkland to travel so far while in bad health.

But the man who walked in the door was not the aging vicar of St. Mark's. It was, instead, a much younger man of moderate height and unassuming appearance. Not the vicar, but the vicar's only son.

"Belle!" George Kirkland's broad grin transformed his appearance. There was nothing distinctive or memorable about his features in themselves, but his smile made him downright charming. Maybe that was the effect of his crooked left eyetooth, which somehow added to his appeal.

The sight of that familiar grin automatically put an answering smile on Arabella's face, too. She was used to that effect, but she did not expect the little flutter of happiness that knocked her heart out of rhythm for a few beats. It had been far too long since she'd seen her old friend.

"I hadn't realized you were visiting Caro, too. What a pleasant surprise!" George's face was a little paler than she remembered, and the distinctive splash of freckles across his nose and cheeks had faded. Apart from that, he looked much as he always did.

"Uncle George!" Charlie promptly abandoned Arabella to rush towards his uncle. George, wise to the ways of four-year-olds, caught Charlie and scooped him up before the child could barrel into him. Then he promptly turned the boy upside down and held him by his legs. This elicited both a fit of giggles and a shower of pebbles falling from Charlie's pockets.

Arabella cringed, thinking of the tidying the housemaid would have to do. That, she supposed, was why some parents preferred to confine their offspring to the nursery or schoolroom. Pebbles and sticks might belong in small boys' pockets, but not in formal sitting rooms.

"How's my favorite nephew?" George addressed the child as if there was nothing unusual about him hanging upside down.

"I'm your *only* nephew!" Charlie gleefully reminded him. "Swing me around, Uncle George!"

Arabella cringed and covered her mouth with her hand, horrified by the suggestion. The morning room at Newton Park was much smaller than the drawing room, and any attempt to swing a child around by his ankles was likely to end in breakage, injury, or both.

"Sorry, Charlie. I don't think your mother would like that." George sounded regretful, but when he caught Arabella's eye, he winked. Then, to her great relief, he turned his nephew upright and set him back on his feet, thereby averting a potential disaster.

"Pick me up again! Again, please!" Charlie lifted his arms up hopefully, but his uncle shook his head.

"I've been traveling for hours," he explained, "and I could really do with a cup of tea."

Arabella brightened. She could help with that! "I shall ring for it, since Caroline is resting."

"Resting? At this hour?" He glanced at the mantel clock and arched one eyebrow. It would be time to dress for dinner soon, since the Grays did not keep fashionable hours.

Arabella tightened her lips and tried to signal a warning with her eyes. Unfortunately, she did not have her mother's talent for conveying silent messages. Either George did not recognize her warning or he chose to ignore it.

"Don't tell me she's in the family way again," George began, "not after what happened last time—"

Arabella's meaningful glance turned into a fierce glare. She glanced pointedly down at Charlie, then caught his uncle's eye and shook her head. After the horrific miscarriage Caroline had suffered with her second pregnancy, the family did not want to openly discuss her delicate condition. They would wait until she quickened to share the news.

Caroline had told Arabella the news the moment she arrived, both because they were good friends and because her morning sickness and fatigue would have been difficult to conceal from a houseguest. But no one else outside of the household knew. Caroline and Leland had not even told Charlie yet, as they did not want to get his hopes up.

"I see." George's smile faded as he collapsed onto the sofa and stretched his legs out in front of him. "If you ask me, Leland ought to be happy with the child he has instead of risking my sister's life—"

No one asked you! Arabella did not say the words out loud, but George must have correctly interpreted her expression, as he let his voice trail off rather than finish the sentence.

"It is a rather personal decision, after all." Arabella struggled to keep her voice steady and calm instead of stammering. It felt awkward to have a conversation about childbearing with a young gentleman, even one she had known all her life. There was only one way Caroline could have fallen pregnant, and it involved a subject not fit for discussion in mixed company.

But George did not take the hint. "I suppose so, but Leland has a perfectly good heir already—"

As if he realized that he was under discussion, Charlie bounded across the room, climbed onto the sofa, and pounced on his uncle. "Uncle George, did you bring me a present? Last time you forgot!"

This time, when Arabella put a hand over her mouth, she did so to hide a smile. "It's not good manners to beg for a present the moment you see a relative," she reminded Charlie. He had said something very similar to her when she arrived last week, hadn't he? Fortunately, she had come bearing a children's paint box as a present to her godson.

"Isn't my presence gift enough?" George suggested. "I'll wager you didn't expect to see me today. Now, did you?" He arched his eyebrows theatrically.

"Nooo," Charlie admitted. "But I still want a present." His lower lip hung down in a pout. "But I'm a big boy and I won't cry even if you didn't bring me anything."

"Hmm, a big boy, are you? I suppose big boys are old enough to buy their own present, if they have the money. If only I had a shilling to give you!" George dug about in his coat pocket. "Alas, my pockets are to let!"

"That's all right, Uncle George," Charlie began to say, but his uncle interrupted him.

"Wait! What's this?" With a flourish, he pulled a shiny silver coin out of his pocket. "For my favorite and as-yet-only nephew."

Charlie shrieked with delight and grabbed the coin. "Hurray! I'm so glad you came to visit, Uncle George!"

George grinned and ruffled his nephew's hair. "So am I," he agreed. "Now, why don't you go put that in a safe place?" They both watched Charlie scamper off, probably bound for the nursery. Then George turned back towards Arabella and sighed. "Being an uncle is exhausting."

"You have made Charlie very happy." Arabella sank down into an armchair. George was right: playing with small children was quite tiring. She had not realized until she sat down just how weary she had grown after an afternoon of playing hide-and-seek.

She wished she could lounge comfortably, leaning against the back of the chair, as George did. But that would be unladylike. According to her old governess, a lady always sat up straight. Arabella had left the school room years ago, but she still heard Miss Trafford's voice in the back of her head, correcting her posture any time she slumped.

"Well, at least some good will have come from my visit." Unwonted bitterness laced George's usually cheerful voice.

Arabella studied him for a moment. In addition to looking paler than usual, he had shadows under his eyes, ink stains on his fingers, and scruffs on his boots. "Is something wrong?"

"Not really." He shifted position and rolled his neck from side to side. "Too many hours in a crowded stagecoach today, that's all."

"Did you leave London this morning?" she guessed.

He shook his head. "I didn't come from London. I was in Bath, visiting my uncle. A matter of family business." The frown on his face made her wonder what sort of business had taken him all the way to Bath. "I just stopped here as it was on the way home, and . . . I thought I could use Caro's advice."

Parker entered the room, preventing George from saying more. "Very sorry about the delay, Miss Canning, Mr. Kirkland. Is there something I can do for you?"

"We should like tea, if you please, Parker." Arabella spoke so softly that Parker had to put a hand to his ear to catch her words. She flushed, embarrassed by this betrayal of her shyness. She had been at Newton Park for a week, but she still hesitated to give orders to the servants. They were not, after all, *her* servants. She was only a guest here.

Arabella wondered if she had been remiss in not waking Caroline from her nap the moment George arrived. Was it even proper for an unmarried lady to be alone for so long with a young man? To be sure, he was related to her hostess, so perhaps they were not violating any rules by meeting together. She hoped so. Even country society could be very unforgiving of young ladies who broke the rules of propriety.

Now that she felt all the awkwardness of sitting alone with a young man, Arabella could think of nothing to say to break the silence. When Charlie had been here, he made a natural focal point for their attention. He was George's nephew and Arabella's godson, and they both loved him. With him gone, Arabella was left to sit in increasingly painful silence, wondering why it was taking so long for the butler to bring their tea.

"Is something wrong, Belle?" George spoke quietly, but in the hushed room, his soft baritone might as well have been a gunshot.

Arabella blinked. "What do you mean?"

"I know you are a quiet girl," he explained, "but you were not used to be so shy with *me*."

She dropped her gaze, feeling embarrassed. Implicit in his gentle voice, she heard all the old complaints. She spoke too softly. She said too little. She should be more gregarious. She should smile more. She should not hide in corners "like a frightened mouse"—to use her father's phrasing.

Arabella clasped her hands together anxiously. "I am sorry." George was right, of course. There had been a time when she could have talked to him as easily as with her own brother. But though they had grown up as neighbors, she rarely saw George now. It would have been an exaggeration to say that he had become a stranger to her, but the easy camaraderie of childhood had faded over the years.

"You owe me no apologies," he said at once. "I only wondered if something had upset you. Had you rather I left you alone?"

"Oh no!" She could not eject him from his own sister's morning room. She had no authority to do so, even if she'd wanted to. And she did not want to. She merely wished she could think of something to say to him. Something polite and unexceptionable. Something more meaningful than a comment about the weather.

But all she could think to say was, "I hope you had fair weather for your travels."

"So-so." He pulled a face. "We had a touch of rain, but not enough to make the roads impassable. At least we've not seen as much rain as we had last summer!"

"Yes, it is nice to see the sun now and again! I am sure the farmers are happy, too." Last year's unseasonably cool weather had ruined crops in some parts of England, leaving people hungry. Everyone was glad that 1817 seemed to be a warmer, dryer year, but Arabella could think of nothing new to say about it.

George cast his eyes around the room, looking as if he had no clue what to talk about either. Then his face brightened. "I say, do you still collect those little china figurines?"

Now, there was a topic she could discuss! Her nervous fingers relaxed. "Not as often as I used to." She wrinkled her nose and grinned at George, remembering the days when she spent her pocket money on any pretty bit of porcelain that crossed her path. Her younger brother, who typically spent his allowance on candy or adventure novels, did not understand her taste at all.

"Really?" George looked surprised. "You used to love those things!"

"My mother kept complaining that my room had been overtaken by porcelain shepherdesses, and I finally admitted she was right. I decided to focus only on the fairy tale figurines, since those are my favorite. I gave away some of the others. Now I only buy figurines in keeping with that theme."

Parting with some of her collection had been hard, but Arabella could not deny that her curio cabinet looked much better now that it was no longer cluttered with too many figurines of different styles and themes. She loved porcelain and bone china. They were beautiful, and thinning out her collection allowed the beauty of each individual piece to shine more brightly.

Someday, maybe, if she had a home of her own, she could set up displays of china throughout the house, rather than confining her entire collection to a single cabinet. But who knew if that would ever happen? Arabella had already spent too much time watching as friends and cousins her own age married and set up their nurseries.

"Do you still have the 'Little Bo Peep' figurine, then? The one you bought in Hillchester?" George pulled his pocket watch out of his pocket and played with it idly.

The corners of her mouth lifted up in pleasure at that memory. "I'm surprised you remember that! That must have been a dozen years ago." Little Bo Peep had been her very first porcelain figure. She stumbled across it in a curiosity shop, and being short of pocket money that day, had borrowed from both Caroline and George in order to buy it.

"How could I forget how anxious you were all the way home? You wouldn't let anyone else hold your parcel, for fear they'd drop it." He looked as if he had more to say, but he never got around to saying it, as his pocket watch slipped from his grip and landed on the floor. He scrambled to pick it up and return it to the safety of his pocket.

Before Arabella could say anything more about her porcelain collection, Parker returned with the tea tray. Having to make the tea and then serve it kept her too busy for conversation. Then there was a blessed pause in which she nibbled a slice of lemon seed cake while listening to George's complaints about the fare at the inn he'd stopped at on the journey down to Bath.

Before they finished with the tea, Caroline came down from her chambers, her face wreathed in smiles. "George! You ARE here! I thought Charlie might have been bamming me when he said you had come for a visit."

"No jest!" George rose to his feet and embraced his younger sister. The two siblings were nearly of a height, though Caroline took her darker coloring from their mother. "I am here, alive and well, albeit rather the worse for travel. But what's this I hear about you being indisposed, Caro?"

That, Arabella decided, was her cue to exit so the siblings could discuss family matters. "If you will excuse me, I believe I shall go rest before dinner." She rose to her feet and turned towards the door.

"You need not make yourself scarce on my account, Belle," George assured her. "You are quite one of the family here."

Arabella shook her head. "I am sure you would like to have a word with your sister alone. And I do need rest." That much was true, if by "rest" she meant "a chance to be alone." After such an eventful afternoon, she needed a moment to herself.

George's arrival threw off the easy comfort she'd settled into. If there were rules for how to treat an old friend when you and he were both houseguests at his sister's estate, she did not know those rules. That made every interaction fraught with the risk of a social *faux pas.*

George furrowed his brow thoughtfully. "I *would* like to have a chat with Caro. I had an odd visit with my Uncle William in Bath, but I needn't bore you with the details, Belle."

Arabella suppressed a sigh of relief at this clear dismissal. "I shall see you at dinner, then."

She tried to gracefully glide across the floor and out the door with all the poise that proper ladies like her mother (or Caroline, for that matter) displayed. Instead, she stumbled over nothing and let the door shut behind her with a bang. A passing housemaid stared at her in surprise.

Arabella flushed with embarrassment. *Three and twenty, and still stumbling about like a gawky schoolgirl,* she chided herself. Not that it mattered, since there was no one here to impress. Her friends did not care whether she was graceful. Even so, it would be a relief to spend a quiet hour alone in her room with a pencil, her sketchbook, and no one around to observe her blunders.

Chapter Three

THOUGH GEORGE HAD already drunk two cups of tea, he didn't mind sitting down and having another with his sister. With Arabella's hint in mind, he scrutinized Caro's appearance carefully, but could not see any signs of illness. On the contrary, she appeared to be in blooming health. He relaxed and let his body slump against the back of his well-padded armchair. He hadn't exaggerated about being exhausted by his travels.

"When's the blessed event to be, then?" he asked.

Caro's lively face froze, and she hunched her shoulders up. *Blast!* He ought not have worded it that way.

"Ah, sorry," he corrected. "I mean. . ." He glanced away as he mentally scrambled for the right words.

The lines of worry smoothed out of Caro's face. "It's all right," she said quietly. "You needn't apologize. I hope to be confined in January. But it could be later." Her lips tightened. "Or never. It is early, you know." Her blue-gray eyes—usually sparkling with humor—looked dispassionate and remote.

"I know." George stared into his teacup, wishing he had some comfort to offer his sister. When they were children, he'd often had to reassure her after a tumble or bump that left her in tears. His parents taught him that such was his responsibility as an older brother, and he had taken his duty seriously. But this wound was neither a scratch that could be easily plastered over, nor a pain that could be soothed with a sweet biscuit or a cup of chocolate. He felt thoroughly useless in the face of Caro's continued grief.

"I am doing quite well at the moment." The cheer in Caro's voice sounded forced, but the way her face softened as she met his gaze looked genuine enough. "But enough of that! What are you doing here? We did not look to see you again until September."

George grinned. "Am I that predictable? I must take advantage of your hospitality too often." His parents owned no estate of their own, and thus had no hunting rights, but his brother-in-law maintained excellent coveys. George generally visited Newton Park during the first sunny weeks in September or October, joining in Leland's shooting parties. But he had no such excuse this time. "No, the fact of the matter is that I had to pay a visit to Uncle William, and I thought I'd stop here on my way home."

"Well, it is good to see you." Caro handed him a fresh cup of tea. "I hope Uncle William is not doing poorly?"

George snorted. "Only if by 'poorly' you mean 'taken a new crotchet.' He invited all the young men of the family to dine with him, he wants to bribe one of us to get married posthaste."

Caro had taken a sip of her tea and the expressions that flitted across her face as she tried to avoid choking or spitting it out were priceless. "And why would he do that?"

He shrugged and took another biscuit. "I believe he is worried about the Kirkland line ending." Now that he was away from Uncle William, he could afford to be amused about it. The Kirkland family had always been respectable, but they were hardly an illustrious or noble house. They were only the cadet branch of the Kirklands of Cheshire. What did it matter if their family line died out? There would still be plenty of more distant Kirkland relatives! "But you'll never believe what he promised to whichever of us marries first."

"Half his fortune?" Caro suggested. "Or, even better, an estate with an immense pinery?"

"Why a pinery?" George's eyes widened. Where had that come from?

"I've been craving pineapple," Caro admitted, "but no one I know keeps a pinery. At least, no one who lives nearby. My friend Eustacia sent me one, but by the time it got here, it was half rotted away." She scrunched her face up at the memory.

"Ah. Well, I am afraid I cannot help you with that." George took another bite of his biscuit, still amused. Then, rudely talking around the food in his mouth, he added: "But I suppose whoever wins Dogwood Cottage will have all the cherries and apples a man could want." Assuming any man wanted sour, wormy apples.

"Uncle William's giving Dogwood Cottage away?" A line formed between Caro's dark brows. "But he loves that house! I can't believe he'd part with it."

"He says his health is too bad to use it himself, so he wants to see a young family growing there. Or something like that. He's hoping treasure seekers will stop breaking in if the cottage is occupied."

Had the cottage had always attracted so much attention from treasure seekers? Certainly, George and Caroline had grown up hearing stories of treasure hidden in the kitchen, but he didn't remember anyone breaking into the house to find it. Maybe Uncle William was right about the house needing occupants to protect it.

George chased down the biscuit with the last of his tea. He pondered the teapot for a moment, but decided he'd had enough. The tea had already worked its usual magic, clearing the cobwebs out of his mind.

"You don't think he could be growing senile, do you?" Caro looked genuinely worried.

George shook his head and put his empty plate back on the tea table. Uncle William had not seemed the least bit senile to him. On the contrary, he'd looked and acted like a man who was vastly entertained by the game he wanted his young relatives to play.

"I believe he is just having fun in his own eccentric way," he told Caro. "And I suppose it is harmless fun, more or less. But I regret that one of Ambrose's boys will win the wager, or whatever you call it." His stomach soured as he imagined Augustus or Benedict lounging by the fire in the front parlor, snacking on a plate of home-grown fruit.

"And why should they win?" Caro raised her brows, a question in her eyes.

"Vincent refuses to play," George explained. "He says it's immoral to encourage people to marry rashly. And of course, I'm out of the running. It's not as if I know anyone who would marry me in a hurry." There might have been women willing to marry George for the sake of twenty thousand pounds and a comfortable home, but he did not want to marry a stranger. He might spend the rest of his life in a miserable marriage! "Maybe Vincent has the right of it after all," he conceded.

Caro frowned. "It is a pity though. I always liked Dogwood Cottage. We made many happy memories there, didn't we?" The line between her brows deepened. "Do you really not know anyone you could marry, George? Surely there must be some agreeable young lady of your acquaintance you could ask!"

George chuckled bitterly. "A man who earns his living by his pen does not have many chances to circulate in good society," he reminded her. "It's not as if I spend my afternoons squiring young ladies about Hyde Park, like a young nobleman." Getting solicitations from streetwalkers was more like it, but he could not say *that* to his sister! A few of his friends did have sisters of marrying age, but none that he knew well, or particularly wanted to know better.

"No, I'll have to leave it to Augustus and Benedict. But you're right that it is a pity. I would have liked . . ." His voice trailed off. What point was there in talking about what he would have liked to do? He would do better to try to forget about Uncle William's ridiculous contest. "So, anyway, how is Leland?"

To his surprise, Caro did not answer. She stared down at the floor, tapping her foot restlessly. The expression on her face made him uneasy. She looked deep in thought, and he suspected he was not going to like whatever she was thinking.

"Caro?" he prompted.

"George." She lifted her chin and fixed him with a steely gaze. "Why don't you ask Belle?"

He stared blankly at his sister. "Ask Belle what? How Leland is doing? But wouldn't you know that better than she would, what with him being your husband?"

"No," she said impatiently, "ask Belle to *marry* you."

It was a good thing George no longer had a plate in hand, because he probably would have dropped it in shock. As it was, the only thing he could drop was his jaw. Which he did, while he continued to stare at his sister.

"Oh, stop gaping at me," she grumbled. "It's the perfect solution. You are both of marrying age. She has no prospects at the moment, so it might be a good thing for her. And you can hardly object to her, since you have been friends all your life."

George finally found his tongue again. "Belle was your friend, not mine!" Even as he said it, though, he knew it wasn't true. Not so very many years ago, he had played cricket with Caro, Arabella, and Joshua Canning on the village green at Norton Combe. They had all been friends together, though Joshua was nearly four years his junior.

"Don't be silly." Caro dismissed his objection with a wave of her hand. "You like her well enough, don't you?"

Well enough for what? Well enough to have a comfortable chat with her, yes. Well enough to trade family gossip or listen sympathetically to her current troubles and cares. Well enough to call her by an old nickname, even. But well enough to *marry*? Well enough to…? His ears burned with embarrassment as he considered some of the duties marriage entailed.

"Caro, you ought to stop matchmaking," he said sharply. "You will spoil our old friendship. Belle does not fancy me, and I do not fancy her."

"But you don't have an aversion to her, do you?" Caro pressed.

"An aversion?" His whole face felt aflame with embarrassment. "This entire conversation is improper. I am certain that Belle would not want to marry me." He hated the priggish tone in his voice, but he needed to nip this in the bud.

"How can you be sure of that if you haven't asked her?" Caro retorted. "I believe she is fond of you. The two of you might suit very well." A smile crossed her face. "And it would be pleasant to have such a dear friend as my sister-in-law."

"Caroline, that is enough!" He glared at her, hoping his use of her full name would silence this nonsense.

It worked. She bit her lip and averted her gaze. "It was only a suggestion!" She used much the same tone she might have used to soothe Charlie in the middle of a tantrum. "You may take it or leave it."

"I will most certainly *not* take it!" George glanced at the mantel clock. "But I *will* take my leave, if you do not mind. I'd better dress for dinner. Assuming, of course, that I am invited to dinner." He grinned at his sister. He was, after all, an uninvited guest.

She dismissed his concern with a wave of her hand. "Of course you are invited, foolish boy!"

Foolish boy, indeed! He was a whole year older than her! He refrained from pointing that out, since he did not want to start another quarrel with his sister. Instead, he dressed for dinner, resolving to put his conversation with Caro out of his head. What nonsense it was to think he should marry Arabella Canning just because they'd been friends in childhood!

Unfortunately, it wasn't easy to set aside Caro's proposed solution. He could not get the suggestion out of his head at dinner, because Belle sat beside him at the round dining table. Every time their eyes met, he wondered what Belle would say if she knew about Caro's matchmaking attempt. He knew she would turn him down if he proposed, but would she be offended? Hurt? Amused?

Fortunately, Belle seemed to have gotten over her shyness of the afternoon. She talked readily about books and essays they'd both read. He discovered, rather to his surprise, that she had read his reviews of *Guy Mannering* and *Emma*, though she disagreed with his assessment of the latter novel. They spent much of the evening arguing about which heroine was worse: Emma Woodhouse or Fanny Price. George found Fanny insipid and too moralistic, while Belle thought Emma Woodhouse's wealth and status sheltered her so much, she didn't understand the world around her.

"Perhaps I am partial to Fanny Price because I fade into the background just as she does." Belle stared down at her half-empty plate, looking bashful again.

"No, you do not! You have much more personality than she does!" George insisted. Then he caught his sister watching him from across the room, a knowing smirk on her face. He glanced away, embarrassed. He lowered his voice, not wanting his sister to overhear. "She is defined only by her judgment of other people's amusements."

"And by her concern about her family's well-being." Belle lifted her eyes from the plate and looked George full in the face as she argued. "As well as her love for Edmund."

"I consider her love of Edmund to be one of Fanny's flaws," George explained, "because it prevented her from pursuing a more advantageous match. If she had accepted Henry Crawford, he might have become a reformed character. He was an intelligent man who only needed a little moral guidance."

Belle vigorously shook her head. "It ought not be a woman's job to reform a man. Or to guide him. Men are responsible for their own lives, just as women are. And why should Fanny give up the man of her heart merely because she might have helped improve Henry Crawford?"

"I suppose women want every marriage to be a love match."

George glanced out of the corner of his eye at his sister, hoping she overheard *this* part of the conversation. Maybe Caro would realize there wasn't the least chance of Belle accepting George. Clearly, Belle was a romantic at heart. She would not want to marry for the sake of a fortune.

George meant to put the whole question of matrimony aside after dinner, but that was easier said than done. Tonight, everything reminded him of marriage. When he picked up a copy of yesterday's paper, the wedding announcements promptly caught his eye. Even after he set the paper aside, he had the example of his sister and her husband sitting cozily on a sofa together, talking privately.

When Caro laughed softly at something Leland said, George had to glance away. He did not want to observe his sister's domestic happiness, given how unlikely it was that he'd experience the same happiness any time soon. It could take years for a literary man to establish his career well enough to support a wife and family. Normally, that did not bother him, but Uncle William's ridiculous absurd offer made him think wistfully about what might have been.

"You look unhappy, Mr. Kirkland," Belle observed. "I hope you have not met with some disappointment." She sat in the armchair by the fire, a tea table separating her chair and his.

George's frown deepened. "You did not used to call me Mr. Kirkland. When we were children, you called me 'George.'"

"We are not children anymore." She studied the piece of needlework in her hand. She was embroidering the borders of what looked like a blanket for Caro and Leland's hoped-for baby.

"I suppose it would be most proper for us to address each other formally." George ought to call her "Miss Canning" rather than "Belle" now that she was a grown woman. How strange that sounded! But it ought not bother him that she called him "Mr. Kirkland." Why *did* it bother him? The corners of his mouth turned down in disgruntlement, and he shifted uneasily on his chair.

"Have I said something to distress you?" Belle's eyes looked soft with concern as she put down her embroidery.

They were, George grudgingly admitted, very lovely eyes. Belle's eyes were gentian blue—not quite purple, but the closest to it that he'd ever seen. He had never met anyone else with eyes that color. Framed with thick lashes of dark gold, they beautified Belle's whole face, making her otherwise unremarkable features sweetly appealing.

Sweetly appealing? He caught himself in horror. He would never have thought such a thing if Caro had not made that ridiculous suggestion about marrying Arabella Canning! Before, those eyes and lashes were just part of Belle's face. Never before did they have the least effect on George's breathing, heart rate, or blood circulation.

Not that he had ever been completely oblivious to his friend's appearance, mind you. He generally noticed when a new dress or hat Belle wore was particularly becoming. And if anyone asked him, he would have said that Arabella Canning was a rather pretty girl.

But though he might have described her as an attractive girl, he had never paused to consider more specifically whether *he* was attracted to her. He did not want to consider the question now. He would rather keep Belle neatly labelled as a neighbor, a childhood playmate, and his sister's good friend. He did not want to think of her as a girl who might be courted, kissed, or bedded. It was one thing to fantasize about bedding a flirtatious barmaid; it was another thing entirely to imagine such things about one's own friend.

"Is something wrong?" Belle asked innocently.

George's face flushed, not so much in shame as in horror at what he had just pictured. Or maybe the horrifying thing was how much he liked what he saw in his mind.

"I am not feeling my best, but I'm probably just tired. It has been rather a long day, you know." He set down his book and got to his feet. "If you will be so kind as to excuse me." He could not bear Belle's look of wide-eyed innocence. How shocked she would be if she had any clue what he'd just contemplated doing with her!

Caro sent a questioning look across the room. "I believe I ought to turn in early," he announced. "Good night, then." Perhaps he would be able to curb his unruly imagination once he was away from Belle.

That night, he dreamed he was a child again, playing in Dogwood Cottage. He and his sister were searching the house from the root cellar to the attic, looking for the treasure that locals claimed had been hidden in the cottage centuries ago. In real life, the treasure was nothing but a legend. Though George and Caro had looked for it many times, they succeeded only in getting dust and cobwebs all over themselves, to the dismay of their nurse.

In his dream, however, the siblings found the treasure chest: not buried beneath the kitchen floor or behind a wooden panel but simply tucked under a bed. But when George opened up the box, it contained only a plain gold wedding ring. He picked up the ring and promptly woke with a jolt. He sat up in bed, his heart pounding as if he'd just had a nightmare.

But the solution that came to him was not terrifying. It was *brilliant.* There might be a way he could win Uncle William's contest without the risk of spending his entire life in an unhappy marriage. What could it hurt to try?

Chapter Four

SUNDAY MORNING DAWNED cool and cloudy, and Arabella feared they were in for another rainy day. But while the family attended religious services, the sun peeped out from behind the clouds. By afternoon, most of the cloud cover was gone, leaving behind a sunny June day.

Finally, a break from the overcast skies! This was the kind of weather Arabella had hoped to see during her visit. She stood in the breakfast room, gazing out the window at the formal gardens in front of the house. The brightly colored flowers finally showed to advantage.

"Caro," she said, "I believe I will go for a walk on the grounds. Will you come with me?" Such a fine day should not be spent indoors.

Caroline covered a yawn with one hand, then shook her head. "I am afraid I already need a nap." She flicked her eyes towards her brother, currently hidden behind the day-old newspaper he was reading. "George?"

"Hmm?" He peered over the top of the newspaper. "Did you need me for something?"

"Arabella spoke of taking a walk while the sun's still out. Why don't you join her? I am sure you rarely get proper exercise in town. It would do you good to explore the grounds."

George grinned. "I think Belle is quite capable of taking a

walk on the grounds without an attendant. Newton Park is perfectly safe! But if you wish me to accompany her, I will." He hesitated for a moment and looked towards Arabella. "That is, if Miss Canning does not object?"

"Of course, you are welcome to join me." She did not understand why he looked so uncertain about it. True, she generally preferred to walk with no other company than her own thoughts, but she rarely had a chance to speak to George now that he lived in London. She was willing to sacrifice the pleasure of a solitary walk for the sake of his company, given how rarely she experienced the latter. "Just let me grab my things."

Though Midsummer was only a week and a half away, Arabella did not trust the weather. She donned a spencer as well as her hat, in case there was a breeze. For once, though, the day felt as temperate as it looked. Yesterday's rain left the ground as soggy as a marsh, but as compensation, the rain also left behind a fresh, clean sent.

She need not have worried about her solitude being disturbed, because George was uncharacteristically quiet today. He idly kicked the gravel ahead of him as he walked, and swung at flowers with his walking stick, beheading some perfectly innocent lupines. In another man, she might have interpreted this as a sign of irritation or uneasiness, but George had always liked to be in motion.

They took the longest graveled walk around the park. This one led to a ha-ha, beyond which lay a pasture full of hungry dairy cows. They paused to watch the grazing cattle. At least, Arabella watched the cattle. George occupied himself by tossing bits of gravel over the sunken fence.

"Did Caro tell you about this ridiculous plan my Uncle William hatched?"

She nearly jumped at the unexpected interruption to the silence. "No." The word fell into the quiet landscape like a stone tossed into a well. "Which uncle is Uncle William?" As she recalled, the Kirkland family had a superfluity of uncles, and she had no idea which one he meant. "Is he the one who lives in Preston?"

"Yes. Or rather, he used to live there. He lives in Bath now. Says the waters do him good." George smiled wryly. "And maybe they do, for all I know. Problem is, his summer house in Lancashire—Dogwood Cottage—is empty now. And he thinks it ought to be inhabited."

"Ah. He is looking for tenants?" She spoke doubtfully, she could not imagine why the emptiness of someone else's cottage was so important that George would interrupt the comfortable silence of their walk to tell her about it.

George snorted. "That would be the reasonable thing to do, wouldn't it? Ninety-nine landowners out of a hundred would either lease the place or sell it outright if they did not intend to use it themselves. But no. Uncle William likes to think more creatively. He wants to give it to one of his nephews so it stays in the family."

"How generous!" she said politely. Then it occurred to her that there might be a personal application to this seemingly random observation. She turned away from the pasture and tried to read George's expression. But he was a closed book to her. "Do you mean to say that he is giving it to you?" That would certainly be a great change for George after his years in London.

He shrugged and looked away from her. "Not exactly. Maybe. It depends."

She waited for him to elaborate, but he merely continued to swing his walking stick back and forth, though there were no flowers at hand for him to behead. "On what does it depend?" she asked at last. It was none of her business, but he'd piqued her curiosity.

George sighed. "His plan is very silly, in my opinion," he said apologetically. "But he means to give to whichever one of his nephews is first to marry. We are all bachelors, you see. . . and. . . I suppose he wants the cottage to go to a family rather than to a single man." He looked down at the toes of his boots. To her amazement, his ears had turned red.

"Goodness, that *is* unusual." She frowned as she searched his face, trying to find the source of his discomfort. Finally, it dawned on her. "I see. You are engaged to marry someone now, are you?"

She wouldn't have predicted that George would feel bashful about announcing such good news, but maybe the engagement was very recent. Or perhaps there was something objectionable about his chosen bride. Surely, he would not propose to someone simply in order to obtain the cottage, would he? He had too much good sense for that!

His blushed deepened. "No, I am not betrothed to anyone. Not yet." He lifted his head to stare into the pasture, though she doubted he actually saw the placid Jersey cattle. "But I was thinking. . ." His voice trailed off, and he looked askance at her. "I was wondering. . . if you would be so gracious as to help me?"

"Help you do what?" Her frown deepened. If he wanted help proposing to the object of his affection, wouldn't his brother-in-law have better advice? Or his father? It made no sense for him to ask Arabella's advice. *She* had certainly never proposed to anyone! Nor did she have any positive proposal experiences to share.

The only proposal Arabella had ever received came from the drunken son of a neighboring squire. He cornered her in the hallway during a country ball and inarticulately declared his love for her. He'd vomited at her feet immediately after she rejected him, making the occasion even more memorable than it would otherwise have been, but she could hardly recommend that course of action to her friend.

George turned to face her fully, giving her an extremely shaky smile. "The fact of the matter is, I'm hoping you can help me gain the inheritance." He squared his shoulders and lifted his chin, as if he expected opposition. "I mean, by marrying me."

Arabella's eyes widened, and she sucked in her breath. But she could say nothing. All her life, she had struggled to find the right words in unexpected social situations. When other people talked about a surprise having rendered them "speechless," they seemed to mean only that it took them a moment to find their words. But Arabella had found that in pivotal conversations she was sometimes left speechless, producing only at best a monosyllabic answer.

This was such a moment. The urgency with which George swished his walking stick back and forth hinted at his anxiety. His warm brown eyes remained locked with hers, and she could not look away. But she also could not, for the life of her, find any words with which to answer him. If her mind were a library full of reference books, every book she opened contained only blank pages, with nothing to help her respond.

"Perhaps I should clarify," George said hesitantly, "that I do not mean that we would *really* be married in any but a legal sense. I am not asking you to keep house with me, at least not for any length of time. I have no intention of permanently altering your life! I wouldn't ask that of you!"

Arabella's jaw dropped. She closed it with a snap, and furrowed her brow as she tried to make sense of his words. How could marrying someone *not* alter her life? "I'm afraid. . . I don't . . . understand." The words came out broken and halting, but at least they came to her lips. She still weltered in a sea of confusion, but she was no longer struck dumb.

"Let me explain." George stopped swishing his cane back and forth, resting some of his weight on it instead. "All I'm asking you to do is go through the marriage ceremony with me, then allow me to present you to Uncle William as my wife. That should be enough to do the trick." He smiled hopefully.

"I don't understand!" Arabella repeated the words more forcefully this time. She thought she was *starting* to understand, but if so, she didn't like what she was hearing. "If I went through the marriage ceremony with you, we would be really and truly married, whether we kept house together or not! There would be no way to back out of it afterward."

At least, not so far as she knew. Perhaps saying the marriages vows without intention of keeping them was grounds for annulment—but even if that were true, such legal recourse would be an expensive, uncertain prospect. Even for the very wealthy, divorce and remarriage was only permitted in cases of infidelity.

"But we would not *behave* as husband and wife to each other," George explained. "At most, we would act the role for only a short time. After Uncle William made the property over to me, you could go back and live with your parents just as you did before, with no harm done. Or, if you preferred, I could give you an allowance, and you could take up residence on your own. So you see," George concluded, "I am not really asking much. Just a couple of weeks of your time, and—"

"Not asking much? You are asking for *my whole life!"* Arabella did not yell, a proper lady never raises her voice. But she hissed the words with such intensity that George took a nervous step backwards.

Most unfortunately, that step backwards sent him tumbling over the edge of the ha-ha. Arabella lunged to grab his hand, but she didn't move quickly enough. Fortunately, he struck his head against the earth on the opposite side of the ditch rather than against the stone wall. Unfortunately, the ditch was full of mud. All the cows in the pasture lifted their heads and stared at him with concern.

George gingerly hauled himself to his feet, looked down at his muddied clothing, and sighed. "I don't suppose you could give me a hand?"

He had dropped his walking stick and lost his hat. He wore his hair cropped too short for it be terribly mussed, but he looked considerably worse for the wear. In Arabella's opinion, he deserved it. Nevertheless, she knelt on the wet grass and reached a hand down to help George scramble up over the wall and back onto the garden path.

"Thanks." Once he regained his feet, he put his battered hat back on his head and wiped ineffectually at his clothing. It took him only a moment to give up and accept that it would take a thorough scrubbing to remove the coating of mud.

By this time, Arabella's temper had cooled. "Are you quite all right?"

"Only my pride is hurt." He looked up from his muddied topcoat and caught her gaze. "I am very sorry. I did not mean to upset you so. But Belle, why on earth did you get so angry?"

All her anger bubbled back up to the surface. "I would rather you not call me 'Belle,'" she snapped. "Because if you can make a proposal like that to me, you are not the friend I thought you were."

His jaw dropped open, but at least this time he didn't stumble over anything. Instead, he merely rubbed his forehead, thereby smearing dirt across it. "Perhaps my fall addled my brain. Can you explain yourself?"

Arabella wasn't sure that she *could* explain. She couldn't remember the last time she'd felt such wounded fury. Words did not seem adequate for the emotions shaking her body. She did not know whether to growl, to scream, or to cry. She closed her eyes and shook her head. Then she counted to ten backwards, as her governess had long ago taught her to do when she was overset. It helped a little.

"Maybe it would be best if we simply pretended this conversation never happened," she said at last. "I will forgive you, and you can find someone else to whom you may propose. And"— she pulled the words out grudgingly, feeling she owed it to him— "we will still be friends. But I don't want to hear any more about this ridiculous plan. Let us walk about to the house and speak no more of this. Can we agree on that?"

George lifted his hat and scratched his head. "But Belle—Miss Canning, I mean—I really do want to understand. I did not mean to offend you. I thought . . ." He grimaced. "Maybe I didn't really think it through. But I wish you would explain yourself more fully."

Arabella rubbed her hands along her skirt, wishing that she too had a cane to swish, a bracelet to fiddle with, or a quizzing glass to raise. She needed something with which to occupy her hands.

"I will see if I can put my thoughts in order as we walk back to the house." She pulled her mouth into a wistful smile. "I cannot promise to be any clearer. I have never been good at explaining myself, you know." Sometimes her strongest sentiments were the most difficult to articulate.

"As you like." George offered her his arm, and she accepted, though it would likely mean getting mud on her spencer.

For several minutes they walked in silence. This time, the blooming flowers were safe from carnage, as George had ceased swinging his walking stick. The nervous energy he'd displayed before his proposal was gone, replaced by a look of quiet dejection. Maybe Arabella wasn't the only one who had been hurt by their conversation.

When they reached a covered bench, she paused. She really had much rather never speak of the subject again. But if she *had* to explain herself, she would prefer to do it here, away from other ears.

"I would like to catch my breath. And then I will try to elucidate the matter." If she could. She had her doubts.

Chapter Five

B Y NOW, GEORGE suspected Belle might be right that they would do better to simply forget about his ill-planned proposition. To say he felt like a fool would be a massive understatement. He felt like the King of Fools. Worse, he vaguely felt that he'd behaved badly, though he could not have said how. Clearly this had all been a colossal mistake. Why had he listened to his sister in the first place? Caro must not understand Belle as well as she thought she did.

But much as he would have liked to pass the blame for his blunder onto Caro, George knew he was the one who'd decided to act on his sister's suggestion. She might have given him bad advice, but he was responsible for acting on it.

"Listen, Belle, I am very sorry to have. . ." He waved his hand in an ineffectual gesture. "To have mucked things up so much. I do hope you will forgive me." Even if he didn't entirely understand why he needed to be forgiven.

"Yes, of course." Arabella rested her hands in her lap and stared off into the distance. This bench provided a good view of the roses in the center of the garden, but she did not seem to be looking at them. "I am sure you did not mean to. . . to. . ." She closed her lips tightly and turned her face away.

He wanted to ask "to what?" but he remembered that Belle could not be rushed. If she had trouble articulating something, pushing her would only make the problem worse. So he waited patiently, pretending that he found the garden fascinating. In reality, he might just as well have been staring at a patch of weeds for all the attention he paid to it.

But the moment Belle said his name, he flicked his eyes back to her. She looked much calmer now, and she met his gaze unflinchingly. When she spoke, her voice was low but firm.

"George, back there, you said that you were 'not asking much.' I don't understand how you could think that! You're asking me to make a commitment that would bind me for the rest of my life."

He opened his mouth to protest, to remind her that he didn't expect her to be his wife in any but a legal sense. She forestalled him with a raised hand.

"Let me speak, please." She waited until he nodded his acquiescence before continuing. "Don't you see what I would have to give up in order to help you win this inheritance? If I marry you, I can never marry someone else. Even if I found the love of my life, I would have to watch him marry someone else, since I would be legally bound to *you*. I could never have a real husband, or children of my own. I might play the role of Mrs. Kirkland for only a few weeks, but all my own dreams would be gone forever. How could you ask me to do that?"

To his horror, her voice broke, and tears glistened in her eyes. George's heart sank. Feeling like he'd been the greatest ass imaginable, he hung his head in shame. "Belle, I'm so sorry. I never knew you wanted those things." The excuse sounded flimsy even to his ears.

"You never knew I wanted those things? But why *wouldn't* I want them?" She did not raise her voice, but she spoke so fiercely that he cringed. "Why wouldn't I want everything other girls want? Other women my age have homes of their own, husbands in their beds, and babies in the cradle. Is it so surprising that I might want all that too?"

George's eyes widened. It was not like Belle to speak so plainly. When they were children, she had let the others decide what games they would play, or where they might ramble on their walks. She usually insisted that it was all the same to her. If she had desires, she hid them well. Perhaps that was why he'd expected her to agree to his plan.

He fumbled over his words, attempting to explain himself. "It's just that, well, you came out of the schoolroom nearly five years ago, and in all that time, you never made a match. You are three-and-twenty and still unmarried, so I thought. . ." *I thought you were on the shelf*, he finished silently. He squeezed his eyes shut, knowing his words would only give her more pain.

"So you assumed I would never marry, is that it?" Belle's voice was hoarse with unshed tears. "I am no longer in my first bloom, I should jump for joy at any proposal that comes my way, even if it's for a fake marriage?"

George flinched at the bitterness in her voice, but he could not deny a word of what she said. It was true. He had assumed she must not be interested in matrimony, why else would she still be unmarried? Belle was the daughter of a baronet, she had a comfortable dowry, and she was pleasing to the eye. If she wanted to marry, surely she would have done so by now.

"Were there never any suitors, then?" That baffled him. Belle had spent at least two Seasons in London. The Cannings regularly attended local balls and assemblies and traveled to more distant house parties. Belle must have had many opportunities to meet young gentleman far more eligible than George.

She shook her head and blinked her eyes rapidly, setting her lovely golden eyelashes fluttering. "There *were* suitors," she admitted, "but none of them seemed to understand me at all. They were interested in the girl they thought I should be, not the one I actually was. No one has ever wanted me for who I actually am."

Then, to his horror, the tears standing in her eyes spilled down her face in a slow, sad trickle.

Hellfire and damnation! George dug around in his waistcoat pocket for a handkerchief, but when he pulled it out, he discovered it was filthy. He'd soiled it trying to clean mud off his coat. And he had no other handkerchief. For a brief and frantic second, he considered unwinding his cravat and offering that to Belle. But he didn't think starting to undress in front of a proper young lady would make this situation any less awkward.

Instead, he wiped Belle's tears away with his thumb: first her left eye, then her right. She closed her eyes. When he finished, she leaned her cheek against his hand.

"I'm sorry," he said, though he knew that couldn't even begin to make up for the pain she'd just displayed. "I didn't know. Of course, you deserve everything other women want! I—" He froze before he could complete the sentence, shocked at what he had been about to say. *I could give you those things, Belle. If you married me.*

George closed his mouth and tightened his lips, frightened by his own impulsivity. He didn't really mean that! Did he? He swallowed uneasily, then gently drew back the hand cradling Belle's face. Touching her seemed like a bad idea, the feel of her soft, warm cheek against his hand made him want to trespass further. A comforting touch might easily lead to an affectionate caress, and who knew where *that* would end? He'd best keep his hands to himself, lest he do something he would later regret.

Belle blinked again, and her eyes widened. She shifted back further on the bench, as if she had only now realized how close together they sat. She wiped her eyes and audibly sniffed. Then she forced her lips into a stiff smile.

"You needn't worry about me, George. I am all right now. I suppose we had better go back inside." She stood up, but he caught her hand before she could walk away. She looked back over her shoulder, surprised.

"Wait, please," he begged, though he had no idea what he was going to say next. He always produced his best writing under the pressure of a looming due date, and he hoped the very different social pressure of this situation might inspire his words now.

Belle sat back down and wrinkled her brow in confusion. "Really, George, there is nothing more you need to say."

He shook his head. "Yes, there is. You see, I was wrong and you were right." In George's experience, it was easier to reconcile after a quarrel if one began with those words. Most people liked being told that they were in the right.

Belle's eyes widened, but she did not interrupt him, for which he was grateful. It gave him the confidence to keep talking. "You were right to say that marriage is permanent. Of course it is. I should have realized how steep the cost would be for you. . . and for what reward? The marriage would only benefit me!" The more he said, the worse he felt. How could he have been so selfish?

"It is all right. I forgive you." She patted his hand, then left her gloved hand resting over his. "We need talk no more of this. I am sorry I cannot help you win the cottage, though. It must matter a good deal to you."

"Yes. I mean, no. I mean, it does matter, but not as much as you. As your friendship does, I mean." Every word he uttered made the situation seem more ludicrous.

"We are still friends." She squeezed his hand reassuringly, but the deepening line between her eyebrows hinted at her concern. "I think you are fretting yourself unnecessarily over this. Would it not be best if we went back into the house?" She looked down at his soiled clothes and wrinkled her nose. "You might wish to change out of that clothing."

George sighed. "Yes, you are right. We ought to go back inside and pretend none of this ever happened." For one dizzying moment, he had toyed with a different possibility, wondering what would happen if he proposed to Belle in earnest. But after the fiasco of his proposal, he thought it best to say nothing more. There were some decisions that ought never be made on an impulse.

He trudged back to the house alongside Belle, trying to talk himself into a happier state of mind. If her rejection disappointed him a little, that was undoubtedly because he'd lost his chance to win Dogwood Cottage. Ah, well. *C'est la vie*, no? It wasn't as if he *needed* a cottage in Lancashire. In fact, he probably wouldn't like living so far away from London's publishing world.

No, his only regret was that Augustus or Benedict wouldn't fully appreciate Dogwood Cottage. But the cottage was only stone and mortar. A house didn't care whether it was loved or merely used. And those apples really *were* inedible.

Chapter Six

THE MOST AWKWARD thing about George's farcical proposal was that he intended to linger at Newton Park for a few days before returning to London. Selfishly, Arabella hoped he might change his mind and go home early. He seemed determined to return to their original footing, but his continued presence could not be anything but an irritation now.

Every time she saw George, she remembered him saying "I never knew you wanted those things." Every time, those words stung all over again.

To her, George's words implied that other women were allowed to have dreams and desires, but not her. As if she were so different from everyone else that she could not expect to participate in the usual rituals of a woman's life: courtship, marriage, childrearing, grandparenthood. She resented the implication all the more because it came from a friend. She'd thought George both understood and respected her despite her eccentricities. It hurt to find out otherwise.

For the next few days, Arabella avoided George as much as possible. Fortunately, he seemed to want to avoid her, too. He probably felt every bit as embarrassed about the whole incident as she did. Maybe he realized how fortunate it was that she had not agreed to the charade. After all, if they exchanged vows before the altar, he would be trapped as well, never able to marry and have a family, either. But it was rather like George not to think very far ahead when making decisions.

George's planned departure date finally came around, but so did another heavy rainstorm. Leland took one look at the flooded carriageway in front of the manor, laughed, and told George to stay a few days more. Caroline smiled and pointed out that Charlie would be happy to have his uncle visit for a little bit longer. Indeed, Charlie capered with joy at the news.

But Arabella quietly despaired. She had looked forward to George's departure, as it would free her of the new awkwardness between them. She was relieved when Leland and George retreated to the billiard room for some manly bonding, or whatever it was that drew men to such sports.

Since the rain kept her indoors, Arabella brought her sketchbook downstairs, intending to use Charlie as a subject for her drawing. She planned to draw a crayon portrait of him to give to Caroline as thanks for hosting her. So far, though, she had not been satisfied with any of her pencil sketches of him.

Getting Charlie to sit for a portrait proved more difficult than Arabella anticipated. She handed him an illustrated book of Mother Goose rhymes, hoping it would keep him occupied while she sketched him. But Charlie could not sit still. First, he pushed a toy wagon around the morning room, periodically trumpeting in imitation of the mail coach. Then he ran around in circles. Finally, he persuaded Caroline to take him up to the attic to look for a hoop, so he could roll it up and down the hallway.

"Sorry," Caroline said, shrugging her shoulders. "It can be hard to get a four-year-old to hold still. You'll see for yourself someday." She chuckled softly as she followed her son out of the room.

Arabella sighed as she set aside her sketchbook. Would she find out someday, though? At her most despondent, she feared George might be right. Maybe she *was* already on the shelf. Maybe she really was so different from other people that she had no right to expect an establishment, a husband, and a family of her own.

As she'd told George, there had been suitors in the past. A well-born young lady with a good dowry was not likely to be completely overlooked when she entered the marriage market. There had been men Belle admired, too. She liked a set of broad shoulders and a handsome face as much as anyone. More than once, she had been certain that the object of her affection had shown some sign of partiality for her. Always, she'd been disappointed, the supposed partiality having existed only in her own mind. She lacked the ability to discern whether the men who danced with her or took her down to dinner meant anything but courtesy by their attentions.

On the other side of the ledger, there'd been times when Arabella unwittingly encouraged a suitor when she only meant to be polite. Apparently, some men took a cheerful smile and a kind word as signs of favor. Even worse, they sometimes grew angry when they learned they were wrong.

The worst case, of course, had been poor John Thurston. He proposed to her after fortifying himself with entirely too much alcohol. When he finally got it through his inebriated head that Arabella was refusing his offer of marriage, he became physically ill. After that humiliation, he grew vengeful. He went about telling everyone in Hillchester that Arabella Canning was a shocking coquette, a girl who toyed with men's feelings.

John's mother had never forgiven Arabella, not even after he married a perfectly acceptable young lady he met in Bath. Since the Thurstons lived within easy visiting distance of Oliphant Hall, this made life rather awkward for Arabella's parents. After that incident, she spent months afraid to even smile at an eligible gentleman, lest he draw the wrong conclusion.

But if she ignored all the attractive young men, she could not be surprised that they ignored her in return. She saw no way to change that pattern. Her opportunities for making a respectable match were limited, too. At three and twenty, she had only a few years left before being considered a confirmed spinster.

Even so, that was no reason to enter into a sham marriage. She shook her head as she remembered George's ridiculous suggestion. How could he have thought she would agree to something so foolish? What could she gain from such an arrangement?

"Miss Canning?" The footman interrupted her dismal meditations. "This letter arrived for you this morning. It ought to have been given to you at breakfast, but it was mislaid. I am very sorry."

"Oh, thank you!" Arabella's spirits lifted. She saw at a glance that it was a letter from home, addressed in Mama's tidy handwriting. She broke the seal and opened it, eager to read all the family gossip. This was precisely what she needed to interrupt her gloomy reflections on matrimony.

At first, the letter answered all her expectations. Mama began by describing the well-being of everyone in the family. Joshua was home for the Long Vacation, and Mama thought he looked "peaked." She wanted to make him drink bone broth every day, for strength, but Papa thought all he needed was more exercise.

Arabella grinned, thinking Papa was likely right. There was probably nothing wrong with her brother that a few country walks or horseback rides could not cure. She thought wistfully of her own saddle horse, Sparta, who undoubtedly needed exercise, too. Maybe she could ask Joshua to take him out sometimes.

Then she came to a paragraph that gave her pause.

Your father and I have been discussing our plans for next year, my dear, and we think the time has come to launch Lavinia into Society. We are agreed that she is ready to attend this year's Hunt ball. Her manners are everything we could wish for, and both her dancing master and music master are pleased with her progress. She does not have your skill with a pencil, but of course that does not signify. We have some hopes that she will make a good match here in the neighborhood, but if not, your father is determined that she will have a season in London next spring, despite the expense.

You would be welcome to join us in London if you wish, but I know you do not care for the social engagements of the Season. We would not wish to leave you home by yourself, but your cousin Dinah wonders if you might care to visit her instead. Her children are rather a handful, you know, and you could be of great service to her. It will be months before you need to decide, but you might do well to begin thinking on it now.

Arabella stared at the paper, reading that paragraph over and over again. Up until now, Mama and Papa had insisted that Lavinia stay in the schoolroom, despite being nearly eighteen. Though they had never said it outright, it had always been assumed that Lavinia would come out once her older sister married. But now they were bringing Lavinia to London, and sending Arabella off to Cornwall—which, at the moment, seemed like the ends of the earth.

I don't like London, Arabella reminded herself. *I don't like the Season. And I do like Dinah and her children.* But she discovered that she also did not like being set aside. Left behind. On the shelf.

"I say, Caro, have you seen—oh!" George stood in the doorway, looking puzzled. "I thought Caroline and Charlie were in here."

Arabella folded the letter neatly shut and tucked it inside her sketchbook. "They went upstairs to look for a toy." She forced a smile. "I believe Charlie is tired of having to play indoors, and your sister is trying to find ways to distract him."

"I'm tired of having to stay indoors, too!" George stood in front of the window, peering out into the rain. "Rain doesn't look like it's planning to stop anytime soon, does it?" He frowned, then shrugged. "Well, we're comfortable enough here. But I don't suppose you've seen the book I'm supposed to be reviewing, have you? It's a book of poems by some lady who fancies herself as good a poet as Mrs. Barbauld."

"The one with the red cover, you mean?" She remembered seeing him with it last night. When George nodded, Arabella cast a cursory glance about the room, though she struggled to focus on her surroundings.

She looked back at George and shook her head. "I'm afraid I haven't seen it. Perhaps the maid moved it while tidying." The other day, that had happened to the novel Arabella was reading, too. She'd looked about the house forever before she thought to check the bookshelves in the morning room.

Still, she scanned the room once more in case the book was hiding in plain sight. When her eyes landed on the sketchbook containing her mother's letter, her face fell.

"Belle? Is something wrong?"

Arabella lifted her chin to look him in the eyes. "Oh, I had a letter from home that made me a little melancholy." When he furrowed his brow in concern, she hastened to clarify. "Nothing is wrong at home, mind you; it merely reminded me that time passes. Lavinia will be making her come out this year. Next spring, she'll have her first Season in London." Her lower lip began to tremble, and she lowered her gaze to the floor so George couldn't see her eyes tearing up.

George must not have been fooled by her smile, because he pulled a chair closer to hers and sat down next to her. "Is that really all? Because that sounds like a good thing to me. You and Lavinia will have so much fun in London. Since I live in London, I'll be able to call on you when you are not gallivanting about!"

That was the final straw. Tears prickled at the corners of her eyes, and she blinked quickly in an attempt to hold them back.

"Belle?" George took her hand in his, stroking his thumb back and forth soothingly. "Are you upset about having to spend the Season in London again? I know you do not care for Town, but—"

"I am not to go to London," she blurted out, as the tears finally escaped her eyes. She reached up to scrub her face, wishing she had a handkerchief in hand. George reached into his waistcoat pocket and handed her a white cotton handkerchief that had been worn into softness. Arabella wanted to thank him, but she could not speak.

"Why are you not to go to London, then?" George asked.

"Did you *want* to go?"

Ah, that was the irony, wasn't it? Under other circumstances, she would have very much preferred not to suffer through another miserable Season.

"No," she said thickly. To her embarrassment, her nose was running. She wiped her face, hoping George didn't notice. She must look a mess. "But I didn't want to be left behind." It might have been a mistake to state the situation so baldly, because her eyes teared up again.

"Why would they leave you behind?" There was an uncharacteristic edge to George's voice. "Don't you deserve a chance in London every bit as much as Lavinia?"

"I already had my turn," she said in between sniffles. "I had two seasons in London and one in Bath, and I didn't take in either place. I suppose they thought I might as well be useful. I'm to be sent off to help tend my cousin's children."

"As if you were already an unwanted spinster who could be passed around from relative to relative as needed? What rubbish!" George's tone contained equal parts incredulity and indignation on her behalf. Arabella found the combination oddly soothing.

She sniffed as hard as she could, wanting to be able to speak clearly. "It is as you said the other day, though. I am already past my prime. If I were going to make a match, I ought to have made one by now."

"Nonsense." The incredulity had vanished, leaving only anger in George's voice. "I was a fool to imply any such thing, and your parents are fools if they believe it. I have half a mind to write to them so I can tell them so!"

That elicited a shaky laugh from Arabella. "It is very kind of you to offer, but I assure you, it is not necessary. I do not like London, and I had rather not stay up all night at balls and crushes and routs. I am only a little melancholy because. . . because. . ."

"Because your parents don't want to bring you with them? I ought to have words with them." George scowled impressively, though she could not imagine what he thought he could do to help her. It was not as if he could defeat her father in personal combat. Papa was taller and broader than George, and he kept quite active for a man of his age.

All this time, George kept holding her hand. Now she gently squeezed his fingers and drew her hand away so that she could give him a grateful pat on his cheek. "It is very sweet of you to take up my cause, but there is nothing you can do about it, George."

He drew a deep breath and squared his shoulders. Arabella frowned, she recognized the determined look in his eyes. This was the way George looked before he made a bad decision. That glint had shown in his eye the day he convinced Joshua and Arabella that there were too many piglets at the Canning home farm and Sir Michael wouldn't mind if his children and their friends took a few of them to market, sold them, and put the money in the Poor Box. Somehow, he'd made this all sound like a very good idea—a noble and charitable deed.

"There *is* something I can do about it," he argued.

Arabella buried her face in her hands. She could not guess what George was about to say, but she knew it would be terrible. So many of his plans ended badly! Papa had been furious about the stolen piglets, and for *weeks* afterward, the vicar preached sermons about the evils of theft and the need for children to obey their parents.

After that incident, there had even been talk of sending Joshua and Arabella to boarding school, to get them away from the pernicious influence of the Kirkland children. If Mrs. Kirkland and Lady Canning had not both possessed a talent for smoothing things over, the friendship between the two households might have ended then and there.

She sighed and lifted her head once again, thinking she had better confront his folly straight away. "What is it you think you can do to help, George?"

"I can marry you, that's what!" he announced. "And then they'll see how wrong they were to think you were past prayers."

Chapter Seven

GEORGE DID NOT understand why Arabella looked so unenthusiastic about this plan. He'd expected her to immediately see the advantages such a union offered both of them. She was usually quick to catch hold of a new idea. But she did not react as he'd anticipated.

After she shut her gaping mouth, she shook her head. "George, we've already been over this, haven't we? I have no desire to enter into a sham marriage. I am rather surprised that you brought it up again." For once, those gentian eyes looked hard rather than soft as she glared at him from beneath lowered brows.

His shoulders stiffened, and he swallowed nervously. This was not an auspicious beginning. But she was not rejecting him. She merely misunderstood him. Best to start by clearing that up.

George leaned forward, trying to hold her gaze. "Belle, you misunderstand me. I am not suggesting a sham marriage again. This time, I am suggesting a *real* marriage."

Her eyes widened, and she cringed away from him. He shifted back in his own chair, fearing that he might be crowding her. Belle never did like being pressed too close to other people. When they had been children visiting a crowded town square on market day, or gathered to watch some sporting contest, the others often had to shield Belle from accidental bumps or jostles.

"George, you have windmills in your head! You and I do not"—her cheeks turned pink as she stumbled over her words—"we do not love each other as a husband and wife should. Which is not to say I don't care about you, but caring for a friend is not the same as loving one's husband."

"So what?" George dismissed that argument with a shrug. "People get married for terrible reasons every day, don't they? Plenty of people marry someone they can't stand just for the sake of a dowry or an income. At least you and I like each other! And we know each other quite well. In some ways marrying an old friend would be better than marrying anyone else, because one knows what to expect from them."

She looked unconvinced, so George tried his most winning smile, hoping to expel that doubtful line from between her brows. "For example, I would know better than to expect you to host large parties."

Not that Dogwood Cottage had room for large parties. The dining room and parlor had been built for family use rather than for entertaining. For that matter, George himself had never cared for events that crammed too many people into too small a space, making too much noise. What mattered was the principle at stake.

"And you would know better than to interrupt me while I'm working." At least, he hoped she would. As a boy, he'd been famous for snapping at people who disturbed him. But a childhood spent growling like a bear who'd been poked with a stick did not stop Caro from bothering him with questions while he was trying to work on an already-overdue book review.

Even worse was when Caro kept chatting with George while he worked on his newest secret project. Thanks to his father's critical literary opinions, George had to keep some of his work *sub rosa*, at least for now. After only a few days at Newton Park, he'd already grown tired of trying to cover up his work anytime someone passed him by. That always resulted in smeared ink, sometimes forcing him to start the page all over again. At least

Leland knew better than to interrupt a man who was only trying to do his job!

George thought he'd made some excellent points, but the frown remained firmly fixed on Belle's face. "I am sorry that I cannot help you win that cottage you want, but it really is rather selfish of you to ask such a thing of me. I have my own life to live."

His whole body drooped in despair. So that was it, then. Perhaps this idea had been as mistaken as his original plan for a sham marriage. He swallowed uneasily, hoping that would soothe the ache in his chest. Dogwood Cottage was only a house, after all. He ought not be so disappointed by Belle's response. He could have no reason to feel hurt. She had not really injured him. If anything, *he* was the one in the wrong.

Meanwhile, Belle turned her face away from George and picked up the leather-bound sketch book on the tea table. When she opened it up, a folded paper fell out. For some reason, the sight arrested her. Her eyes widened again, and her soft, plump lips tightened into a hard line.

Wanting to at least be helpful, George stooped down and picked up the letter. He pasted a smile on his face as he handed it back. "I suppose it was foolish of me to think I could give you what you wanted," he confessed.

She stared at him blankly. "Give me what I wanted? How would—"

"You know," he interrupted. "The things you said you wanted." Her words in the garden sprang easily to his lips, as if he had memorized them. "A home of your own, a husband in your bed, a baby in the cradle. I could give you those things, Belle. But of course, you wouldn't want them from *me*." His throat tightened alarmingly, but he forced the words out. "I hope you find someone more to your liking."

Geroge got to his feet, thinking it best to end this conversation. He might have no reason to feel injured, but rejection always stung, and he didn't trust his ability to control his voice or facial expressions.

Before he could walk away, Arabella caught hold of his hand. "Oh, *George*. You foolish boy. I have hurt you, haven't I?"

He drew a deep breath, intending to tell her that she was talking nonsense. Of course he wasn't hurt—not seriously, anyway. But before he could assure her of his uninjured state, she rose from her chair. Then, to his intense embarrassment, she stepped forward and folded him into an embrace, as if he were a child in need of comfort.

"It was sweet of you to offer for me, but you know it would never work. When you think it over, you'll realize how much better it would be if you married someone you fancied." She stood on tiptoe to press a kiss against his cheek in much the same way Caro might kiss Charlie after he'd banged his head or scraped his knee.

Maybe to Arabella, kissing George felt like kissing her brother. But it did not feel that way to him. Even the casual brush of her lips left a point of heat on his face. He suddenly felt very aware of every place Arabella's body met his: her arms around his back, her face brushing against his, her bosom pressed against his chest. This close, he even caught a whiff of the rosewater with which she washed her face.

He wanted her to stay there forever. He wanted to pull her closer to him. And he wanted to press his mouth against hers in an extremely unfraternal way. Was she really oblivious to all of that? How could she not feel it too?

"Belle, do you have any idea how much I desire you right now?" The unsteadiness of his voice surprised even him. He gently freed himself from her embrace and stepped back.

"How much you *what*?"

This close, he could see the flutter of Belle's eyelashes as she blinked. Her lips parted slightly with surprise. He stared at her sweet, soft mouth, nearly overcome by the outrageous desire to show her what he meant.

"How much I desire you," he repeated. Irritation colored his voice. Or was it frustration? "I could kiss you right now! And I don't mean a brotherly peck on the cheek. I suppose to you I am merely an old friend from your childhood, but. . ." He paused to draw a deep breath. "Truth be told, I think I rather fancy you."

He wouldn't have thought it possible for her eyes to widen any further, but they did. He was a little surprised himself. He had not intended to say that. Only a few days ago, he'd told Caro that he did not fancy Belle. But he was fond of her, and he desired her, and what was fancy but a combination of attraction and affection? If the word fit, why not use it?

"Oh." She gulped audibly.

He had messed things up again, hadn't he? George closed his eyes in despair, steeling himself for another apology. A tiny part of his brain whispered that he should pack his bags and catch the next stagecoach back to London. If it was too late to leave today, maybe he should retreat to an inn to make things less awkward. It would be easy enough to pretend that he only wanted to be on hand to catch the earliest coach.

"*George*. Look at me!"

He instantly obeyed, opening his eyes in time to see Belle step closer to him. She tilted her chin at a determined angle. Some strong emotion glinted in her eyes, but he didn't recognize it. Thus, he was entirely unprepared when she stood on her tiptoes and pressed her lips against his.

It was, to be honest, a terrible kiss. Clearly, Belle had no idea what she was doing. She kissed much the way she spoke in unfamiliar company: shyly, uncertainly, with occasional pauses as if to make sure of her footing. But George did not let that deter him. He took her face in his hands and kissed her back, catching and teasing her lower lip. He moved his mouth slowly, giving her ample time to figure out how this worked. Though he would have liked to taste her more thoroughly, he kept his tongue in his own mouth, not wanting to startle her.

As far as physical sensation went, this kiss would not have made it into George's top ten. But in terms of emotional depth, kissing Belle felt worlds apart from most of his previous experiences with the fairer sex. The only time George had felt anything like this combination of hesitancy and hope during a kiss was when he kissed Priscilla Brooke for the first time. That brief entanglement had ended badly for him. He could only hope that history would not repeat itself with Belle.

With what little of his attention he could spare, George frantically wondered what Belle meant by this. Was her kiss a sign that she accepted his proposal, or something else? But what else *could* it mean? Maybe she wanted to say "yes," and could not find the words. Maybe—his thoughts skittered to a halt when he felt her teeth gently nibble his lower lip. Whatever Belle meant by kissing him, her technique was certainly improving. She had real potential, by Jove!

Belle ended the kiss by lowering her head and burying her face against George's shoulder. He wrapped his arms around her as it seemed the natural thing to do. When he brushed his lips against her golden hair, he again caught a whiff of rosewater. She clung to him tightly, and he thought that might be a good sign. Unless, of course, she was currently in a state of shock and needed to lean on him for support. He couldn't rule out that possibility.

"Well?" he prompted. He couldn't remember which of them had spoken last, but he wanted to hear her explanation before he said anything he would regret. Or rather, any *more* things he'd regret. He had already said too many regrettable things over the past few days.

Belle muttered something that he couldn't hear, since her face was still muffled against his shoulder.

"I didn't quite catch that," he admitted.

She lifted her head and stepped back from him. This meant he could see her face, which he supposed was an advantage, but his arms felt empty without her.

"I said, that didn't work the way I intended." Her eyes shone brightly and her cheeks were flushed.

George cocked his head to one side as he tried to make sense of that. "What did you intend, then?"

She hesitated, fidgeting with the little gold cross that hung on a chain around her neck. "I intended to prove you wrong. I mean, I intended to demonstrate that there was nothing between us but friendship; that we did not desire each other as. . . well, as man and wife. But it didn't work out quite the way I expected." Her already-blushing cheeks turned two shades pinker.

"Ah." George had no idea what he should say. *I was right and you were wrong* did not seem an appropriate response, under the circumstances. *I want to stop talking and go back to kissing you, we could get even better with practice* would have been honest, but not necessarily helpful. And it was probably not yet time to say *Why don't I pay a call on the bishop to see about getting a license?* After all, Belle had not accepted his proposal.

Seconds ticked by as he waited patiently. Belle stared at the floor for a long time. When she finally lifted her head, the corners of her mouth were still turned down, and a puzzled line had formed between her brows.

"Very well," she said slowly. "I suppose we might do worse than to get married."

It might not have been the most unflattering acceptance in the history of matrimony, but it probably ranked in the top ten percent. Even so, George's heart bounded with joy. He caught Arabella's hand, lifted it to his lips, and kissed it.

"I will make certain that you never regret this." In his initial burst of happiness, it seemed like a perfectly reasonable promise to make.

Chapter Eight

A N HOUR LATER, Arabella found herself staring at a piece of stationery, her mind just as empty as the sheet of expensive notepaper. Normally, she found it easier to express herself in writing than in speech. She was rarely at a loss for words when she had a pen in her hand, and more than one of her friends had remarked that Arabella was far more talkative in a letter than in face-to-face conversation.

But the news she needed to share now felt too momentous to be contained in words, even written ones. She had to explain to her parents why she was getting married almost immediately—as soon as she and George could return to Derbyshire and obtain a license. Somehow, she would have to make her hasty marriage to George seem advantageous rather than baffling.

She very much feared that she had set herself an impossible task. The moment she thought of a possible opening into the subject, she also thought of a handful of objections. She had not even written the date or the salutation, because she was afraid that unless she worked out the wording for the whole letter in advance, she might have to scrap the paper and start again. She knew that was silly; almost superstitious, in fact. But she could not bring herself to put pen to paper.

"Aren't you finished yet?" George, who had dashed off a note to his own parents in just a few minutes, peered over her shoulder.

"I don't know what to say," Arabella whispered.

She felt ashamed of having been caught loitering over the task, but she also felt hyperaware of George's proximity. Maybe it was her imagination, but she thought she could feel the warmth of his body as he leaned over her shoulder, though he was not touching her.

A week ago, she would have thought nothing of it. She might not even have noticed how close he stood as he looked over her shoulder. Now it was all about which she could think. She wanted to lean her head against him. She wanted to feel his hands in her hair, making a mess of her chignon. She wanted to bury her face against his coat again, so she could smell the mixture of strong soap and faint musk that made up his scent. She wanted other things, too, that she wouldn't let herself think about in too much detail, because thinking about them made her heart pound and her body flush.

Arabella shifted uneasily in her chair, not sure how she felt about these carnal sensations. She wished she had some control over her physical response. She did not like feeling like a cat in heat! Wouldn't it make more sense if her desire for George could be turned on and off at will? She could switch it off until after the wedding, when they would be in the privacy of their own bedchamber. Then it would be safe to want all the things she could not yet have.

This line of thought did not aid her epistolary efforts in the least. It was a relief when George pulled a chair up and sat down next to her instead of hovering behind her and making her want things she was embarrassed to name. At least, it was a relief until he caught sight of her frown.

"What's wrong, then?" He took hold of her right hand, gently freeing the quill from her fingers.

Oh. She had gripped the pen so tightly that it left marks on her fingers, and she had not even noticed. She forced herself to relax every tightly clenched muscle. She immediately felt better.

Even her incipient headache retreated.

But she could not bring herself to admit the actual cause of her discomfort. How could she explain to her intended husband—and childhood friend—that she simultaneously wanted him to touch her and felt uncomfortable with the new ways her body reacted to his? Instead, she told George about her other problem: "No matter what I say in this letter, Mama and Papa are going to be shocked."

She could not predict how her parents would feel about the engagement. On the one hand, George was not particularly well-to-do, and his family did not have important social connections that might have made up for his lack of fortune. On the other hand, her parents knew and liked the Kirklands, and his uncle's gift would make George financially independent, if not wealthy. Mama and Papa could have few legitimate grounds for objection to George.

But even if her parents accepted her choice of groom, they would not understand why she wanted to marry in such a hurry. She could be certain of *that*.

"Do you want me to write to your parents instead?" George offered. "I can explain everything, and you can just add a personal note at the end."

"Yes, please." She slid the notepaper over to George and watched as he immediately began writing. The fluidity with which his pen scratched across the paper amazed her. How did he know what to say without taking so much as a moment to think about his wording first?

It took him less than five minutes to finish the note. "Here, take a look." He offered her the letter, which nearly filled the entire page.

As she read it, the corners of her mouth lifted up. It sounded so characteristically George: enthusiastic, optimistic, friendly. Where Arabella would have begged for her parents' approval, he simply assumed that Sir Michael and Lady Canning would be delighted to hear that their daughter was betrothed to someone they already knew very well. Most of the letter was taken up with a concise explanation for why George and Arabella were going to marry as soon as possible, by bishop's license, rather than calling the banns.

"I asked my father to get the license for us as soon as he gets my letter," George explained. "That way we need not waste time once we get back to Norton Combe."

Arabella nodded, though she suspected her mother might be disappointed not to have time to help choose a wedding dress or order a trousseau. With no time to purchase clothing, Arabella would have to wear one of her existing dresses for the wedding. Perhaps the white muslin with lilac trim? Though that one had a tear in one sleeve. Her maid had done a good job of mending it, but it might be better to wear something newer.

"Are you sure we need to marry in such a hurry?" she asked. The seamstress the Cannings patronized could usually make room in her schedule for a rush order if the price were right. If given a week's notice, she could probably whip something up for Arabella to wear.

But George shook his head. "I have no idea what my cousins are up to," he reminded her. "One of them may have already found a bride. I'd hate to lose the race because we tarried too long." He rubbed his forehead, looking more somber. "The worst scenario would be us marrying and then finding out that Augustus or Benedict had already claimed the prize."

A cold, sick feeling spread outward from the pit of Arabella's stomach. "That would be the worst case?" In that scenario, he would still be married to her. She swallowed, trying to stuff her rising misery back down as she faced the implications of his words. "I suppose that since you are only marrying me in order to get the prize, it would be terrible to be stuck together if we lost." She ought not be so surprised by that. He had made it clear from the beginning that Dogwood Cottage was his goal. But she had thought, or hoped, that—

"No!" George looked properly horrified. "It's just that without the money from Uncle William, I couldn't afford to marry." He twisted his mouth into a bitter line. "I do not make enough by my writing to support a family, you know."

"I have a dowry invested in the Funds," she reminded him. "We would have the income from that to live on."

George dismissed the suggestion with a shake of his head. "Not comfortably. You shouldn't have to make do with shabby rooms on Grub Street." He scrunched up his face in disgust. "Believe me, you would not like that. If we are too late, I suppose I will just have to seek ordination after all and look for a position as a curate. That would at least make my father happy." He smiled wryly. "I suppose your father would be pleased to have you living at Norton Combe someday."

Arabella nodded. George's father had always intended his son for the church, and Sir Michael would have perfectly willing to hand the Norton Combe living on to George when the time came. It had been a surprise and a disappointment to both families when George announced that he was not going to pursue a career in the church.

"Why *did* you decide not to be ordained?" she wondered aloud. Curates generally had tiny incomes, but the pay would probably have been steadier than what he made as a writer.

"I realized that I was not fit to be a clergyman." He looked down as he fidgeted with the quill pen, passing it from hand to hand and thoroughly inking himself in the process. Evidently, he would rather not discuss this.

Arabella tugged the pen out of his hand and slid the notepaper away from him. "I had better add a note for my parents, so they know I am still in my right mind." She meant it as a joke, but maybe it wasn't funny. Her parents were going to be very surprised by this news. Probably very confused, too.

She could already imagine her mother saying "But I had no idea that you and George had any sort of understanding. Why did you not tell us earlier?" Or maybe it would be her father who spoke first: "Are you sure this is what you want, Jelly-Belly? You might yet do better." She cringed as she imagined it, because Papa *would* keep using that nickname, though she'd told him many times that she hated it.

All her fears rushed back to overwhelm her. "What if they're mad at me?" Or worse, disappointed.

"They *couldn't* be mad at you, silly." George said this with such confidence that she almost believed him. Almost. But how could he be so certain? He did not know Mama and Papa as well as she did.

George must have seen the doubt on her face because he ruffled her hair affectionately. This would have been a sweet gesture if she'd had short, cropped hair of the sort that could stand being ruffled. But since she wore her long hair swept up in a chignon, the gesture resulted in the collapse of her coiffure He laughingly tried to help her repair it, while only making it worse, he knew nothing about women's hair arrangements.

"This is hopeless!" she wailed, which only made George laugh harder.

When she glared at him, he put his hand under her chin, tipped her face upwards, and lightly kissed her. The tense muscles in her jaw relaxed again. Even more amazingly, she ceased fretting about her parents in order to focus on the pleasing sensation of his mouth against hers.

If anyone had told her yesterday that she would find comfort in kissing George Kirkland, she would not have believed it. If anything, she would have expected a kiss from a young gentleman to send her into a panic. Perhaps it would have done so if she had kissed the wrong man. But she *liked* kissing George.

She would never have expected someone as impulsive as George to kiss so tenderly and thoughtfully! Maybe *thoughtfully* wasn't the right word, but she could think of no other way to describe the slow, gentle way he teased her mouth, or the moth-wing-soft kisses that he left on her nose, her eyelids, her jawline, and the space just behind her ear. That last kiss sent a shivery thrill—unfamiliar, but not unpleasant—from her head to her toes.

Her body temperature seemed to rise a degree or two in response, though that must have been her imagination.

She gasped with surprise, and George immediately drew back. "Sorry." His voice came out rougher and thicker than usual, and that, too, sent a shiver down her spine.

Arabella reluctantly opened her eyes. She vaguely felt that they must have been doing something wrong, though she could not have said what. There was no impropriety in a young lady kissing her fiancé, but the sensations she'd just experienced seemed downright decadent. Surely proper ladies were not supposed to enjoy being kissed that way! Arabella had always tried her best to follow all the rules her mother taught her, but perhaps she had somehow been corrupted. She frowned as she pondered that.

"Belle? Is something wrong?" George stroked the furrow between her brows with one gentle finger. "Did I frighten you?"

"No, I frightened myself." She could see from his face that her explanation puzzled him. "You didn't do anything wrong," she assured him. It had not been his ardor that startled her, but her own fervent desire. That would take some getting used to.

"I suppose I had better seal this letter," George suggested, "and it put out for the next post. And then, I wonder if I ought to ask Leland if I can borrow one of his saddlehorses."

"Saddlehorses?" Arabella repeated. "Aren't we going to rent a chaise?" Her parents had sent her to Newton Park in the family coach, but it had long since returned home. She did not want to impose on the Gray family by requesting they send their coachman to escort them back to Norton Combe.

"You can rent a post chaise," he agreed, "but I will get there faster on horseback. And I cannot travel with you anyway, Belle, unless we have a chaperone. I suppose if my sister were willing to come with us, it would be right enough, but otherwise, it would look bad."

"Oh, yes." She lowered her head and stared fixedly at the toes of her slippers, ashamed that she had not thought of that.

Naturally, an unmarried man and woman could not travel alone together for two days, not even if they were betrothed. She cleared her throat, hoping her suggestion hadn't scandalized George. "When will you leave, then?"

"Maybe tomorrow." He restlessly tapped his fingers against his leg. "Or the day after. It depends on how quickly we can make the travel arrangements. I suppose we'd best talk to Caro about it all."

At that moment, the door to the morning room swung open. Caroline stood there, wearing a charming dove-gray morning gown and a look of intense, wide-eyed interest. "Talk to me about what?"

George scowled at his sister. "How long were you eavesdropping?"

Caroline looked back and forth between George and Arabella. "Long enough to know that something interesting is in the wind. Why are you leaving so soon George? I thought you were going to stay out the week." The corners of her mouth tipped down slightly.

George caught Arabella's eye and raised his eyebrows, asking a silent question. Arabella gulped, clasped her hands together, and nodded. Then she looked at Caroline and smiled uncertainly.

"I think I had better go and . . ." And do what? What could she possibly be planning on doing at this hour? She frantically tried to think of a task that might take her away from this awkward conversation, but the tablet of her mind had gone blank. "I have some things to do before dinner."

She waved her hand vaguely and scurried out of the room before Caroline could ask any more questions. Let George explain matters to his sister. Such a task lay well beyond Arabella's powers of speech just now.

When she reached her guest room, she looked about, wondering how long it would take her maid to pack her things. At present, her possessions were scattered all over the room—not in a mess, but neatly placed on shelves, in drawers, or hanging in the wardrobe. She had settled into the room, because she'd expected to stay at Newton Park for at least a month. She so rarely got to see Caroline that she'd wanted to make the most of this visit.

All her summer plans would be altered now, wouldn't they? Arabella sank down onto the bed, struck by the enormity of the changes that lay before her. In just a day or two, she'd be on her way home, for the last time ever. She would undoubtedly visit her parents in the future, but Oliphant Hall would never be her home again. She would live at Dogwood Cottage with her new husband.

Arabella tried to imagine her new home, but she could not form a clear picture of the cottage or its setting. She had been to Lancashire before. In fact, she'd attended an unexpectedly eventful Christmas house party in Lancashire a year and a half ago. That was where she first made the acquaintance of her friend Rose. But she had never visited the town of Pendleford. She had no idea how big it was, whether it was pretty or ugly, old or new. Would there be nearby cotton mills belching black smoke into the air? She wrinkled her nose at the thought.

Well, she'd find out soon enough! Pendleford would be her home. And George Kirkland would no longer be simply her best friend's older brother. He would be Arabella's husband. She would be Mrs. Kirkland of Dogwood Cottage.

She shook her head, struggling to imagine taking such a large step forward. Since Arabella was a creature of habit, changes often unsettled her. But this would be a change for the good. She would finally have an establishment of her own, a husband of her own, and one day, perhaps, children of her own. At the very least, she would be able to kiss George as much as she wanted without fear of impropriety. That prospect assuaged some of her anxieties, though it also put a blush on her cheeks.

In the meantime, she'd better finish that portrait of Charlie now, while she still had the model in front of her. It might be years before she next visited Newton Park, and by then, Charlie would have grown and changed. She picked up her box of crayons and went in search of her godson. The prospect of creating art put a spring in her step and a tune in her mouth, making it easy to lay aside any doubts and anxieties about the decision she and George had made today.

Chapter Nine

FOUR DAYS AFTER Arabella accepted his proposal, George Kirkland walked into the vicarage at Norton Combe and drew a deep breath. The house smelled of lemon-scented furniture polish and something delicious baking in the oven. The familiar scents felt like a balm to his soul.

The upper housemaid, Mary, greeted him in the foyer. "Master George! Your parents will be quite surprised to see you." The inflection in her voice turned it into an implicit question.

"I am sure they will, Mary. It's been a week full of surprises." George grinned as he imagined how the Kirkland elders must have reacted to his letter, assuming they'd already received it. It was possible that he'd beaten it home. "Are my parents at home?"

"Mrs. Kirkland is out paying sick calls," Mary told him. "She should be back before dinner, though. Mr. Kirkland is in his study."

"Right." George handed Mary his hat and walking stick, then headed up the stairs to his father's study.

The previous incumbent had used a room on the ground floor as his study and library, but Mr. Kirkland found the ground floor too noisy on a normal day. He had taken over one of the bedrooms on the first story, building bookshelves along the walls at his own expense. No one was allowed in the study without explicit permission from the vicar, who guarded his space as fiercely as a watchdog.

George tapped lightly at the study door, ready to retreat if his father was in the wrong mood. But he was again in luck, for the elder Mr. Kirkland called "Come in!" in a voice that was, if not welcoming, at least not forbidding.

"Hullo the Pater!" As usual, George found his father buried in scholarship. A stack of books sat on the left side of his writing table, and a mess of inked-up papers sprawled all over the right side. "Working on a sermon?"

His father sat up straight and pushed his spectacles higher on his nose. "It's a letter to the editor of the *Derby Daily Mail*," he explained. "A complaint about the local circulating library."

"What's wrong with the circulating library, then?" George leaned against one of the glass-fronted bookcases. The room contained only two chairs, one of which was occupied by his father. A box of old periodicals took up the other chair. He could have moved the box to sit down, but he had been seated in a carriage for two days, and he preferred to stand.

The look of pleased interest on his father's face morphed into a scowl. "Circulating libraries promote nothing but the most frivolous of modern literature."

Ah, that old complaint! His father had very old-fashioned views on the subject of novels. The Reverend Mr. Kirkland made allowances for religious tracts that used narrative to teach religious principles, but he had little tolerance for works of pure entertainment. George drew a deep breath, preparing to steer the conversation away from dangerous waters, but it was too late.

"For every one good book of information, there must be at least a dozen novels!" His father's voice grew louder as he launched into a tirade that George had already heard many times before. "And not just any novels. The sickliest flights of fancy ever written! Half of them written by uneducated scribbling women, the other half by gentlemen who ought to know better."

"Indeed?" George interrupted. "How terrible! It is a good thing the people of Derbyshire have you on hand to warn them of the danger, sir. By the way, did you get my letter—"

"I wish that you would write a good, scathing review of books like *Clermont* and *Mysteries of Udolpho*," Mr. Kirkland continued. "Young people continue to read such nonsense, though many volumes of better work have been published since then."

"I'm afraid Gothic novels are not my line, Pater." George used his most soothing voice. At least he could afford to be sincere about that. Though he'd written any number of things that his father would have disapproved of had he known about them, George had never tried to write a Gothic novel. "But you might like the essay I'm writing about Dr. Mesmer's legacy."

He hadn't thought about that article for days, not since Uncle William's fateful dinner party. Wasn't it due in a few weeks? Or... his whole body stiffened, except for his heart, which pounded as if he had just galloped up a flight of stairs.

"I say, do you know what day today is?" Please let his calculations be wrong!

His father wrinkled his brow. "It is Thursday, the twentieth of June. The day before Midsummer. Why do you ask?"

A chill ran down George's back. He had promised Robert Halsey that he'd hand him the essay no later than the twenty-fifth of June. But he had barely started it. All he had was a page of scribbled notes. Those notes—and all his research materials—were back in London. *Damn.* Halsey was a good sort, but the last time George turned in an article a few days late, the editor had very drily reminded George that that sort of thing just wouldn't do when a man had a journal to get out on time.

The essay on Mesmer was going to be more than a few days late. George hoped to marry Belle next week, and he meant to take her to Bath to visit his uncle immediately after the wedding. How on earth was he going to finish the essay? He covered his mouth with his hand as he faced reality: he was *not* going to finish the essay. It would not get to Halsey in time to be published as scheduled. And he would probably never be asked to write an essay for *The Current Review* again. His heart sank. He'd liked working with Halsey.

"Is something wrong?" His father cocked his head to one side, clearly puzzled.

"Just remembered a task I have to do," George replied. "It has nothing to do with our conversation. Very sorry to have lost focus." He swallowed, trying to get the lump out of his throat. *It does not matter*, he told himself. If Uncle William gave him the cottage and the promised funds, George would no longer need to write essays about quack physicians in order to keep himself fed. *If.*

Perhaps, after all, George should have gone into the church, despite knowing he lacked the moral character for it. But would he have done any better at writing sermons? If he'd become a curate, he probably would've spent the rest of his life burning the candle at both ends every Saturday night while he tried to finish his sermon. Not for the first time, he wondered how other people managed to get their tasks done on time. Ahead of time, even!

"Anyway, Pater, enough about my writing." He did not want to think about how colossally he'd messed up with regard to that essay. He'd dash a note off to Halsey with his most fervent apologies. Surely a man could be forgiven for such an error when he was about to be married? George would have been more sanguine about his chances of being forgiven if turning in an article past the promised time had been an aberration rather than his habit.

He cleared his throat and changed the subject. "Did you get my last letter? Dated this Monday last?"

Mr. Kirkland's face brightened. "Ah, yes! How could I have forgotten? Congratulations on your betrothal. Your mother and I are quite pleased to hear you are settling down."

George's shoulders relaxed. There had been no real reason for him to fear parental disapproval over this engagement since his parents had always liked Belle. Even so, he'd been a little anxious.

"What does Sir Michael say about it, though?" his father asked.

That put the tension right back into George's spine. "I haven't spoken to him yet," he admitted. "Naturally, I wrote to him. We both did, Belle and me. But I came straight here when I got into town, and I haven't called at the Hall yet."

His father's smile faded a little. "You had best do that without delay. Sir Michael may be displeased that you did not ask his permission before proposing. I am sure the Cannings were no more expecting this announcement than were your mother and I. Sir Michael will not want to be kept waiting."

"I suppose not." George glanced down at his travel-worn clothing. "But I think I'd better change my dress first." And perhaps fortify himself with a cup or two of tea. He had no idea how Sir Michael would react to the news. Was it too much to hope that the baronet would be as pleased as the vicar was? He feared it might be.

George's visit to Oliphant Hall was further delayed, not only because the cook insisted on serving him a slice of fresh-baked cake along with his tea, but because his mother returned home from her sick calls. Mrs. Kirkland collapsed onto the uncomfortable settee in the parlor and gratefully accepted a cup of tea.

"George, how on earth did you convince Arabella Canning to marry you?" she demanded. "I thought she meant to stay a spinster, given the way she's rejected every other suitor."

"Have there been many suitors, then?" George mumbled through a mouthful of cake.

"I should think so." His mother brushed an errant strand of hair out of her eyes and took a sip of tea. "I know that John Thurston was quite broken up when Arabella turned him down, some two or three years ago. And there have been other men who pursued her over the years. But she is so reserved, it's hard for anyone to approach her. Some of the gentlemen find her standoffish."

George followed his bite of cake with a gulp of strong, black tea. "There you are then," he said cheerfully. "It isn't at all hard for *me* to approach Belle since we have known each other all our lives. Hence, I succeeded where others failed." In truth, he did not know why Belle had accepted him when she had turned down a man like John Thurston, who stood to inherit a comfortable manor and at least two thousand a year.

"Well, I wish you both all happiness in the world," his mother said, "but you have not given us much warning. If you really intend to marry within the week, I had better talk to Lady Canning about the wedding breakfast. Have you spoken to the Cannings yet?"

George swallowed his last bite of cake so abruptly that he nearly choked. He had to pour himself another cup of tea to wash down the morsel. "That's where I'm going next, after I change out of these clothes." And, perhaps, after another cup of tea. He would need all his fortitude for this conversation.

Half an hour later, George sat in the least comfortable chair in the Blue Salon at Oliphant Hall, restlessly bouncing one foot up and down. The butler had ushered him into the room, blandly informing him that Sir Michael would see him as soon as he finished meeting with one of his tenants.

To George, the wait seemed interminable. He was astounded when he checked the clock and saw that he had only been in the room five minutes. It felt like a quarter of an hour. He got to his feet and paced back and forth, only to discover that the room was too small for pacing. He could cross from one side to another with just a few strides. Why couldn't the butler have sent him to the drawing room? There would've been room for a man to move about there! He hardly had room to breathe here.

"Ah, Mr. Kirkland." Sir Michael stepped into the room, wearing the country version of morning dress: buckskins, top boots, and a waistcoat that was serviceable rather than fashionable. "Thank you for waiting. Won't you sit down?" He gestured toward a chair by the fire.

"Yes, thank you." George did not want to sit down, but he

could scarcely hold a conversation with his future father-in-law while walking back and forth across the room. He thought more clearly while moving, but he had long since learned that other people generally preferred to be stationary during their conversations.

The moment he sat down, his brain, which had been feverishly working out what he wanted to say, promptly quit working. In an attempt to gain time, he looked down at the floor, pretending to admire the handsome Axminster carpet.

"I like that rug. It's new, isn't it?" He wanted to put Sir Michael in a better frame of mind if he could, the current expression on the baronet's face did not look promising.

Sir Michael looked at the rug, too, and frowned. "Not really. We must've had it for at least two years. But I suppose you have not visited during that time."

George flinched at the hint of rebuke in Sir Michael's voice. "It *has* been some time since I last visited," he admitted. "I came home the Christmas before last, but you all were away."

That year the Cannings had gone to a Christmas house party at some nobleman's estate. At the time, it had not seemed to matter that Belle was away. Now he wondered what would have happened if he'd spent time with Belle before Uncle William announced his "race" to win the cottage. Would George have considered…?—But it was no good pondering what might have been.

"Indeed." Sir Michael nodded, but his stiff posture did not relax in the slightest. "And last summer, you were home for a week, but did not even call on Belle, did you? Strange, since the two of you claim to be so attached to one another." He stared at George until George dropped his gaze. Sir Michael's blue eyes were an icy pale shade, nothing like the rich violet of Belle's eyes.

Heat flooded George's face, sweeping all the way to the tips of his ears. He'd hoped this would be a friendly meeting. He'd known that he might have to listen to boring details about settlements, but he had not come prepared to defend himself.

"When two people have known each other as long as Belle and I have, they can pick up the threads of friendship even after the passing of time." He risked a quick glance at Sir Michael's face, and inwardly cringed. Judging from the set of Sir Michael's jaw, he did not like George's use of a childhood nickname. Or maybe he did not like George.

"And yet," the baronet said, "never, in all of that time, has my daughter mentioned any romantic attachment to you. On the contrary, when we asked her if there was any suitor she favored, she always told us that her heart was free. You can imagine my surprise when I learned that the two of you wished to be married so suddenly." Sir Michael propped his chin up on his hand as he continued to fix George with his icy stare.

George swallowed, trying to reduce the uncomfortable dryness in his mouth. "I suppose our engagement *was* unexpected." He could hardly deny that. Everyone who knew either George or Belle must be surprised at the news.

On the journey home, he'd toyed with the idea of claiming that he had long been in love with Belle, and only waited to propose until he had the means to support her. That would have made for a romantic, touching story. But he did not trust his own acting ability. Besides, as he knew from past experience, once one started to tell lies, the work of maintaining those lies grew heavier and heavier.

Instead, he stuck to the facts. "Belle and I will deal very well together." Sir Michael's face looked more thunderous than ever, so George hurried on before he could be interrupted. "Thanks to my Uncle Kirkland's generosity, I can provide a comfortable life for her."

"My daughter deserves more than a *comfortable* life," Sir Michael argued. "She has been raised in the lap of luxury. And her definition of comfort may be quite different from yours, Mr. Kirkland. She is used to socializing with the best families, you know." He looked George up and down, the scowl on his face suggesting that he found fault with everything about George's appearance, from the scuffs on his boots, to the ink stains on his right hand, to the fact that his topcoat was out of date.

By this time, George's nerves were making him jittery. He rested his hands on his knees to keep from tapping his foot. "I understand that I may not be the suitor you would have chosen for Arabella," he acknowledged. "But she has chosen me. That is, she has accepted my offer of marriage. Don't you think she should have what she wants?"

Sir Michael shook his head. "I simply do not see why she wants to marry you, Mr. Kirkland. She could have done so much better."

George's face flushed scarlet again, but this time, he forced himself to keep steadily meeting Sir Michael's gaze. "Perhaps she felt more comfortable marrying an old friend than a suitor whom she'd only encountered at balls and parties. I imagine she knows me better than she did any of her other suitors."

Sir Michael snorted. He leaned back in his chair and crossed one booted leg over another. "You've made your point, Mr. Kirkland. I will respect my daughter's decision, even if I do not understand it. But I wish you could explain to me why the two of you must marry in such a hurry."

George licked his lips nervously. He did not want to reveal all the details of Uncle William's ridiculous challenge. That would not reflect well on the Kirkland family. But he was perfectly willing to let his uncle shoulder the blame for the hasty wedding. George would never have rushed into matrimony like this if not for his uncle.

"My uncle is in ill health." Best not to admit that "ill health" meant "gout," and that Uncle William hadn't had a bout of the gout in years. "I believe he wants to make sure that he lives to see. . . ." His voice trailed off as he realized that talking about the "next generation" of Kirklands might be a mistake. Sir Michael might not like being reminded that after the wedding, George would take Belle to bed.

Sir Michael raised one eyebrow. Since his eyebrows were

thicker than George's, the expression looked far more effective on his face. "Well? I am waiting to hear what your Uncle Kirkland's ill health has to do with marrying my daughter."

Fortunately, inspiration struck George in the nick of time, as it so often did. "My uncle wants to meet her. In fact, we plan to visit Bath immediately after the wedding." He smiled hopefully. "You must know how it is when one has demanding relatives."

He *had* written to Uncle William with the news of his betrothal, but he had not yet received an answer. How could he, given that he'd left Newton Park the day after posting the letter? But it would be very like his uncle to want proof that George was married, so he did plan on taking his new wife with him to Bath.

Besides, Belle would probably expect some sort of wedding tour. And, in any case, George had no home to which he could take her yet. He could certainly not expect her to live in his cluttered chambers in London! He had no idea how quickly they could move into Dogwood Cottage. All he had was a vague hope that spending a week or so in lodgings in Bath would give him a chance to work out their new living arrangements.

"I see." Sir Michael narrowed his eyes. "Do you have some sort of expectations of this uncle of yours?"

"Yes," George said baldly. "He is being quite supportive. I don't know what I'd do without him." Well, that wasn't true. He did know what he would do. He would be back in London, working on that very boring article about Franz Mesmer. He might even have finished it on time, if not for the hasty wedding. "Have you any more questions for me?"

"I suppose not," Sir Michael reluctantly concluded. "I can only say that I hope you and Belle know what you are about."

A genuine grin split George's face. "Belle is far more level-headed than I am," he confided. "You can trust her judgement, even if you don't trust mine."

The baronet shook his head, but a rueful smile tugged at the corner of his mouth. "That is not exactly reassuring, young man. But I suppose Belle must know what she is doing." He cleared his throat. "Now, as to the settlements, I am meeting with my solicitor this afternoon. He will likely call on you tomorrow. I certainly hope we can work things out to our mutual satisfaction."

"I am sure we will," George said quickly. Though, in fact, he had no idea how he could promise Belle set amounts of pin money, when he was not certain how much of an income he would have. If only there were time for him to meet with Uncle William before the wedding to talk over financial matters! But it could not be helped. He could only trust that everything would work out.

Everything *would* work out, wouldn't it?

Chapter Ten

O N A SUNNY day in late June, Arabella Canning and George
Kirkland stood before the altar rail at St. Mark's Church and
vowed to "love, honor, and keep each other in sickness and in
health."

There was something simultaneously dreamlike and mundane about the wedding ceremony. The church itself was a
familiar space, smelling of beeswax, old wood, and cool stone.
Mr. Kirkland's rich, clear speaking voice filled the small sanctuary
as loudly as it ever did. There were only a handful of people in
the congregation today, but most of them were people whom
Arabella had known all her life.

Other things made the day seem as ordinary as any other.
While Arabella listened to Mr. Kirkland leading the congregation
in prayer, she noticed an enormous horsefly buzzing around the
sanctuary. Its rapid movement back and forth, up and down, kept
drawing her eyes, distracting her from the momentous ceremony
taking place. It distracted George, too. His eyes followed the fly
around the room until his father cleared his voice and gave his
son a pointed look. Then George snapped to attention. She did
her best to focus, too, but part of her wanted to giggle at the way
the insect brazenly interrupted what was supposed to be a solemn
moment.

At first, Arabella had been afraid she would stammer and

stumble her way through the vows, since she felt painfully conscious of all the people watching her. But before Mr. Kirkland began reading the marriage service, George leaned over and whispered in her ear, "Just pretend it's a play, like the ones we put on when we were children. You were always the best actress!"

Arabella drew a deep breath. George was right: she had always been good at reading aloud, telling stories, or acting a part. Speaking did not pose the same difficulties when she had a script to follow. She took her betrothed's advice and pretended that she stood on a stage, performing for her audience. It worked perfectly. She did not flub a single line, and her voice rang out clearly in the little church.

She kept up the act as she and George exited the church, accompanied by the sound of church bells. This part of the performance was easier because she did not even have to speak. She merely smiled and waved at the handful of villagers and tenants who made up most of the congregation.

George handed her into the carriage, then turned to throw a handful of shiny coins at the little crowd milling about the entrance to the church. This elicited a cheer. But the crowd cheered even more when George turned back to Arabella and gave her a hearty kiss on the cheek.

Her face flushed and she turned her head away, embarrassed. Though family members and friends might sometimes greet each other with a kiss on the cheek or hand, she knew very well that kisses between lovers were supposed to be saved for private moments. Were the rules different on one's wedding day? Perhaps brides and grooms enjoyed a dispensation from the usual rules against public displays of affection. She hoped so.

The carriage began to roll the short distance from the church to Oliphant Hall. George stopped waving and covered Arabella's hand with his own. "In case I haven't said it yet, you look beautiful today. Those violets on your dress match your eyes."

Arabella did not stop blushing, but the corners of her mouth turned up. She glanced down at her white muslin gown.

Embroidered violets bordered the neckline and sleeves, and the skirt displayed the flounces that had become so popular. Her seamstress had put the dress together almost overnight, based on the measurements from her last fitting. Such speed must have cost a good deal of money, but Mama refused to admit how much. She would only say that Arabella deserved a new dress for her wedding day.

"My eyes are blue, not purple." If her goal had been to choose embroidery that matched her eyes, forget-me-nots would have been a better choice.

"Well, purple or blue, the color suits you," George said cheerfully. "And now we are married!"

"It doesn't seem real yet," Arabella admitted. Today, she had irrevocably bound herself to another human being. Nothing would be the same after this, whether for good or for bad. And yet, she felt the same as she did yesterday. Shouldn't the world feel different now?

"You could pinch me to find out if it's a dream," George suggested.

Arabella giggled, covering her mouth to hide the unladylike laughter. "That might prove that *you* were not dreaming, but it would not prove that *I* am not dreaming. You would have to pinch me back to make sure of that."

"Pinch a lady? Never!" Mock horror infused George's voice, and when she met his gaze, his grin broadened. "If this is a dream, it is a pleasant one." But the smile in his eyes slowly faded, replaced by unfamiliar intensity. He tipped her chin up with one finger, and before she understood what he meant to do, he kissed her on the lips.

Or rather, attempted to do so. Unfortunately, he misjudged the angle and crashed into the wide rim of Arabella's straw bonnet. It nearly knocked his own hat off.

Arabella burst into a fit of giggles. Once she got herself under control, she scolded her husband. "You shouldn't do that in public, anyway. People might see."

George snorted. "No one would be the least surprised to see a bride and groom kissing on the way home after their wedding! But if you prefer, I will wait until we are in private to kiss you." An unusually wolfish smile crept across his face. "I look forward to being alone with you, my wife."

A shiver composed of equal parts anticipation and anxiety ran down Arabella's spine, as she suspected George had more than kissing in mind. He was probably thinking about the wedding night. Contemplating that prospect made her own heart beat faster.

Yesterday, after Arabella tried on the wedding dress for the last time, her mother sat down with her and spoke very seriously about Marital Duties. Arabella had known a fair amount about human reproduction, but she nevertheless learned a few rather surprising facts about what men and women did together in bed.

George's innuendo now filled Arabella's mind with images that still seemed downright scandalous, despite the ceremony that had just concluded. Picturing what it might be like to go to bed with George flustered her so much that she looked away from him, pretending to admire scenery she'd seen hundreds of times. In reality, she wondered what his hands would feel like on her body. What his body would feel like pressed against hers. What—

"I hope you are not worried about the wedding breakfast," George suggested. "I know you don't like large parties, but this time you know all the guests. There is no need to feel shy."

Arabella had not worried about the breakfast until he reminded her about it. "I will be fine!" All she had to do was keep up her performance as the Gracious and Lovely Bride. Hopefully, she could maintain the act for a few more hours.

As it turned out, George was right that she had nothing to fear. Like the wedding itself, the breakfast afterward was a family affair. Apart from Arabella and George's parents, the only other guests were the Grays. Caroline's family had traveled up to Derbyshire with Arabella so they could celebrate the marriage. Caroline seemed in excellent health, but Leland, still anxious about the possibility of a miscarriage, protectively hovered around her every time she got out of her chair.

That could be me in a few months, Arabella thought, and froze. She sat holding a fork in the air, stunned by the realization of how much her life was going to change.

"Belle? Is something wrong?" George pitched his voice softly, so none of the happily chattering guests around them heard.

"I am not hungry anymore." She put her fork down, its bite of wedding cake untasted. Instead, she took a sip of sweet white wine. That helped settle her stomach. Then someone leaned across the table to ask her a question. In answering it, she forgot about her momentary bewilderment.

She spent most of the breakfast performing the part of a blissfully happy young bride, but the mask broke when her mother hugged her as they said good-bye. She could not act when in her mother's arms.

Mama stepped back from the embrace and wiped her eyes with a dainty scrap of handkerchief. "I can't believe I am losing my daughter already." Her smile quavered as she blinked back tears.

Arabella stared at her in confusion. Not two months ago, her mother had bewailed Arabella's spinster status and rhetorically wondered what she would do with a daughter who couldn't say boo to a goose. Shouldn't Mama be glad that Arabella was finally married? Now her parents could focus all their attention on launching Lavinia into society. Wasn't that what they wanted?

"I thought you would be happy that I finally got married," Arabella said.

"Oh, sweetheart!" Her mother pulled her into a hug so tight it threatened to destroy Arabella's new bonnet. "I *am* happy! I'm delighted that you will finally have a home of your own! But we will miss you so much."

Papa embraced her next. There were no tears running down his face, but he had flushed an alarming shade of red. That could have been a result of too much wine, but Arabella suspected it had more to do with strong emotions.

While he had her wrapped in a tight hug, Papa whispered: "Remember, Belle, you can always come back home if you need to."

Arabella's eyes widened and her mouth fell ajar. Why on earth would she need to come home? She could not imagine George mistreating her. Annoying her with his impulsiveness, perhaps. But harming her? No.

She had no chance to ask her father for clarification, as George was waiting to assist her into the carriage they'd borrowed for the first leg of the journey. After their first stage, they would travel by hired post chaise.

The carriage door swung shut, leaving Belle alone with her new husband. The situation still felt unreal. Maybe she should pinch herself, if George wasn't willing to do it for her.

"Tired?" George rested his arm along the back of the seat, casually embracing her.

After all those tearful farewells, Arabella had to clear her throat before speaking. "A little." But mostly, she felt peculiar. She sat alone with George Kirkland in a carriage, and for the first time in her life, there was nothing scandalous about their being alone together.

"Isn't it strange?" she whispered.

"Isn't what strange?" George wrinkled his forehead.

"Being married," she explained. "Nothing will ever be the same again."

His face cleared at once. "Ah, that. I suppose you're right. But everything will be better now. Or at least, life won't be any worse than before. If nothing else, marriage will be interesting." He smiled at her. "It's good to try new things, isn't it? No doubt matrimony will prove very educational."

Arabella's mouth twitched. She pressed her lips together, trying to restrain a grin, but it broke out anyway. She would not have chosen the word "educational" to describe matrimony.

"What if we try it and don't like it?" she asked. "Marriage

vows can't be undone."

The smile faded from his eyes. "No," he said more seriously. "The vows cannot be undone. But I am not your jailor. If you find you cannot live with me, you are free to go your own way. You need not fear that I will trap you in an unhappy situation."

Arabella frowned. Separation was not as scandalous as divorce, but society looked down on husbands and wives who lived apart. "I suppose the same is true for you," she replied. "If you are unhappy, I do not mean to hold you to your word." What would happen, though, if they had children? That might complicate things.

"Why the frown? You ought not be unhappy on your wedding day." George stroked her lower lip with a feather-light touch.

Arabella lifted her eyes. George's warm brown eyes were soft with concern, and a line had formed between his brows. Her mouth slowly relaxed back into a smile. Then, feeling simultaneously affectionate and shy, she kissed the tip of his finger.

"Ah, that reminds me." George's eyes darkened as he leaned closer. "There was something I meant to do once we were alone."

"Wha—oh!" Before she could even ask a question, he'd begun to fumble with the ribbon tying her bonnet on. When she realized what he intended, her heart sped up again. She untied the knot in the ribbon with shaky fingers so she could set the bonnet aside. Then she tipped her chin up to be kissed.

Arabella thought she knew what a kiss felt like. Now she discovered that she was mistaken. This time, when she opened her mouth a little, George slipped his tongue inside. She drew back, startled.

"What's wrong?" For some reason, his voice sounded hoarse.

"I don't know why you're doing that," she explained. In her experience, people generally kept their tongues to themselves.

He stared blankly at her. "Because it feels good?"

She wrinkled her nose. "It does?"

The corner of his mouth quirked up. "Why don't we try it, and if you don't like it, I will keep my tongue out of your mouth." His smile turned into a smirk. "But I think you might like it."

Arabella wasn't so sure about that. But George was her husband now. Tonight, he would do even more intimate things than slipping his tongue into her mouth. She swallowed uneasily, but nodded. "I suppose it wouldn't hurt to try," she whispered.

When their lips met again, she opened her mouth to George, eager to explore the unfamiliar terrain of passion.

Chapter Eleven

Less than a month after the eventful dinner party at which William Kirkland announced his plan to give away Dogwood Cottage, George Kirkland once again stood at the doorway of his uncle's townhouse in Bath. This time, Belle stood by his side, her arm linked with his. He caught her eye and smiled. Her mouth curved into a shy smile in return, but when he rapped at the door, she winced.

"You look nervous," he whispered while they waited for someone to answer the door.

She wrinkled her nose. "I *am* nervous," she whispered back. "I don't like going to new places and meeting new people. I never know what to expect!"

"But that's what makes travel fun!" George protested. Not that Uncle William's townhouse was at all new to him; he merely wanted to defend the principle at stake. The world was enormous and interesting and the only way to explore it was by seeing new places. Which, yes, did involve meeting new people.

Belle turned her head to frown at him. She opened her mouth, but before she could disagree with him, the butler opened the door.

"Ah, Mr. Kirkland," Baines said. "I believe your uncle is expecting you." He hesitated and studied Arabella for a moment. He caught George's eye and slightly raised his eyebrows.

George caught the hint and made the necessary introduction. "Baines, this is my wife. Mrs. George Kirkland, nee Arabella Canning."

"Very good, sir." Baines's face softened from a marble mask into a genuine smile. "Your uncle will be most delighted to meet Mrs. Kirkland. My felicitations!" His smile faded and he cleared his throat. "Your uncle is currently sequestered in his study with another visitor, but he will see you shortly. Won't you please step into the drawing room to wait?"

George intended to tell Baines that they could see themselves in, but Baines did not give him the chance to do so. The butler led them through the foyer and down the short corridor that took them to the drawing room.

"Mr. and Mrs. George Kirkland," Baines announced.

The hour was too late in the day for morning calls and too early for dinner guests. George had therefore assumed that the drawing room would either be empty or occupied solely by Aunt Betsy. He had not expected to encounter a well-dressed woman who looked to be in her late twenties. She sat in the most comfortable chair, a teacup in hand.

Aunt Betsy's face broke into a smile. "George! So good to see you again! I wish we could have attended the wedding, but I am afraid that William's health did not allow it." She stepped forward to take Arabella by the hand. "We are so very glad to meet you, my dear." Then she glanced to the unfamiliar woman seated by the hearth, and her smile faltered. "I was just telling Miss Buxton about the wedding."

George, remembering his manners, bowed to Miss Buxton. "How do you do, ma'am?"

But the stranger drew back abruptly, as if affronted. Too late, George realized that he ought to have called her "miss" rather than "ma'am." She probably disliked the implication that she was a confirmed spinster.

"Very well, thank you." The unhappy lines of her face belied her words. She looked disgruntled, if not downright angry. "I suppose you are to be congratulated on your marriage, Mr. Kirkland."

Belle responded to the unexpected bitterness in Miss Buxton's voice by cringing and stepping closer to George.

"Thank you," George said blandly. "My wife and I are delighted we could visit my uncle before we move to our new home."

Miss Buxton scowled, but before she could say anything further, the door was flung open and Uncle William walked in. His gout must have reoccurred because he limped heavily. But his face, like Aunt Betsy's, was wreathed in smiles. He did not content himself with a handshake, but clasped George on the shoulder affectionately.

"I am glad to see you, my boy." Uncle William directed an odd sideways glance at the unhappy Miss Buxton, then turned toward Belle. "And *very* happy to meet you, my dear. We are pleased to welcome you to the family." He leaned towards Belle and dropped his voice conspiratorially. "Though I shouldn't say it, you've managed to hook the best of my young nephews."

Belle's face flushed a bright red. George faked a cough so that he could hide his face behind his hand. But the most interesting reaction came from Miss Buxton, who audibly gasped.

Uncle William turned back to her. "I mean no offense to your fiancé, ma'am. Benedict is a fine young man too. He will make you an excellent husband. But you must understand, I am not as well acquainted with Ambrose's boys as I should like to be. George, on the other hand, practically grew up at Dogwood Cottage."

That was an exaggeration, but George better understood why Miss Buxton was so unhappy. Benedict must have hoped to win the matrimonial race and secure Dogwood Cottage for himself. He and his fiancée would not enjoy meeting the couple who had beaten them to the altar.

"I am very pleased to meet a future member of the Kirkland family," George said, hoping to soothe some of Miss Buxton's discontent. He did not particularly like Benedict, but that was no reason to be rude to *her*. "How long have you known Benedict?"

Miss Buxton flushed and shifted in her chair. "Not so very long," she admitted. "We were introduced by a mutual acquaintance who knew that we both wished to be married." She straightened her back and stopped fidgeting. "And we found that we suited each other so well that there was no reason to wait before becoming betrothed."

"What a charming story!" George hoped his smile did not reveal that he found the story amusing rather than romantic. Benedict must have been willing to rush into matrimony merely for the sake of securing Dogwood Cottage. To be sure, George had done the same, but he at least chose to marry someone he already knew and liked!

"I am not sure what our plans will be now." Miss Buxton's lower lip began to tremble alarmingly.

George surreptitiously patted his waistcoat pocket, looking for a clean handkerchief. Aunt Betsy moved more quickly, passing a dainty, lace-trimmed handkerchief over to Miss Buxton before George had even located his.

Sure enough, Miss Buxton burst into rather noisy tears. George handed her his handkerchief, anyway, guessing that Aunt Betsy's would not be adequate to stem the tide.

Meanwhile, Uncle William looked on the verge of an apoplexy. "Now, now, there's no need to carry on that way." He probably meant to soothe Miss Buxton, but his panic filtered into his voice, which sounded more likely to alarm than to calm.

When Benedict Kirkland walked into this chaos, his eyes widened and he paused to dither in the doorway. "What's going on here?" He glanced at his fiancée and nervously licked his lips. "Lucretia, is something wrong?"

She was crying too hard to reply and could only shake her head. Benedict cautiously approached her and awkwardly patted her shoulder. "We'll figure something out." He hesitated, then added, "My dear," as if it were an afterthought. "My father hasn't filled the position I left, you know. We shan't starve."

"But you shan't be a gentleman, either," Miss Buxton sobbed.

Ah, so that was the trouble, was it? Miss Buxton did not want to marry a man who helped manage the family's cotton mills. She wanted to marry a man of leisure who lived off the income from his investments. Unfortunately, she and Benedict had not acted quickly enough to secure the prize.

George glanced sideways at Belle, curious how she was taking all this. Her face had paled, and she covered her mouth with one hand as she observed the tumultuous scene before them.

"I wonder," George suggested to his aunt, "if we could have a cup of tea. Mrs. Kirkland's nerves are rather worn after our travels, you know." They'd had time only for a short rest after arriving in Bath. He knew he'd said the right thing when Belle directed a grateful look at him.

Uncle William looked frankly relieved to have an excuse for abandoning his fruitless attempt to comfort Miss Buxton. "Of course, of course. You are staying to dine, naturally, too?"

"That is our intention." George glanced at Belle again, hoping for some clue as to how she felt about that.

Belle had woken up with a headache this morning, and she'd been rather out of sorts all day. She attributed this to the stress of travel, but he worried that he might have inadvertently contributed to her ill humor. One thing he'd learned over the last few days was that eating, traveling, and sleeping with a single person nearly twenty-four hours a day was quite different from being a guest in the same house with her. Marriage might be harder than he'd expected.

"I would be delighted to dine here, Mr. Kirkland. Thank you for the invitation."

Belle spoke politely, but the stiffness in her voice suggested her head still pounded. They might do better to dine privately at their hotel. But it would be terribly awkward to change their plans immediately after accepting Uncle William's invitation.

"We will probably not be able to linger after dinner," George warned.

"But aren't you going to stay here tonight?" Uncle William's face fell. "I could have the yellow room made up for you in a trice."

"Oh, there's no need to impose on you," George said hastily. "We've secured comfortable lodgings for our stay."

He very nearly made a joke about honeymooning couples preferring their privacy, but he remembered at the last second that Belle would be mortified if he said any such thing. On some issues, she remained shy even with George. They'd shared a bed every night since their marriage, but she still preferred to undress under the cover of darkness.

In any case, there were other reasons for not staying with Uncle William. A visit could not be anything but awkward if Benedict and his fiancée were also guests. As it was, their presence made dinner a tense affair. Miss Buxton ceased her tears, but her eyes remained bloodshot. From time to time, George heard her softly sniffle.

Throughout the meal, Benedict ignored George and Arabella entirely, speaking only to his fiancée, Uncle William, and Aunt Betsy. At first, George was surprised to hear his cousin conversing so amicably with Uncle William even after the latter made it crystal clear that Dogwood Cottage would be signed over to George. Then it occurred to him that Benedict might be hoping to wheedle money or some other piece of property out of their uncle. Benedict could not afford to alienate the wealthiest member of the family.

George did not mind being snubbed by his cousin, but it irked him that both Miss Buxton and Benedict snubbed Belle, too. As a new-married bride, Belle should have been treated as the guest of honor rather than being left to sit in silence for most of the meal. At first, Belle tried to talk across the table to Miss Buxton, but after a handful of laconic answers, she gave up. By the end of the evening, she kept her eyes focused on her plate, speaking only when Uncle William addressed her.

If it had been up to him, George would have departed as soon as the meal ended. But Belle assured him she would not mind if he lingered in the dining room to have a glass of port.

"For I know that you rarely get to see your uncle," she explained.

George watched with anxious eyes as his new wife left the room, trailing behind Miss Buxton and Aunt Betsy. Then he turned towards Uncle William. "I really cannot stay long," he said firmly. "We both of us need rest."

"But you will dine here again tomorrow night, won't you?" Uncle William wheedled. "I am sure you are eager to settle into your new home, but Betsy and I would love to see you again before you go."

"Of course. We plan to spend a little time in Bath." After traveling for days to get here, George was not particularly eager to hop into another post chaise and travel north again. He had done enough traveling over the last few weeks, thank you very much!

"Don't stay away for too long, though," Uncle William advised. "The house needs someone looking after it."

George blinked. "Isn't there a couple living there who look after it?" He could've sworn he'd heard Uncle William say something about a housekeeper and a manservant who kept the place in order.

Uncle William waved that objection away. "Yes, of course. Mr. and Mrs. Hastings. They've done a fine job. But they're not quite up to coping with all the village children who show up looking the treasure."

George, caught in the middle of an overly large sip of port, nearly choked. He put his cup down and hastily covered his mouth with a napkin. "*Again?*"

"Damn kids won't leave the place alone!" his uncle grumbled. Then he paused and shot George an uncertain look. "Pardon my language, lad. But this time, whoever broke in started chipping away at the kitchen walls, as if they thought there was a secret room hidden behind the plaster!"

"*Is* there a secret room hidden behind the plaster? Could that be where the treasure is?" Benedict leaned forward, his face alight with curiosity—or maybe greed.

"Pfft!" Uncle William dismissed the idea with a shake of his head. "Of course not! How many times do I have to tell you boys, there's no treasure there!"

"There's a hidden closet under the staircase," George pointed out. "But I've never seen any treasure in it." More like broken battledore rackets, a pall-mall set with only half the mallets, empty baskets and crates, and other odds and ends.

"Yes, that's the closest thing to a hidden room the cottage contains," Uncle William agreed. "And I assure you, there's nothing of any value in that closet. Not unless Mrs. Hastings has taken to hiding the plate there!" He chuckled at his own joke, though no one else laughed. "People have been looking for treasure in that house for centuries. If it were really there, it would've been found long ago."

Benedict sighed and looked down into his empty wineglass. "But imagine if there *were* treasure—"

Uncle William interrupted before Benedict could get any further. "If there really is a treasure, I hope to God someone finds it soon, because I've had enough of people making a mess of the place looking for it." He shifted his eyes towards George, and his face relaxed into a loose grin. "Of course, it's no longer my problem. I'll sign the papers making the cottage over to you tonight, George. From now on, *you'll* be the one worrying about treasure seekers!"

"Marvelous." George poured himself another glass of port. He suspected he was going to need it.

Chapter Twelve

July 1817

L AST SUMMER HAD been unseasonably cool, but more typical weather patterns returned this year, and the month of July was as torrid as ever. By the time the borrowed carriage rolled off the high road towards Pendleford, Arabella felt absolutely miserable. She'd felt thirsty for what seemed like hours, and longed for a cup of cool water or iced lemonade. Or even a handful of tepid pond water, she'd grown too parched to be choosy.

Though the carriage roof shielded the travelers from the rays of the sun, the cabin also blocked out most of the breeze. Even with the windows opened, the inside of the carriage felt like an oven. Sweat trickled down Arabella's back, making her chemise cling to her and causing itching in the most impossible-to-reach places. The heat drove her frantic with discomfort, but all she could do to combat it was fan herself and pray the torture ended soon.

She glanced out the window at the Pendle Water. The opposite bank was lined with trees, and the shaded stretches of the river looked particularly inviting. What would happen if Arabella stopped the carriage, bolted outside, and threw herself into the river? She swallowed, imagining how cool the cool water would feel. Would it really be so terrible to jump in if no one saw her do it?

"Almost there!" George interrupted her fantasy of cool water by affectionately resting his hand over hers. The gesture would have been comforting if she hadn't been sweltering. Instead, the warmth of his hand added a new, unwanted layer of discomfort.

Don't touch me! Arabella bit her lip to keep from snapping at her new husband. But she must not have adequately hidden her distress, because George removed his hand and turned his face to look out the window.

Had she hurt his feelings? Probably. But right now, she felt too miserable to try making amends. She turned her head to stare out her window again. She at least had a good view of the river limpidly flowing between high banks. George only had green fields to observe. Given how much traveling up and down the country he'd done over the last few weeks, she doubted he found that view interesting.

"Ah! There it is!" George said eagerly.

"Where?" All Arabella could see were trees. Once they reached the end of the field, an orchard began. But the coach horses jogged along at such a slow pace that it might as well take an eternity to reach the shade of the trees.

"You can see a bit of the chimney there." George pointed in the direction of the orchard.

"Oh." He was right. A bit of red brick peeked out from between the trees. "Is there something special about the chimney?"

George chuckled. "Only that it's the chimney of our very own home!" He turned to grin at her, his eyes alight with sudden joy. "I haven't been here for years," he confided, probably for the dozenth time over the last three days. Then his smile faded. "I hope everything has been kept in order."

"I am sure the Hastings have done their job well. Your uncle would not employ them if they were incompetent." Arabella might have been able to respond to his anxiousness with more sympathy if she had not already delivered that line twice today.

"Poor Belle." George brushed a strand of hair away from her sweat-dampened forehead. "Don't take this the wrong way, but you look miserable, sweetheart."

"I *am* miserable," she admitted. "I *hate* being overheated."

"I would've thought you inherited a stronger constitution," George suggested. "I mean, your great-grandfather lived in India for decades, didn't he? Seems like if he survived the heat, you should, too."

Arabella wrinkled her nose at him. "I can only suppose that I didn't inherit my sensitivity from him. Maybe my mother's blue blood is to blame!" All the Canning wealth came from East Indian trade, but her mother's family, the Hallingstones, had the superior family background. Arabella's great-grandfather on *that* side of the family had been a baron, and her Hallingstone relatives never let anyone forget it.

"In any case, you won't always be overheated here. The breeze off the river usually keeps the gardens cooler than this," George assured her. "Today's heat is not normal for July."

"That's a relief!" Though it did nothing to assuage her discomfort now.

But the even bigger relief came when the carriage turned off the country lane onto a private drive. As the carriageway curved past a gnarled old tree, the changing view revealed a cottage garden and a large, pale, half-timbered house.

"Is that it?" She knew her question was foolish. Obviously, this must be their destination. The dogwood trees that gave the cottage its name lined both sides of the carriageway. In spring, this short drive must be breathtakingly beautiful.

"Yes! Isn't it smashing?" Geoge leaned forward, as if he could not wait to get out.

"It's bigger than I expected." To Arabella, the word "cottage" suggested a tiny, charming little house with a thatched roof. This wattle-and-daub house was certainly charming, and it did have a thatched roof, but it was much bigger than what she had pictured, falling in between the size of a large farmhouse and a small manor house.

But the front garden was everything a cottage garden should be, with vegetables and old-fashioned flowers mingled together. Pink and cream roses wended their way up a trellis near the doorway, promising a familiar sweet odor. The homely beauty of the flowers inspired Arabella's artistry for the first time that day. She woke up from her heat-induced stupefaction and began to really *see*.

I shall have to sketch this! she thought happily. A pencil sketch first, and then some experiments with colors. Arabella had little skill with a paintbrush—watercolor and oil paints never behaved quite the way she wanted—but she liked using Conté crayons. She wasn't sure crayons could capture the color and mood of the garden, but she wanted to try.

"I hope I can find my art supplies right away." She probably wouldn't have a chance to work on the sketches today, but tomorrow morning might be the perfect time to start. At least, if she could find her paper, pencils, and colors. "I hope nothing got left behind. What if. . ."

"Belle, you insisted on packing the art supplies yourself," George reminded her.

"Oh, you're right." Her body sagged with relief. Then she wrinkled her brow in confusion. "How did you know that?" George hadn't been present when she packed up the boxes that were sent ahead of them.

"How could I not remember?" he retorted. "You wouldn't stop talking about it the day after the wedding. You were worried that Jenny wouldn't remember where she put it, or that she'd pack it poorly and your clothes would get ruined." His affectionate grin removed any trace of criticism from the reminder.

Yes, that was right. She had given her maid a hard time about the packing, too. Poor Jenny! In hindsight, Arabella suspected that what had really been troubling her was the marriage itself rather than the fate of her trousseau or her art supplies. But so far, she'd found that she enjoyed married life, at least if she ignored the discomfort of so much traveling. George could be a lot of fun, both by day and by night.

"I'm glad you remembered that," she told George. With the end of their journey finally at hand, much of this afternoon's crankiness slid away, and she managed a genuine smile. "I can't wait to start drawing the house." She could send a sketch to her sister Lavinia, who was very curious about what Arabella's new life would be like. Was there by any chance a pencil in her reticule? "I don't suppose you have any paper on you . . .?"

George chuckled. "I always have paper in one pocket or another! Unfortunately, I think the pages in my notebook would be too small for sketching. And it's full of my notes, anyway."

"I suppose I shouldn't steal your notebook." She ought to have brought her sketchbook with her, instead of packing it in a trunk. When she was out of sorts, nothing helped her recover faster than taking up a pencil and doodling or sketching.

"Besides, you won't want to stand around drawing when we have exploring to do." George opened the carriage door almost before the vehicle had come to a full stop. "Come on! I want to show you the house."

"Can we begin in the parlor, with a glass of water?" she suggested hopefully.

"Whatever you need," he promised.

She expected George to offer her a hand stepping out of the carriage, but instead, he lifted her out, as if she were a child. As he let her slide to the ground, her body brushed against his. She noticed the precise moment when he registered the contact, his eyes widening and darkening. Instead of letting go of Arabella when her feet touched the ground, he wrapped his hands around her back in a loose embrace.

The flush burning in Arabella's cheeks was no longer due to the July sun alone. She hadn't expected to see *that* look in George's eyes right now. How on earth could anyone contemplate amorous congress in this heat? The mere thought turned her stomach.

She drew in a sharp breath. "I do need to rest," she said gently. "Travel wears me out."

"Of course." If George was at all disappointed by her response, he hid it well. "Let's see what refreshments Mrs. Hastings can offer us. Perhaps you'd like a moment to repair your toilette as well?"

"Yes, please." She needed a cold drink, she needed to take off this miserable walking dress and put on something lighter and cooler, and she needed to rest in a darkened room for at least an hour. Maybe after all that, she could respond to the implicit suggestion in George's eyes.

Getting that chance to rest required getting past the housekeeper, Mrs. Hastings. It transpired that Mrs. Hastings had been a young housemaid at the cottage when George was a child. She not only remembered George, but remembered a few rather disreputable stories about him, all of which she wanted to relate when she brought refreshments into the parlor.

Or ought this sitting room be called a drawing room? Whatever one called the room, it had been furnished with both elegance and a good deal of money. Arabella might have been mistaken, but she thought one of the landscape paintings on the wall was a genuine Gainsborough. Another painting—a view of the sea during a storm—looked like the work of Mr. Turner. The whole house was an artist's dream!

While Mrs. Hastings reminisced, Arabella closed her eyes and fanned herself. She had taken a chair near the open window so she could catch the full effect of the light breeze wending its way into the room. She would not exactly use the word "cool" to describe the room, but it was a considerable improvement over the stuffy carriage.

George gently interrupted before the housekeeper could begin another story. "I am very sorry, Mrs. Hastings, but I am afraid Mrs. Kirkland is not in any condition for a chat at the moment. She requires rest."

A grateful smile lifted the corners of Arabella's mouth, and she opened her eyes. "My husband is right. The journey here has quite exhausted me. I would be all the better for a chance to rest."

"You poor dear!"

To Arabella's horror, Mrs. Hastings affectionately patted her on the shoulder, as if they were long and very close friends rather than having only just met. It took the greatest willpower to keep from physically recoiling from the unwanted touch. Fortunately, Mrs. Hastings didn't seem to notice the negative reaction at all. Even more fortunately, when she bustled back into the room with a glass of water, she contented herself with merely handing the glass to Arabella and leaving.

By the time she'd finished her drink, Arabella felt approximately forty percent recovered. She put the glass down on the tea table and sighed. Her skin still itched in half a dozen places, and she felt sticky and grubby. For a moment, she toyed with the idea of asking for a bath. But that would make extra work for the housemaid. Besides, getting into a tub of hot water did not appeal at the moment.

"I had thought to take you on a tour of the house and garden, but perhaps I had better simply show you to your bedchamber?" George suggested. "So you can rest?"

"Yes, please," she promptly replied. "I do want to see the place, but I need. . ." She hesitated, "rest" was not exactly the right word for what she required. Sometimes when she retreated to her room, she napped. More often, she simply needed time alone in a quiet, comfortable, familiar space. It would not be possible to find a familiar space in this strange building, not yet. But she hoped for quiet and comfort. "I need a chance to collect myself," she concluded.

"You shall have whatever you need," George assured her. He offered her a hand getting up from her chair, then led her up a steep, narrow flight of stairs. "You must watch the steps at night. It is easy to stumble. My Aunt Helena once broke her leg coming down in the dark."

"Watch the steps at night," Arabella repeated. She seemed to be losing the capacity for complicated thought. Once she began moving, she realized how very tired she really was. Just hauling herself up the staircase seemed almost more than she could manage.

Fortunately, she did not have to go far to reach sanctuary. George led her to the door nearest the staircase. He flung the door open, revealing a room papered with a pattern of blue tree branches and yellow birds. Arabella squinted at the birds, trying to figure out what they were. Chaffinches, she thought. The yellow color wasn't even remotely realistic, but she could not deny that it made a pleasing pattern.

"How pretty." The words were decidedly inadequate to describe the room, but Arabella could not articulate her opinion more clearly.

"My Aunt Helena decorated this room," George explained. "She liked bright, cheerful colors."

"This was her room, then?" Arabella guessed. The pretty paper suited a lady's bedchamber.

"She shared it with my uncle." George spoke matter-of-factly, probably with no idea of how his words affected Arabella.

She cast her eyes about the room again, slowly taking in more details. A sawtooth quilt, thick white stripes alternating with yellow, covered the bed. The quilt had been pulled back to reveal crisp, white sheets and thick pillows. Two pillows, for two people. This was not, as Arabella had initially thought, a lady's bedchamber, but a room for a married couple to share.

I don't even have a room of my own? After a long, exhausting day, this was the final straw. She blinked her eyes quickly, hoping to prevent open tears. But she could not hide her distress from George.

"Belle?"

For some reason, the gentle concern in George's voice tipped her over the breaking point. Her shoulders began to shake, her throat tightened, and she clapped her hands over her mouth in an attempt to hold back undignified sobs. She hated revealing such weakness in front of her new husband, but she could not seem to control the distress welling up.

"What's wrong?" George slipped one arm around her waist and drew her into an embrace.

For a moment, she resisted. She was not a cranky toddler whose distress could be hugged away. On the other hand, in a setting where everything looked strange and new, George was a familiar face—and a familiar voice, scent, and touch. At this moment, when her body and her heart both seemed out of control, she needed that.

So she buried her face against his shoulder, breathed in his familiar scent, and let him comfort her as she wept.

Chapter Thirteen

GEORGE'S FRIEND POTTER, who had five older sisters, liked to say that women were incomprehensible. He used this theory to explain everything from the vagaries of fashion, to the scandals in the society pages, to improbable plot elements in the works of lady novelists. George had never concurred with Potter. In his experience, the women in his life—his mother, sister, cousins, and friends—all made about as much sense as the men. Which was to say, not that much. Other people's thoughts and motives often *were* unintelligible to George, but their opacity had nothing to do with gender.

But as he held his weeping bride, George reconsidered his earlier stance. He had no idea why Belle was crying. Having seen how much travel exhausted her, he'd expected her to be happy, or at least relieved, that they had reached their journey's end. He'd hoped she would be pleased with this house. He knew that he saw Dogwood Cottage through nostalgia-colored lenses, but surely it wasn't as bad as all this?

He studied the room, trying to see it through Belle's eyes. Everything about it looked clean, tidy, and in good condition. The only flaw he could see was that the wallpaper was a couple of decades old. Personally, *he* thought it still looked charming, but perhaps his wife would prefer something more modern? Brides often did like to redecorate a house when they married. He'd forgotten that.

George sighed as he wondered how much it would cost to repaper some of the important rooms. The dining room and parlor retained the paneled walls of days of yore, but surely that could be changed if necessary.

Belle drew away from him and wiped her eyes with the back of her hand. By now, George had learned that he needed to keep more than one clean handkerchief in his pockets. He pulled the first one out, intending to wipe Belle's eyes. But she took it away from him and wiped her face herself.

He cleared his throat. "I hope you understand that we can afford to replace the furnishings in here if the chamber is not to your liking. I know the paper on the walls is old-fashioned, but—"

"What?" Belle stared at him with wide eyes. "I love that design, and the colors! I have no desire to change it." Her eyes roved about the room again. "The whole room is quite charming. Your aunt had good taste."

He heard an implicit "but" following that praise. He waited for her to explain her objection, but she only lowered her gaze, staring at the toes of her half boots. He cautiously cupped her face in one hand, afraid that she would pull away from him again. Instead, she leaned her head against his hand and sighed very softly.

"Can you explain to me what's wrong, then?" George might not be a particularly observant man, but it did not take much perspicuity to see that *something* had upset his wife.

"I am merely tired out from travel," she murmured. "You know how delicate my nerves are, don't you?"

George might have believed her if she'd said that while looking him in the eye. But the way Belle kept her eyes fixed on the floor suggested she was keeping something from him.

"Is that really the only problem?" He didn't want to push too hard, but he felt certain this was more complicated than mere exhaustion.

"The thing is. . . what I mean to say is… the fact of the matter…" Belle twisted her hands together as she stammered over her answer. "The fact of the matter is that I am used to having my own chamber. To go when I need time alone, I mean."

George drew his brows down. "Your own chamber?" It took a ridiculously long time to make sense of that. "Oh! You wanted your own bedroom?" That would never have occurred to him. His parents shared a bedroom, of course, the vicarage was much too small to have separate rooms for the vicar and his wife. "If you prefer, I can move to one of the other bedrooms, and leave this one for you. Or I can put a bed in the dressing room."

He walked across the room and opened the door into the dressing room. "See? There's plenty of room." He stepped aside, giving her space to take a look. The dressing room was at least as large as most servant's bedrooms, though it was narrower than it was long. A rather worn-looking *chaise longues* lined the longest wall, and there was a comfortable chair in front of the dressing table, but apart from that, the room had been furnished with utility in mind.

Open storage shelves and a narrow closet had been built into the shortest inside wall, and there was a window seat with storage beneath it along the outside wall. An old-fashioned close stool had been tucked into one corner, though Uncle William's updates to the cottage included a modern water closet downstairs. Perhaps most surprisingly, the room contained a small fireplace that shared a chimney with the adjoining bedroom.

"I could sleep here if you prefer," he suggested.

Belle peered through the doorway. She twirled a strand of hair around her index finger as she studied the room. "I could see myself using this room. That window seat might be a good place for reading or drawing. And one could write letters at the dressing table."

"I suppose so," George said doubtfully. He preferred to do his writing in a room large enough to pace in. Sometimes he could only get his mind working properly by walking back and forth, much to the annoyance of the gentleman who lived in the flat below his London chambers. "If you like, we can replace the *chaise longues* with a proper daybed." He looked askance at her, wishing he knew what, precisely, she was thinking. "That way, you could sleep alone when you wanted."

"Oh, it's not so much the nighttime that's the problem," Belle clarified, "but rather the daytime hours." Belle drew a deep breath and gave a final tug to that poor abused strand of hair. "Sometimes I need to be alone. I don't know why, but I need a quiet space where no one will interrupt me. For when I'm working on my art, or when I need to . . . collect myself."

"Ah!" George finally got it—at least some of it. He didn't understand what she meant by "collecting herself," but the rest of it made sense. "I can't work when people interrupt me, either. I snap at people if they bother me." Especially when he was working on one of his secret projects!

"Good to know." A tiny smile briefly lit Belle's face, like a stray sunbeam breaking through gray clouds.

Seeing that promise of sunshine, George breathed more easily. "This house is not big enough to have a private sitting room for its mistress, but you are welcome to furnish one of the other bedrooms as your work room. Or you could have the study downstairs, and I could take this room—"

"No. Let me have this room, if you please." She walked past him to peer out the window. "This window faces north, so it would provide good light. And I like the window seat. It would be a comfortable place to curl up with a book, a cup of tea, and a plate of biscuits." This time, the smile that crossed her face lingered longer.

George wrinkled his nose. "When I eat biscuits at my desk, I end up getting crumbs everywhere! On the papers. On the floor. Even in the inkwell." His charwoman had often expressed her distaste for his snacking habits.

Belle glanced back over her shoulder, looking on the verge of laughter. "How do you even get crumbs in an inkwell?"

"It's a gift." He shrugged his shoulders and tried to look modest. "But if you want to use this room for your work, you are welcome to it. I can move a wardrobe into the bedchamber for my clothes." He did not have as many clothes as she did, anyway. "Would you like to see the rest of the house, or should I leave you here to recover from the journey?"

"I had rather have some time to myself, thank you." She spoke as formally as if they were strangers. Another time, that might have annoyed him, but just now, he found it endearing.

"I shall leave you to it, then." He stepped forward, intending to kiss her on the cheek, but she flinched. It was so slight a movement that he might have missed it if he had not already been concerned.

George drew back immediately and a puzzled furrow formed between his eyebrows. He opened his mouth to ask what was wrong, but then he thought better of it. His wife had already made it clear that she needed to be left alone. He ought to do as she asked. So he turned and walked away, though a niggling voice at the back of his head wondered if he had done something to displease her. They were still in their honeymoon. What would he do if she took a dislike to him so soon?

He worried about that all the way down the stairs, but when he got to the ground floor corridor, a delicious smell diverted his attention to the kitchen. As children, both he and his sister had been quite at home in this room. Caro had often "helped" Cook with the baking. George had limited his work to taste testing. The kitchen had changed little in the intervening years.

He found Mrs. Hastings seasoning a chicken in preparation for roasting it. The good smell he'd detected came from the bread oven, where a cake of some sort was currently baking.

"Is that a seed cake?" he asked hopefully.

"Currant cake," Mrs. Hastings said. "But I daresay you'll like it, Mr. Kirkland." The smile on her face slowly faded into a frown. "I really must ask you to stay out of the kitchen while we are working, sir. We don't want you getting hurt."

And they probably didn't want him getting in their way,

George reasoned. Fair enough! He wouldn't like it at all if Mrs. Hastings or one of the maids wandered into his study while he was writing.

He turned to go, then paused to stare at the wall surrounding the bread oven. "What on earth happened to the plaster?" A series of deep holes, spaced at roughly equidistant intervals, ranged more than halfway up the wall.

"Near as we can tell, someone poked a bunch of holes into the plaster, hoping to find something hidden behind the wall." Mrs. Hastings wiped her forehead and scowled at the wall. "Don't have any idea how they got into the house without breaking any windows or unlocking any doors."

George gaped as he stared at the wall. This must be the damage Uncle William had mentioned, but it was worse than what he'd imagined.

"It's lucky they didn't bring the whole wall down!" He shook his head, awed by the lengths someone had gone to in attempt to find treasure that did not exist. "How did they get away with this? Was everyone out of the house?" He could not imagine why the servants would be away all at once, unless perhaps to attend church.

Mrs. Hastings shook her head. "We were sound asleep upstairs and didn't hear a peep!" Unexpectedly, she chuckled. "I suppose if I can sleep through Ezra's snoring, I can sleep through anything, so perhaps I ought not be surprised."

"Ah." George glanced up at the exposed ceiling beams, as if he expected to see all the way to the attic rooms the servants occupied.

"But you need not worry, Mr. Kirkland. We're taking precautions now."

"Oh? What kind of precautions?" Did she force Mr. Hastings to sleep in the kitchen so his snoring would frighten away treasure seekers?

His guess proved disturbingly close to the truth.

"Young Peggy there beds down under the kitchen table."

Mrs. Hastings jerked her chin in the direction of the kitchen maid busily chopping onions. "She's a light sleeper. If anyone starts pounding on the walls, she'll hear."

"'Deed I would, sir." Peggy looked up from her work and grinned at George, displaying crooked front teeth. "At home, my ma always said I could be woken by a kitten's sneeze."

"Let us hope there are no sniffling kittens about the place." A frown formed on George's face as he studied the hard paving stones beneath his feet. "Isn't it rather an uncomfortable place to sleep, though?"

"I s'pose so," Peggy agreed. "But there's folks what don't have a roof over their head, aren't there? So I can't complain."

"I see." Privately, George thought she had plenty of grounds for complaint. The existence of less fortunate people did not make her suffering more tolerable. There must be a better way to secure the kitchen from intruders! "I think we must add a bolt to that door," he decided. "The lock is clearly not enough."

"Aye, that's a good plan," Mrs. Hastings agreed. "We can't have riffraff breaking in now that the family's back." She pronounced the phrase "the family" with a distinct note of pride.

Did it make so much of a difference to have the cottage occupied? George did not quite understand why. The Hastings lived here year-round, regardless of whether any Kirklands occupied the cottage. Their safety ought to matter just as much as George and Arabella's. Though, naturally, he did not want to put his wife at any risk.

"I will think on the problem," he promised Mrs. Hastings. "There must be other security measures we can take." It ought not be so easy for anyone to wander into the house and chip away at the walls! Such destruction ought to be reserved for the youngsters of the Kirkland family.

George found himself grinning as he remembered some of the trouble he and Caro had gotten into back when they were young. He had not realized it at the time, but Aunt Helena must have been a saint to tolerate their hijinks as she did. Some years,

Vincent and his sisters had visited too, and the house rang with children's voices from morning to night. Uncle William had occasionally grumbled about the noise, but Aunt Helena rarely lost her smile. George supposed she must have loved her nieces and nephews all the more because she had no children of her own.

His grin faded as he looked back over Aunt Helena's life and wondered if she'd been lonely. She'd always had rather poor health, at least as long as he could remember, and Uncle William believed that living in the country was better for her than living next to his factory. But that meant she spent many long days alone, often seeing her husband only on the weekends. No wonder she had been so happy to have guests staying for extended visits!

Well, there might be children disrupting the quiet cottage soon enough. If nothing else, George hoped to persuade Caroline to visit once she was past the worst of her morning sickness. Having Charlie about would certainly liven up the place! Perhaps someday there would be other young Kirklands in the cottage, undoubtedly making a mess as they tried to catch the family ghost or find the legendary treasure. He could only hope.

Chapter Fourteen

ARABELLA WAS RIGHT about the garden being the perfect place to sketch. In the days immediately after their arrival, she sketched the house from two different angles, and drew a rough picture of the barn and the pasture occupied by a single elderly dairy cow. She planned to begin creating some crayon landscapes, too, but she wanted to wait until she'd figured out the best views.

A week after they moved in, the weather changed. At first, Arabella welcomed the cooler breeze that chased away the oppressive heat. When storm clouds rolled in, though, she lost some of her enthusiasm. She had planned to spend a day outside, reading under the shade of a tree. Instead, she stood in the parlor and stared out the window, watching the rain fall in wind-driven sheets.

Normally, she liked storms. There was a special pleasure in curling up in a well-cushioned armchair and listening to the wind howl. Today, though, she felt restless, unable to sit down to either read a book or write a letter.

Maybe she did not have the right book. Dogwood Cottage did not contain a library. Apparently, William Kirkland had never been much of a reader. His wife had left behind only a handful of old-fashioned novels, all of which Belle had read before. But one of George's London friends had crated up his small library and all his papers. The crates had been delivered yesterday. As a literary man, George seemed to hear about new novels before anyone else. He might have something Belle hadn't read.

Arabella and George had a tacit agreement not to interrupt each other when they were working, but since all of George's new books were in his study, he could hardly blame her for poking about the room a bit. She didn't need to talk to him. She just wanted to rummage around his bookshelves. Surely, he wouldn't mind that?

She half-expected to find George pacing back and forth in the study, since that seemed to be his usual mode of operation, but today he sat at his desk, his quill scratching quickly across a piece of paper. He did not look up from his work when she walked in, so she left him alone and went straight to the bookshelves lining one wall.

To her disappointment, she found only the same old volumes she'd already perused. She had absolutely no desire to read bound copies of old Spectator letters. Nor did she want to reread *Sir Charles Grandison*. Reading that once had been enough, thank you!

"George, haven't you unpacked the books Mr. Potter sent you?" She glanced over her shoulder. George still sat at the desk, frantically writing as if he were in a race against the clock. He did not answer her.

"George?" she prompted. "What happened to the crate of books from London?"

"Mm?" He did not even look up from his work, though he'd clearly heard her. "What's that?"

"What happened to the books your friend Potter sent you from London?" she repeated, a little less patiently.

"Oh!" He pointed with the quill. "Over in the corner, near the fireplace."

Arabella walked around the desk and found two heavy crates full of books resting on an even heavier wooden trunk. Someone had pried the lids off both crates, but George had not even begun unpacking them.

She knelt on the floor and peered into the first crate. To her delight, it was full of books. Thick reference books and slim volumes of poetry mingled with three-volume novels and essay collections. Arabella had never read any of the novels, and she happily spent a few minutes investigating them.

"Do you recommend any of these?" She could not decide between *Rosalind, or The Lady of the Forest,* or *Hunting the White Hart.* She had heard of neither book.

Once again, George completely ignored her. When she glanced back at him, she saw his head still bent over his writing as he dipped his pen in the inkwell. *Are there biscuit crumbs in there yet?* she wondered.

No longer amused by his inattention, she tried raising her voice. "George!"

"What the devil?" He tossed his quill pen aside and glared so fiercely that Arabella quailed under his gaze. "Is there something you need?" A lock of nut-brown hair fell in front of his eyes, and he impatiently brushed it aside, leaving a streak of ink on his forehead.

Arabella tapped her own forehead. "You have ink on—"

"I know I'm probably covered in ink," he snapped. "I usually am when I write. But there is no need to interrupt me just to tell me that. There will be time enough to clean up when I'm done working for the day." He lowered his eyes to the paper in front of him and resumed writing.

Arabella gulped. "My apologies." She glanced down at the box of books. Clearly, this was not the time to ask him about these novels. He would not appreciate her questions. Anxious to leave the study, she grabbed the first book at random. "I will leave you be now," she promised.

Once again, George did not answer her, nor even glance up from his work. It was as if he had not heard her.

She snuck off to her tiny sitting room, reminding herself that she ought not be hurt by the brush-off. George had warned her that he did not like being disturbed. Very likely, he had a looming due date for whatever article or review he was currently working on. She ought to give him space to work as she understood the need for solitude. She would not like being disturbed while at work on her art.

Still, she had not expected to be snapped at so fiercely. At least not by George, who usually treated her with gentleness. Was this how he would treat her now that the honeymoon was over? She sighed, then tried to push the incident out of her mind. She settled down in the window seat and looked at the book she'd chosen.

It turned out that she'd grabbed the first volume of *Rosalind*. She began reading, hoping the story would distract her from her bruised feelings. The novel's title led her to speculate that it might be in some way inspired by Shakespeare's *As You Like It*. It had been years since she'd read that play, but she remembered liking it.

Instead, *Rosalind* turned out to be a comedy of manners about a spoiled wealthy young lady, the daughter of an earl, who disliked the wealthy scion of a merchant house whom her parents wanted her to marry. After only a few chapters, Arabella felt certain she could accurately predict the whole plot. Rosalind (the titular spoiled aristocrat) would discover that her first impressions of the young merchant heir were wrong, and she would end up falling in love with him. Not a particularly original story! The author had a gift for spinning a pretty phrase, but that was not enough to keep Arabella reading.

Eventually, she decided she'd had enough. She set the book aside, wrapped her arms around her knees, and watched the falling rain. The wind had not died down. On the contrary, it gusted and howled as it swept around the corners of the house. She hoped none of the trees would be toppled. It looked as if the dogwoods had not been properly pruned in years. But she was no arboreal expert, and she might have been mistaken.

Enough of this! She ought not let the gloomy weather affect her mood. She pulled out a piece of stationery and began a letter to Lavinia, one full of details about her new home and the drawings she had been working on. She said nothing about the lack of good reading material or about George's bad temper. None of that signified in the least!

At the dinner table that night, George apologized for answering her so brusquely. "But you know, Belle, it would be best if you refrained from disturbing me while I'm working. Once something throws me off the track of an idea, it's hard to find the scent again. That's why I hate interruptions."

"I know," she assured him. "I am sorry. You did warn me ahead of time. I shan't interrupt you again unless it is really important. I only wanted to ask if I might borrow one of your books. I haven't anything to read."

He smiled across the table at her. "Of course! You may read any of my books, so long as I don't need them for an article or a review. When we married, I promised to endow you with all my worldly goods, didn't I? That must include my library."

"I suppose it does." The smile that flitted across her face had as much to do with George's improved temper as with the prospect of raiding his library. "Is there anything you might particularly recommend? Any novel, I mean?" She had nothing against poetry or books of information, but they did not grip her the way a good story did.

"Hmm." He took a sip of wine while he considered her question. "Have you read any of Alec MacPherson's novels? I quite enjoyed those."

The name sounded familiar, but it still took a moment for her to place it. "He wrote *Rosalind, or the Lady in the Forest*, didn't he? I started reading that—" she began.

George interrupted her. "Splendid! That is his most recent novel, and probably his best work. At least, that's what some of the reviewers have said." He smiled broadly.

"Really?" She wrinkled her nose doubtfully. "I must say I was disappointed in the chapters I read. But perhaps it gets better later."

His face fell. "Disappointed? How so?"

She nibbled on her lower lip as she tried to think through how to explain her disappointment. "The plot seemed unoriginal. It was as if *Pride and Prejudice* were combined with *Joseph Andrews*. Not that Lady Rosalind tries to seduce Harold, of course," she quickly corrected, "but there is a similar theme of love across social orders."

A frown darkened George's face. "I had not noticed that." He spoke stiffly, almost as if he were offended. "You may be right about the plot being derivative. That is, I believe some of the book reviews said much the same. But I quite liked the comic touches. The character of Lady Jareth, for example, was well done. Or so I thought." He looked at her uncertainly.

Arabella thought about that for a moment, then shook her head. "She amused me a little, yes, but she seems like a copy of Mrs. Jennings, from *Sense and Sensibility*. I think this Mr. Mac-Pherson must fancy himself as good as the 'lady' who wrote *Sense and Sensibility* and *Pride and Prejudice*. But he is not. He is not good enough to tie her bootlaces!"

George abruptly began coughing, and his face turned a strange shade of red.

"Are you choking?" Arabella rose out of her seat, ready to pound him on the back until he spat out whatever clogged his throat. But George shook his head, covered his mouth, and coughed something into his napkin. She sat back down, relieved.

"Must've swallowed too big of a bite," George rasped. "I shall be all right in a trice." He drained the last of his wine, then dabbed at his mouth with the napkin. "So, you were not impressed by Mr. MacPherson's writing. Shame. He happens to be one of my favorite writers. But no matter." Oddly, he kept his eyes focused on his plate rather than looking at Arabella as he spoke. And he stabbed at his food with unnecessarily violence.

"*De gustibus non disputandum est.*" There was no accounting for matters of taste, as Sir Michael was fond of saying whenever anyone argued about the merits of a carriage horse, a play, or a pudding. "We need not like the same novels merely because we are married," Arabella pointed out. There were bound to be many issues on which she and George disagreed. They had different personalities, after all.

"Quite right!" George lifted his chin, met her gaze, and smiled with his mouth, but not with his eyes.

Arabella frowned, feeling puzzled. She had favorite authors, favorite pieces of music, and favorite foods, just like everyone else. But she would not feel hurt by finding out that a friend did not share her interests. She was, in fact, quite used to people being less interested in things than she was. No one ever wanted to talk about colors and patterns as much as she did. And she couldn't remember George reacting this way in any of their other discussions of literature. He must really love MacPherson's novels, though she could not see why.

Perhaps George would appreciate the chance to talk about his favorites. "Tell me what you like about Alec MacPherson's novels," she suggested. "I would like to know more about your taste in books."

George shrugged. He continued to avoid eye contact. "I don't know that there is much to say. As you point out, people like different things. I happen to like the novels, that's all. I thought perhaps you would, too." He refilled his wineglass. Then he brightened. "I thought MacPherson did rather a good job writing women." He caught her eye and smiled hopefully.

Arabella furrowed her brow. "Really? Rosalind did not seem nearly as well rounded a character as the ones written by many lady novelists, or even by Sir Walter Scott. She wasn't consistently written, either. One minute Rosalind is haughty and rude, and the next she is sympathetic and kind. Her mood seems to change as the plot demands."

George scowled down at his plate. "As you said, there is no disputing over matters of taste. We should simply leave it at that." His voice carried an uncharacteristic edge. He sounded not merely hurt, but angry.

As she stared at him, her hand slowly crept up to take hold of one of her curls. She wound the strand of hair around one finger as if she were winding up a ball of yarn. She could tell she'd upset her husband, but she didn't understand why. And she had no idea what she ought to say. How did one mend such a situation?

George took a bite of his roast beef, then caught her eye and smiled wryly. "You needn't look so guilty, Belle. You said nothing wrong. I suppose I am rather sensitive about. . . my favorites. My literary favorites, I mean. For the future we will know better than to talk about MacPherson's writing."

They fell silent for a moment, then George waved a fork at one of the serving bowls. "Have you tried this cucumber salad? All the vegetables are from our own garden! Isn't that marvelous?" This time, the smile on his face looked genuine.

Arabella forced her stiff face to return his smile. She unwound the tangled strand of hair from her finger, picked up her fork, and dutifully tried the salad. But she could think of little to say for the rest of the meal.

When George cautiously suggested that he might go back to the study and see if he could get a little more work done before bed, she readily agreed. He might insist that Arabella had done nothing wrong, but she knew her words had upset him. She could not help feeling vaguely guilty for that. Besides, if it wasn't safe to talk about books with her husband, what *could* they talk about?

Marriage, she realized, was going to be more difficult than she had expected.

Chapter Fifteen

G EORGE STARED BLANKLY at the manuscript in front of him. His scrawling handwriting filled each page, ending halfway down the paper on the fiftieth page. When he wrote so quickly, other people struggled to read his handwriting. Fortunately, Mr. Sherman, of Sherman and Peabody Publishing, found it reasonably legible. Reasonably. He still sometimes frantically called George into the office to ask what in God's name he'd meant by one of the scribbles.

How was Sherman going to do that now that George no longer lived in London? It was a question George had been evading for the last two weeks. Every time he tried to confront the reality of how his working life would have to change, he ran away from the problem by finding some less knotty intellectual tangle to unravel in its place.

Today, he distracted himself by once again wondering what on earth Belle meant when she said the work he published under his MacPherson *nom de plume* was derivative. Derivative? What did that even mean? All writers drew on the stories and tropes of the past. Even Shakespeare had taken most of his plots from other sources, and no one ever called *him* unoriginal, did they?

I'd like to see her do better! Though George sometimes had the habit of talking out loud while he thought, he kept this particular complaint to himself. After all, he no longer lived alone. He had already spoken to the serving staff about staying out of the study, but at any minute, Belle might take it into her head to come looking for him there. She was the mistress of the house, so he couldn't order her to never enter the room.

Or could he? For one fanciful moment, George toyed with the idea of putting a "No Girls Allowed" sign on the door. But he was no longer a schoolboy trying to avoid an annoying younger sibling. He was a grown man, and his wife was (fortunately) significantly less annoying than his little sister. Since he and Belle were both adults, he should simply ask her to stay out of the study. It should not be hard to make himself clear on that point. Belle already seemed to understand about the need for solitude. Though not, perhaps, about the pain of being interrupted.

Pleased to have resolved the question, George got up from his desk and stretched. He had been sitting for hours—or at least what seemed like hours—and he could stand it no longer. He needed to move more! It could not be good to spend all his time in a single stuffy room, crammed into an uncomfortable wooden chair.

In his old Grub Street life, he would have walked everywhere. Nearly every day he spent in London, rain or shine, involved walking to the nearest street vendor, the local pub, the circulating library, his publisher's office, or, in the not-too-distant past, Priscilla Brooke's bakery and her living quarters above the shop. Once he had been quite at home there.

The thought of Priscilla called up a host of sensory memories: the smell of fresh-baked pies, the taste of iced tea cakes, the prickle of a stiff-backed horsehair sofa, and the rustle of freshly aired sheets. George quickly shoved the latter memory out of his mind. Now that he was married, thinking about Priscilla felt disloyal. That *affaire* was in the past, and he had no cause to think of Priscilla at all. Belle need never know about any of *that*.

George strode more quickly down the short corridor to the back door. No one used this entrance, so far as he could tell. Tradesmen and deliveries came to the kitchen door on the side of the house, not this door. But this was the fastest way to the orchard, and the orchard was the best place for a ramble on a hot July afternoon. The country lane that ran parallel to the river could also be a pleasant place for a walk, but some parts of the lane lacked shade at this hour. The orchard would be cooler.

Once he reached the orchard, George slowed down to enjoy his surroundings. Here, summer light danced with tree shadows. Now and again a bird chirped lazily. This part of the orchard abutted the pasture, so he could smell hot grass and the occasional whiff of cow manure. He walked down one row, then up the next, but too soon he came to the last row. He still had no idea what ought to happen next in the novel he was supposed to be drafting.

He stood at the end of the orchard, wavering. He was of half a mind to go for a longer walk along the river. But could he justify leaving his work for so long in the middle of the day? If Belle noticed his absence, she would ask questions. He preferred not to have to talk about his current writing project if he could avoid it. After hearing her criticisms of *Rosalind*, he wanted to conceal his *nom de plume*, at least for now.

Someday, after he'd earned fame and fortune with his writing, he would reveal the truth to his wife. She would be proud and happy and apologize for ever having doubted "Alec MacPherson's" abilities. George strode up and down the orchard paths a second time, imagining how much Belle would regret her criticism when he finally achieved literary fame. But, given how slowly his writing had been going lately, he might have a very long wait before he could reveal his secret.

No one in his family knew that George wrote novels as well as book reviews and essays. Given his father's dislike for fiction, George could not admit to this side of his literary career, even though it was the kind of writing he liked best. Mr. Kirkland thought it was bad enough that George wasted his abilities merely reviewing novels. He would have been horrified to learn that his son wrote his own novels, too.

George's mother had always been a little more liberal on the subject of imaginative literature. She allowed her children to read Mother Goose rhymes and books of nursery tales as well as more devotional works. But she rarely read novels, in deference to her husband's opinion. She, too, would be dismayed rather than pleased if she ever learned that her son wrote fiction. Caro would not have disapproved of George writing novels, but he didn't trust her to keep it a secret. In his experience, anything confided to one family member eventually reached all the others, too.

On the other hand, the Canning family read novels and loved them. In fact, George used to borrow books from Oliphant Hall, sneaking *Robinson Crusoe* or *Gulliver's Travels* into his room and hiding them under his mattress like contraband. He intended to tell Belle the truth about his writing. He just hadn't found the right time for bringing it up.

Up until their conversation about MacPherson's writing, George had toyed with the idea of waiting until *Ermintrude* was published to reveal the secret. Then he would give Belle the first copy, bound in a ribbon, with an affectionate inscription. He might even dedicate it to her! She would be over the moon.

Except that Belle hadn't liked *Rosalind*, so she probably wouldn't like its sequel, which related the story of Lady Rosalind's younger sister, Lady Ermintrude. Ermintrude was less histrionic and more comical than her temperamental older sister. The humor in this volume would be much stronger, and there were some parodies of high society that George thought very entertaining.

But George had a sinking feeling that Belle would say that Lady Ermintrude, like her fictional sister, behaved inconsistently from one scene to another. In truth, character development was George's least favorite part of writing fiction. He preferred catapulting his characters from one ridiculous situation to another.

Unfortunately, the British book-buying public seemed not to love MacPherson's comedies of manners. Only a few reviewers liked *Rosalind* and the sales had been moderate, at best. Mr. Sherman had delicately hinted that perhaps George ought to study the market a little more and see if he could write something that might sell better.

George had hoped that *Ermintrude* would be the book that made him successful, proving the critics and his editor wrong. He'd spent hours rereading his favorite novels, trying to figure out how those authors succeeded where he always seemed to fail. But none of that would matter if he could not finish writing the book!

Which meant he'd better sit back down and write, hadn't he? He sighed and trudged back to the house, his head hanging down. He couldn't really justify a longer break, given how little progress he'd made today. Or yesterday. Or for weeks, if he was honest. His muse seemed to have deserted him entirely.

He squared his shoulders and marched through the back garden, only to find himself within a hair's breadth of a collision with Mrs. Hastings.

"I am terribly sorry!" he gasped.

"Oh, it's as much my fault as yours," she said cheerfully. "I was so busy thinking about dinner that I didn't look where I was going." She gestured to the basket of fresh-picked French beans she carried.

"Well, we don't want you to spill the beans." George, worried about the way the basket kept tipping, took it out of her hands.

Mrs. Hastings beamed at him. "Indeed we don't. I should hate to have wasted the time picking those." She dusted her hands off on her apron. "Not but what the garden is a pleasant place to be today, aside from the heat."

"Yes, I was just stretching my legs in the orchard." George held the kitchen door open for her, then followed close behind. After a quarter hour spent in the bright afternoon light, the kitchen seemed downright Stygian. He had to wait until his eyes adjusted before he could carry the basket of beans to the table.

"Thank you, sir. Now, was there something you needed?"

George grinned, recognizing the hint. "No, Mrs. Hastings. I'll be on my way."

But as he turned to go, he caught sight of the damaged wall. The gouges in the plaster had all been patched up. The patches were still visible, being a different shade from the rest of the wall, but at least the wall was whole now.

"I see someone mended the damage that burglar did."

"Aye, Mr. Hastings patched it up." Mrs. Hastings had been preparing to wash the beans, but she turned around to face George. "That reminds me, Mr. Kirkland. Have you made any arrangements for securing the door? So as to keep treasure hunters out, I mean?"

"Ah, no, not yet, but I'll be right on it." George had, in fact, entirely forgotten about it. He surreptitiously patted his pockets, hoping against reason that he might have a notebook and pencil on hand so he could jot down a reminder. All he found was a handkerchief in need of washing. How long had he been carrying *that* in his pocket?

"It's no great matter," Mrs. Hastings assured him. "It's only that young Peggy has been complaining about how uncomfortable the floor is."

"I don't blame her," George agreed. "I wouldn't make a dog sleep on that floor." A dog? Now *that* was an idea! Why hadn't he thought of it? Perhaps the security problem would be easy to solve after all. "I say, Mrs. Hastings, do you know anyone who might be selling a guard dog?"

"I don't know anyone who'd part with a trained guard dog," she said doubtfully, "but I believe that Squire Cawley, up at Waterbury Lodge, was looking to sell some bulldog puppies. You might talk to his groundskeeper."

"That's a splendid idea. I'll do that." George particularly liked this mission as it gave him a reason to delay sitting back down to write. He still had absolutely no clue what ought to happen next in *Ermintrude*. Maybe, just maybe, he should've taken Potter's advice and tried making an outline first, rather than diving in headfirst without a plan.

It might not be too late to make an outline of the rest of the novel. His usual method of drafting had not worked so far. Maybe it was time to try something else. But that would be a problem for another day. Today, he was going to go see a man about a dog. He left the cottage, whistling as he headed westward, toward Waterbury Lodge.

This errand proved more successful than his writing session. Not only was Mr. Cawley up to receiving visitors, he seemed quite pleased to meet George. He invited George into his library for a brandy. George accepted, more out of a desire to be polite to his nearest neighbor rather than particularly wanting a drink.

Mr. Cawley handed George an unnecessarily full glass and settled into an armchair near the open French windows. "I believe I must've seen you visiting your uncle back when you were a lad, Mr. Kirkland." He leaned back in his chair and smiled pleasantly.

Mr. Cawley could have been no more than ten years older than George, but he already had the look of a bluff, sporting country squire. His hair had begun to recede, and his tanned skin indicated that he spent a good deal of time outside. George guessed he took a hands-on approach to managing his farmland.

If I wrote a character like Mr. Cawley, Arabella would say it was only a caricature of a country gentleman. George kept his bitterness to himself, instead smiling back at his host. "I seem to recall you driving about the country in a gig drawn by what looked like a circus pony."

As a child, George had envied young Walter Cawley, who seemed to be everything George wanted to be: dashing, athletic, and wealthy. Strange to sit with the man now that Providence had brought them back together. George and Squire Cawley differed widely in both situation and personality, but they now belonged to the same community and would most likely move in the same circles. Uncle William's generosity had made George an independent gentleman, even though he chose to continue his literary career.

Mr. Cawley burst into laughter. "Oh, dear Lord, yes. Poor old Baldwin. He did look like a circus pony, didn't he? He was an excellent carriage horse, though. Good wind, fine legs, lots of stamina. He couldn't help being as spotted as a Dalmatian dog." He took a small sip of his brandy, then set the glass down. "We were all so pleased to hear that Finch's Cottage was to be occupied at last. We've missed your uncle these last few years."

"Finch's Cottage?" George could not remember having heard it called that.

"Ah, forgive me, I know your uncle changed the name." Mr. Cawley quickly explained. "The place used to belong to my family—or rather, my grandmother's family. The Finches. She was the last of the Finches, so the property came to us. My grandfather sold it to pay for improvements to Waterbury Lodge, I believe."

"I did not know that." George studied the older man uncertainly. People could be touchy about selling properties that had been in the family for generations. "I hope you don't mind that the place no longer belongs to the Finches. It really is a charming house."

"Oh, goodness, no, you are welcome to it!" Mr. Cawley dismissed George's concern with a wave of his hand. "If I ever visited the place as a child, it's more than I remember. Even before your uncle bought it, the place was leased out. And my grandfather had a devil of a time finding tenants, too. Most people who want houses in the country prefer to have a park for the sake of hunting. No, we are quite happy to let someone else make use of the place."

"Glad to hear that." If young Mr. Cawley had wanted to reclaim his family's ancestral land, George would have felt conscience-bound to sell it. But he would have been very unhappy about it, and Uncle William might have been downright apoplectic.

Mr. Cawley drained the last of his brandy and sat up straighter. "So, Mr. Kirkland, is this purely a social visit, or was there something particular you wished to discuss?"

"Oh, right!" George leaned forward in his chair and explained about the recent break-ins, the damage to the kitchen, the servants' fears about possible future violence, and his hope that a guard dog might help.

Cawley's mouth gaped wide. "You mean people still believe in the treasure? That's absurd!" He shook his head and cracked a rueful grin. "I admit that when I was a boy, I believed my Aunt Tilly's stories about there being some precious object hidden in the house, but I left that belief behind when I grew up. I had no idea that anyone outside the family had even heard the story."

George chuckled. "Oh, we all heard it when I was a child. I don't know who first told it to me, but I know my sister and I went all around the kitchen, knocking on the walls in search of a hollow space. Never did find it, of course."

"If anyone finds anything of value hidden in that house, I'll eat my hat!" Cawley cheerfully offered. "But enough of that. I should think you do need a guard dog! Why don't you come out to the kennel with me and I'll show you the pups?"

George followed the squire out the door, confident that he'd seen the last of the vandalism in the kitchen. No one would break into the house knowing it was guarded by a ferocious-looking dog.

Chapter Sixteen

ARABELLA DREAMED SHE was being chased by a too-friendly dog. The dog jumped all over her and tore her dress, hassling her until she developed a headache. She woke up with her head pounding and something giving her face a thoroughly unnecessary washing.

"Go away," she grumbled. "It's not morning yet."

"The only reason it's not morning is because it's almost dinner time," announced an entirely too-cheerful voice.

She knew that voice. She opened her eyes, then blinked. Why was she sleeping outside? No wonder her whole body ached! She sat up and looked around groggily. She had fallen asleep in the front garden. She'd originally come here hoping to capture the precise color of lavender leaves. She had lain down, intending to rest for a moment. Now her head hurt, she needed to visit the water closet, and a large brindled puppy was gnawing on one of her charcoal pencils.

"Stop that!" She tried to take the pencil away from the dog, but it mistook this for an invitation to play. It backed away, growling under its breath, and threw a play bow. Arabella looked up at her husband. "Whose dog is that?" she asked, though she was afraid she could guess.

"It's ours!" George looked inordinately pleased with himself.

Arabella closed her eyes and put a hand to her head. The dog came bounding back and licked her in the face again. She shuddered and pushed the puppy away.

"I don't really like dogs," she whispered.

"What's that, love?" George flopped onto the blanket next to her. "I didn't hear you."

Arabella cleared her throat and tried again. "I wish you had asked me before you brought a puppy home, George." She used the gentlest voice she could muster, not wanting to hurt his feelings. "I don't really like dogs."

Her husband stared at her, his forehead wrinkled with confusion. "That's right," he said at last. "You never did care for dogs, did you? I'm sorry, Belle. I forgot that." He gently pulled the puppy away from her. "But Bowser's not really a pet. I got him to guard the house. You know, so Peggy didn't have to keep watch over the kitchen."

Arabella's face relaxed a little, though she couldn't quite smile yet. "That was well thought of you," she said. She had never been easy about the idea of leaving Peggy in the kitchen at night. Not only was it a terribly uncomfortable place to sleep, but it left Peggy in danger if a stranger *did* break into the house. A guard dog would be much better protection against would-be treasure seekers.

"You needn't have anything to do with Bowser," George assured her. "I imagine he'll stay in a kennel when he's not on duty. Or he'll sleep in the kitchen. I'll have to see what Mrs. Hastings thinks." He scratched the puppy behind its ears, sending it into ecstasies.

A genuine smile tugged at the corners of Arabella's mouth. "I don't think Mrs. Hastings is likely to want a dog in her kitchen," she warned.

George grinned back at her. "No, I suppose not. But Hastings can put together a kennel near the house. This dog should be a natural at guarding. His mother's been the watch dog at Waterbury Lodge for years." He kissed the dog on the top of its head and was rewarded by a canine tongue lashing.

Arabella shook her head. Bowser seemed like a charming animal, if one liked dogs. She supposed she couldn't object to George keeping a pet, if he wanted one—though it would have been nice if he'd consulted her first. But she couldn't share George's confidence about the dog's ability to guard the property. Based on the pup's gregarious personality, she suspected it might befriend anyone who walked into the house, regardless of the intruder's intentions.

"Anyway, *that's* settled." Unlike Arabella, George had no doubts about whether so friendly a puppy would actually keep the house safe. "In other news, we've been invited to dine at Waterbury Lodge tonight."

"Tonight?" Her eyes widened with surprise, and nervousness made her voice higher than usual.

George stopped petting the puppy and stared at her. "Is something wrong with that? We don't have any other plans, do we?"

"No, but . . ." *But I can't do a dinner party with no notice!* Arabella closed her mouth with a snap, not at all sure how to explain herself.

"What's wrong, then?" George's soft brown eyes looked as gentle as his voice sounded.

Maybe it wouldn't be that hard to explain. "I like having advance notice when I have an entertainment or dinner to attend." Arabella clasped her hands together anxiously. "If you wish, we could invite them to dine with us next week, instead." Though she had no idea whether Mrs. Hastings could cook a meal fit for the local squire.

That skeptical line formed between George's eyebrows again. "But I already accepted the invitation. It would be very rude to cancel at the last minute. Next time, I promise to let you know ahead of time." His eyes looked downright beseeching. He might have been a needy puppy himself.

Arabella gulped. "What time do they dine?" She had no watch with her, but judging from the position of the sun, it must already be late afternoon.

"At six," George told her. "The Cawleys will send a carriage for us at five thirty, so we need not worry about getting dirty on the walk there."

Five thirty? That did not leave much time to clean up and dress! Arabella licked her lips nervously, trying to decide whether to argue further.

"I am very sorry if you don't like it, Belle." The apology in George's tone sounded sincere. "I thought it would be good to get to know the Cawleys. We may spend the rest of our lives here. We would do well to cultivate good relationships with our neighbors."

Arabella nodded stiffly. She could not dispute any of that. As the daughter of a baronet who preferred country life to London, Arabella knew all about the dinner parties, morning calls, house parties, picnics, private balls, and church fetes that constituted rural social life. George was right: they did need to be on good terms with the Cawleys, their nearest respectable neighbors. If she'd had enough warning to mentally prepare herself for the dinner, she might even have been grateful to George for accepting the invitation.

The problem was that there was *no time*. Even with the help of her lady's maid, she would have to dress in a hurry. There would be no time for talking herself into the right state of mind for dining with strangers. A dinner party where she knew none of the other guests was the very worst kind of social event!

George must have seen how unhappy she felt, because he leaned toward her and pressed a soft kiss against her forehead. "If you don't feel that you can do it, I will send in your regrets. But I would like to go myself, regardless of whether you accompany me."

"Of course." Arabella swallowed the lump in her throat. Would she rather stay home without her husband, or go dine with strangers? Neither option seemed at all appealing. Must they really change their plans at the bequest of strangers?

George studied her face for a moment, then sighed. "I see how it is. I'll tell them you are indisposed, shall I?"

Her heart sank, as she registered the disappointment dripping from his voice. He no more wanted to dine without her than she wanted to dine without him. *I am being childish,* she decided. Dinner parties with the neighbors were a natural part of country life. It was foolish to try to avoid them.

"I will go with you." The grudging words falling from her mouth sounded as heavy as paving stones. "I had better hurry, though. I will need to wash up and dress."

George's face lit up. "Splendid! I am sure you will enjoy yourself." Before Arabella could cast any doubt on his prediction, he added, "If you need to go home early, just let me know."

"I will," she promised, feeling relieved that he understood her well enough to know she might not be able to stay for the whole evening. Dinner parties could last for hours, particularly if the hosts brought out the card table afterward. Arabella could not possibly maintain conversation with strangers for that long. She'd better bring a book.

Her lady's maid seemed far more enthusiastic about the last-minute dinner party. Jenny kept up a stream of cheerful chatter as she arranged Belle's hair into an elegant, restrained knot. Arabella never minded such prattle, because Jenny did not expect a response. Arabella sat with her eyes closed, letting the words flow over her without paying them much mind, until one sentence caught her attention.

"... and of course Mr. Kirkland always looks dignified, even when his clothes are not in the best condition. It is a pity he has no valet. I don't think Mrs. Hastings has any idea how to remove ink stains from his shirt sleeves, you know, but a good valet would have methods—"

She interrupted Jenny. "Does Mr. Kirkland have ink stains on *all* his shirt sleeves?" She was so used to seeing him covered in ink that she hadn't even noticed. Whatever else he might do when he closeted himself in the study, he clearly splashed ink about.

Jenny wrinkled her nose. "He might have one shirt that's still clean," she said dubiously. "But I know Mrs. Hastings was complaining that lemon juice doesn't get all the ink out."

"I see. I will talk to Mr. Kirkland about the possibility of hiring a valet." George had never told her what their income was or how much should be budgeted for servants, so she had no idea whether they could afford a valet. But if they were to circulate socially, he needed to look presentable.

When Arabella met her husband in the front hall downstairs, she scrutinized his appearance, from his polished boots to his rakishly placed top hat. She paid special attention to the cuffs of his sleeves. No sign of ink stains! He looked perfectly respectable, albeit not in the height of fashion. A relieved smile broke across her face.

"Do I pass muster tonight?" George raised his eyebrows and adjusted the angle of his hat the merest fraction. "Or are you ashamed to be seen with me?"

He sounded amused, but heat rushed into her face anyway. George was not always careful about his appearance, and *she* had been worried that . . . well, that his evening wear would not do him credit.

"You look very handsome." Her face burned hotter as her blush deepened. She had only meant to say that he looked well tonight! "I mean, very dashing." Was that any better?

George's grin deepened. "Thank you, my dear. You look lovely yourself. But I don't know why you are blushing like a schoolgirl, when we've been married more than a fortnight." He brushed one gloved hand against her burning face. "I look forward to showing you off to everyone."

Arabella gulped. *Everyone?* "Isn't it only the Cawley family we're meeting tonight?" She reached up, intending to wrap one of her curls around her finger, only to remember that Jenny had arranged a neat coiffure, leaving no loose strands with which Arabella could fiddle. Instead, she took hold of the little cross pendant hanging around her neck.

George shrugged. "I think they might have a few other

guests, but I don't know who. Does it matter?"

Oh, it *mattered*. Arabella had been overwhelmed by the prospect of an unexpected dinner party even when she thought it would involve only a few members of the Cawley household. Now she had no idea who to expect, nor even how many people she would meet. Worse, since it this was her first social appearance in the neighborhood, everyone would be watching her, evaluating her, and finding fault with her.

In the past, Lady Canning had told Arabella that people did not constantly watch her behavior. "They are more concerned about themselves than about you, pet," she would say whenever Arabella felt particularly self-conscious. "If you make a mistake, they won't notice. And even if they do notice, they won't care."

Arabella had never entirely believed her mother on that point, but she knew for a fact that Mama's advice did not apply to this situation. In the country, every new addition to the community mattered. Since the Kirklands had only been here a week, everyone would be curious about them. And they would be particularly curious about Arabella.

George wasn't entirely an outsider the way she was. He'd visited Dogwood Cottage often in the past. Even if no one remembered him, they certainly would remember his uncle. But the people who made up local society would know nothing about Arabella, and they would be curious. They would ask questions, and they would gossip about her answers. If she said or did the wrong thing, everyone would know about it. That was how life in the country worked!

"Belle? Is something wrong?" George tipped her chin up to make her look him in the eyes. His face was creased with worry.

"Nothing is wrong," Arabella croaked. She forced a smile to her lips, even though her stomach had already begun to roil. She could only hope she would not be sick all over the carriage that Mr. Cawley was thoughtfully sending for them. Probably she would, though. That was the sort of thing that tended to go wrong when Arabella dined out.

Please, she silently prayed, *don't let tonight be a disaster!*

Chapter Seventeen

ANYONE MIGHT FEEL a little nervous dining with strangers, so George understood the anxiety that made Belle curl up in the corner of the carriage and fiddle with her necklace during the short drive to Waterbury Lodge. That wasn't so very strange. George himself kept jiggling his leg up and down. He wished he'd refused the offer of a carriage. Walking would have given him something to do with all this nervous energy!

But everything went swimmingly once they arrived at Waterbury Lodge. Mrs. Cawley graciously introduced George and Belle to the other guests. It really was not such a very large dinner party after all. The clergyman and his wife were in attendance, as well as the surgeon, Mr. Arkwright—though Mrs. Arkwright had stayed home with a sick child. The only other guests were an older couple, Mr. and Mrs. Hargreaves. They owned a large estate to the east of Pendleford, and had been on visiting terms with Uncle William and Aunt Helena.

The clerical couple, the Richardsons, were too new to the area to have ever met Uncle William, Aunt Helena, or any of the other Kirklands. But Mr. Arkwright had grown up in Preston and was thus very familiar with the Kirkland Mill. He knew Uncle William only by reputation, but when Mrs. Cawley explained George's relationship to the mill owner, his eyes widened.

"Don't worry," George said breezily. "I'm nothing like as

important as my uncle. Just a run-of-the mill Kirkland, only I write for a living instead of preaching sermons." He grinned, imagining what a terrible clergyman he would have made.

"Ah, but I am sure you are very dear to your Uncle Kirkland," Mrs. Hargreaves suggested. "He loved that house by the river. He would not have given it away to anyone he did not hold in great esteem."

George's face burned with embarrassment. He certainly did not want to admit that he had been given Dogwood Cottage only because he was willing to get married at the drop of a hat. As charming as it might be to believe himself favored by Uncle William, George knew better.

Apart from that awkward moment, the rest of the meal went quite well. The Cawleys served a substantial but unpretentious meal, with a first course that included lamb chops with asparagus and peas, and a second course featuring a curried rabbit. By the time dessert was served, George had eaten so much that he could only nibble on a few fresh strawberries. Belle, he noticed, did not take anything but a handful of nuts, which she left on her plate.

George had been seated next to Mrs. Cawley, far down the table from his own wife, so he could not hear any of Belle's conversation. He noticed that she seemed quiet for most of the meal, but he thought nothing of it. Belle *was* rather shy around people she did not know. Once she warmed up to the other guests, she would do well. So he told himself, anyway.

George ceased worrying about Belle once the ladies retreated to the drawing room, leaving the gentlemen to enjoy their claret in peace. The gentlemen's conversation centered around the replacement of a member of the select vestry at St. Edmund's parish. Apparently, it was the custom in St. Edmund parish for all rate-paying male parishioners to elect the members of the closed vestry, much as in an election for Parliament, though of course the stakes were lower.

As George learned, there were two competing candidates for the open vestry position: a well-respected farmer who always voted Tory, and an "upstart" draper suspected of Whiggish principles. Arkwright, who lived in the busy heart of Pendleford, supported the draper, claiming that he had modern ideas. Richardson, whose vicarage sat at the edge of town, preferred the farmer.

The debate was lively but polite. Hargreaves was the only dinner guest who did not belong to St. Edmund's parish. Since he had no stake in the matter, he leaned back in his chair, filled his wineglass near to the brim, and played the part of an amused spectator. Mr. Cawley, who lived much closer to the town, was more invested in the election, but he also refused to take a side. Instead, he insisted that every argument or counterargument the two debaters made was "an excellent point."

When Arkwright grew flushed (either from wine or from argument), Cawley tried to put a stop to the contentious discussion. "Gentlemen, I believe both of you are right in the main. Let us leave our small differences behind us, shall we?" He smiled as he looked back and forth between the two combatants.

How, George wondered, could both sides be right in such a disagreement? There could not be *two* best candidates for a vestry position!

Much to George's surprise, Arkwright turned to him and appealed for support. "You've lived in London, Mr. Kirkland. You must know how out of touch with the modern world many of these north country folks are." The young surgeon held George's gaze, making him feel like a beetle pinned by an entomologist.

"I . . . well, I ..." How was George supposed to answer that? He lived in Lancashire now, and probably would for the rest of his life. He had just received a house and a fortune in the Funds from a north country mill owner. It would be ungrateful of him to say anything critical about the locals. "I haven't met either candidate, so I have no opinion." That seemed like a safe conclusion.

"Ah, but you will want to pay more attention to such issues in the future." Richardson waggled a finger at him in admonition.

"In times like these, our county needs the support of all right-thinking men."

George blinked, having no idea how to respond to this. What was so distinctive about these times, anyway? In the end, he molded his face into what he hoped was a suitably grave expression and nodded solemnly.

Unfortunately, Richardson kept pushing. "Remind me again, do you live in town?"

"Oh no," George said quickly. "We live a couple of miles west of Pendleford, along the river. In Dogwood Cottage. Some people call it Finch's Cottage," he added, wanting to be precise.

Richardson frowned. "Wasn't there something I heard about that cottage? Some kind of trouble?"

"Burglary and vandalism, perhaps?" George suggested. "Just before we moved in, someone marked up a wall in the kitchen, as if they were looking for a hidden safe or a secret room. Looked like it had been pricked all over with an awl or something." That was only a guess, though. He had no idea what kind of tool made the marks.

Arkwright gaped at him for a moment. "Why on earth would anyone do that? How could you have a local enemy already?"

"Oh, they're probably aren't an enemy, *per se*. I imagine they were just looking for the treasure," George explained. "Silly, really. If no one found it after all these years, it's not going to be found."

"Treasure?" Arkwright's eyes widened. "Was the cottage owned by a pirate?"

Cawley burst into laughter. "It was owned by my grandmother's family, and I assure you, the Finches were not pirates. They were perfectly respectable smallholders." His laughter died down, and he flicked his eyes towards Richardson before pulling a wry smile. "Just not good Church of England members."

"Oh?" It was George's turn to stare blankly. He had absolutely no idea what Cawley meant. Apart from the legend of hidden treasure, George knew very little about the previous owners of the cottage. Until today, he hadn't even known their family name.

Cawley cleared his throat and took a sip of wine. "Mind you, *my* father was a good Protestant. But his mother's family were Recusants. Legend has it that generations ago, the Finches helped smuggle a Jesuit into the area to say Mass."

"So that's why everyone thinks there's a secret room of some sort!" George interjected. Everyone stared at him. Richardson held his glass halfway up to his mouth. Arkwright's jaw hung open for a second before he closed it tightly. They clearly had no idea what George was talking about.

"Because of the priest," George elaborated. "There must've been a priest hole." It made perfect sense! Lancashire had always had a substantial population of Roman Catholics, despite sixteenth- and seventeenth-century penal laws.

"Ah, yes, that might make sense," Hargreaves agreed. Everyone turned to look at him now, taking the attention away from George, for which he was grateful. "Whitland Hall belonged to Recusants, too, and there's a priest hole under the stairs." He snorted. "When my boys were little, they used it as a bandit cave during their games."

That sounded like the sort of thing George would've done, too. "Were there any stories of a priest hole at the cottage, Cawley?" In his haste, he entirely forgot that he ought to address his host formally. They were not on such terms as to use their surnames without titles.

Cawley did not look offended, though. He merely lowered his wine glass and shook his head. "That certainly would make sense, but none of the stories my aunt told ever included a priest hole. She talked about a secret storage space full of family valuables. I always imagined something like a space under a loose paving stone."

George grinned. "Yes, that was what my sister and I thought, too. During one visit, we tried digging up the paving stones in the kitchen and got in a world of trouble."

Hargreaves chuckled. "I should imagine you did! I suppose you never found anything?"

"Not a brass farthing!" George agreed. He turned back to Cawley. "Did you ever get a chance to search the place? Or was it already out of the family by then?"

"Grandfather Cawley sold it long before I was born," his host confirmed. "So my brother and I never had the chance to dig up the floors. Probably for the best, though. We broke enough pieces of furniture here at the Lodge as it was!"

The conversation shifted, then, to a discussion of children. The Richardsons had no children, and the Hargreaves' offspring had already grown to adulthood, but the Arkwrights and Cawleys both had boys in school and girls under the care of governesses. George, having limited knowledge of child rearing, let his mind wander during this part of the conversation. He had completely lost track of the conversation by the time the gentlemen decided to join the ladies in the drawing room.

He could not stop thinking about the possibility of a priest hole in Dogwood Cottage. Despite what Cawley said about the family legend, George thought that was the most reasonable explanation for the stories about hidden treasure. Dogwood Cottage was a pleasant house, but it was not a gentleman's manor. Cawley had described the Finches as smallholders, people of modest means. How would they even have gotten their hands on a treasure? Or why, if they'd obtained it, would they not have used the wealth to advance the family's fortunes?

No, a hiding place for a fugitive priest made much more sense. Except for the matter of whether there was room anywhere in the cottage to hide a whole human being. George spent much of the ride back to the cottage trying to remember the layout of the house. Were there any walls that seemed suspiciously thick, or ceilings that hung lower than they ought?

He did not even think to ask Belle about the dinner party until the carriage stopped in front of the garden gate. As he helped her out, it dawned on him that she had not said a word during the ride home.

"Everything all right, love? You're rather quiet tonight." With only a half-moon for light, he could not make out her expression.

"I am tired," she said. "I have a headache. That is all."

He placed her hand on his arm as they walked up the path to the front door. "I am sorry about your headache. I hope you had a lovely evening apart from that."

"Mm hmm," she murmured. She drew her arm away from his to cover her mouth as she yawned. "It will be good to get into bed. This has been such a long day."

"But a good one." George could not say more, because the moment they entered the dimly lit front hall, a dark blur barreled into him, barking happily. He squatted down to greet the bulldog puppy, who acted as if George had been gone for a long, empty eternity. "Bowser! Look at you, learning to bark whenever people come into the house! Who's a good guard dog?"

Bowser, frantically licking George's hand, seemed confident that *he* was the good guard dog. His stubby tail wagged furiously.

What could be better than being greeted so enthusiastically when one came home? George lifted his head, intending to tell Belle that bringing home a puppy had already paid off. But she had not stopped to greet their dog. She'd walked right past Bowser and was halfway up the stairs already.

Strange that she didn't want to greet their puppy, but it was her loss! George shrugged his shoulders and resumed baby-talking to a delighted Bowser. When he came upstairs, he decided not to ask Belle any further questions about the dinner party or their new neighbors. She did not seem disposed for talking, and he guessed she probably needed her rest.

$$\text{Chapter Eighteen}$$

BELLE DID NOT particularly enjoy the dinner party. Mrs. Hargreaves and Mrs. Cawley spent most of the evening talking about their children. They tried to loop Belle into their conversation by catching her eye and smiling at her occasionally, but the topics they chose never allowed her an opportunity to join in.

Miss Cawley, the middle-aged aunt of the current landowner, seemed sweet, polite, and approachable. During dinner, Belle enjoyed listening to her stories of growing up in Lancashire. She would have been quite happy to sit beside Miss Cawley and listen to her soft, harmless chatter while they waited for the gentlemen to rejoin them. Unfortunately, Miss Cawley settled into a soft chair by the fire and promptly fell asleep.

I should have brought a book after all! Or a sketchbook. Or some kind of needlework. Embroidery did not interest her to the extent drawing did, but she enjoyed learning new patterns, or sometimes even designing them. It could be fun to work on objects that could be used by people she loved. For example, she intended to embroider George's initials on a set of new handkerchiefs, since he seemed to lose handkerchiefs at an alarming rate. She'd left her book at home as she knew some people would think it rude to come prepared for reading, but she could certainly have brought her needlework with her.

Arabella glanced about the drawing room, hoping to find something with which to occupy herself. She would have settled for a lady's periodical, which might have given her fashion plates to study or a story to read. But she saw no reading material of any kind in the room. Perhaps the Cawleys kept all their periodicals in the library.

With nothing to do, she stared into the fire and thought about what color she should use for George's monogram. She had never asked him about the Kirkland family arms. Did the Kirkland family even *have* a coat of arms? George ought to have one, since he was quite clearly a gentleman. She should ask him about it sometime.

"Mrs. Kirkland?" The gentle prompt came from Mrs. Cawley.

Arabella's heart skipped a beat at the sudden interruption. She snapped to attention, feeling vaguely guilty for having let her mind wander so far. "I'm very sorry. I'm afraid I was woolgathering. What did I miss?" She forced the corners of her mouth into a smile that she did not genuinely feel.

"Mrs. Hargreaves was wondering where you were from, and I told her that I thought you came from Derbyshire. Is that right?"

Arabella relaxed. A question that simple carried no threat. "Yes. I grew up near a little village called Norton Combe. So did George. My husband, I mean. Of course he wasn't my husband while we were growing up." She had to stop babbling! "The elder Mr. Kirkland—my husband's father, I mean—is the vicar there."

"Norton Combe, you say?" When Arabella nodded, Mrs. Hargreaves continued. "Do you by any chance know Lady Canning? I went to school with her, more years ago than I prefer to admit, when she was Miss Hallingstone and I was Miss Edwards."

"You went to school with my mother?" Odd that her mother hadn't said anything about having an old school friend near Pendleford! But it had to be her; Hallingstone was too rare a name for there to be any mistake.

Mrs. Hargreaves raised her eyebrows and exchanged a look

with Mrs. Cawley, as if Arabella had said something significant.

"I am Sir Michael Canning's eldest daughter," Arabella added, in case she had been unclear. "My mother's maiden name was Hallingstone."

Mrs. Richardson leaned towards Arabella. "I am so glad to hear that. When Richardson and I heard that Dogwood Cottage was to be occupied by the nephew of a manufacturer, well, we were a little concerned."

"Concerned?" Arabella wrinkled her forehead as she glanced at each of the three women. She sensed undercurrents here that she couldn't quite fathom.

Mrs. Richardson nodded. "You see, the ladies of the parish want to improve the tone of local society. We thought perhaps your Mr. Kirkland had been raised in Preston, among the factories, so we were a little afraid that. . . well, that he wouldn't quite understand our way of life. You know, out here in the country."

"Oh no!" Arabella exclaimed, happy to be able to reassure them on that point. "George worked in London for a few years, but before that, he grew up in the country. In fact, the vicarage is closer to Oliphant Hall than to the rest of the village, so George and his sister played in our park as often as not. . ." She blushed when she realized she'd begun babbling again. These ladies had not asked for her life story!

But her answer seemed to please the other women, particularly the hostess of the party. "Precisely! A vicar's son and the daughter of baronet must always be acceptable in good society." Mrs. Cawley beamed, as if Arabella had done well in choosing to be born the daughter of a baronet rather than a tradesman.

Arabella's whole body stiffened. "I see." Her new neighbors were all relieved to find that she came from the same genteel background they did. What would the surgeon's wife have thought if she were here? Mrs. Arkwright might have provided a different opinion, given that surgery was not considered as genteel as some professions. The wife of a physician could be presented at court; the wife of a surgeon could not.

Eager to change the subject, Arabella asked, "What is the local society like here? Are there assembly rooms in Pendleford?"

Mrs. Cawley wrinkled her nose. "I wish there were," she confided. "The Dove and Rose has a room that used to be used as a ballroom, but the inn doesn't have the proper facilities for large gatherings."

"Inadequate withdrawing rooms," Mrs. Hargreaves explained. "Perhaps the ladies of the previous century did not mind being forced into a little closet for necessary functions, but it would not do today!"

"Unfortunate," Arabella murmured, though in fact she didn't particularly mind. She enjoyed dancing, but had never been particularly good at it. When she did dance, she much preferred an informal hop where she already knew the other dancers. "Do you ever host balls here at the Lodge?" The drawing room certainly seemed large enough for a small party.

"Not formal ones," Mrs. Cawley said. "But at our party last Christmas, we did roll up the rug and dance a few reels." She looked about the room, catching the eyes of the other guests. "Now that there are more genteel families in the area, we might do that more often."

"That would be lovely," Mrs. Richardson proclaimed. "And far better than a public assembly, the company would be more select."

Arabella bit her lips to hold back a sharp retort. A scrap of verse from the Bible popped into her mind, unbidden: *"when thou makest a feast, call the poor, the maimed, the lame, the blind: And thou shalt be blessed . . ."* The clergyman's wife must have forgotten that passage. Or perhaps she did not interpret it literally.

By now, Arabella's head ached from the dual strains of reading between lines of dialogue and holding back her genuine reactions. Instead of arguing about what constituted select society, she restricted herself to saying, "That sounds lovely." After that, the conversation shifted, and she fell silent again.

The rest of the chat remained harmless, as it concerned Mrs. Cawley's indecision about whether or not to try growing orange trees in the conservatory that had just been added to the Lodge.

But the damage had already been done, and Arabella's headache grew worse over the remainer of the evening. By the time she and George departed Waterbury Lodge, she was content to lean back against the squabs of the carriage seat and rest in silence. George did not seem to mind. He, too, was in a brown study.

She left him to greet the overly enthusiastic puppy. Just how big was it going to get, anyway? She could not remember whether it was a bulldog or a mastiff. When George brought it home, she'd been so shocked that he got a dog without talking to her first that she neglected to ask questions about its breed, projected size, or training.

To be sure, this was George's house rather than hers. He was the man of the family. But if George had asked her, she would have reminded him that she did not particularly want a dog in the house. Dogs were dirty and smelly and if they loved you, they got slobber and dog hair all over you. If they did not love you, they might hurt you. She doubted that so friendly a puppy would bite a family member, but it was always a possibility.

Now she wondered about the practicalities of the pet. Would it sleep in the house at night, or in a kennel? Was it housebroken? Would it bark every time a tradesman came to the kitchen door with a delivery? If she and George had children, could the dog be trusted with the children?

That last consideration stopped Arabella in her tracks. She rested a hand on her abdomen, wondering if she was with child yet. She ought to know soon enough, since her courses were due any day now. Either she would spend a day incapacitated with headache and cramping, or her life would change forever. How strange that those were her only options! Not for the first time, she thought there ought to be a better way of managing "women's matters."

As soon as she got to her bedchamber, Arabella rang for her lady's maid. Then she stepped into the dressing room—now her own private studio—to begin the process of removing all the accoutrements necessary for dining out.

Jenny arrived to help her, smothering a yawn beneath one hand. "I hope you had a pleasant evening out, ma'am." She unclasped Arabella's necklace and returned it to its place in the jewelry box.

"Pleasant enough." Had she been alone with Jenny, Arabella might have told her about the awkward moments and strange undercurrents in tonight's conversations. She sometimes used Jenny as a sounding board when she feared she might have made some conversational misstep or other social *faux pas*.

But George had already followed her upstairs; she could hear him quietly singing to himself in the bedchamber. Rather unfortunate that he had so little sense of pitch, given how often he hummed or sang to himself!

Arabella would not have minded confiding some of her social struggles to her lady's maid, but she did not want George to overhear any complaints about the evening's entertainment. He seemed disposed to like the Cawleys. Though he had assured Arabella that he did not expect her to entertain lavishly, she knew he would want to return their neighbors' generosity and have them to dinner.

Or could they get away with a card party after dinner? Arabella brightened as she considered the possibility. She liked card parties better than dinner parties. Card games provided both a common focus for conversation and, when needed, a reason to remain silent. Everyone understood that some players preferred not to chat during an intense game.

Besides, Arabella was quite good at *vingt-et-un*. She won more often at that game than at any other, having learned long ago to school her face so as to hide her true emotions. Whist was more of a challenge, but she might do well enough if partnered with George.

Once she'd donned one of her new, lace-trimmed night rails, Arabella dismissed Jenny. She drew a deep breath and went to face George, hoping he would not be in a chatty mood tonight. Her head still ached and she had rather not lie in bed talking, as they sometimes did.

She found George sitting in bed with his lap desk, a pencil in hand. He frantically scratched something into his notebook, so deep in his work that he did not look up when she climbed into bed.

Arabella watched him write, fascinated by the sight. She had sometimes seen him pull out his notebook to jot down an idea, but up until now, he had done all of his serious writing in his study. She had never seen him working in bed.

"What are you writing?"

He did not answer. His eyes kept following the line of writing as he scrawled whatever-it-was. She leaned over, hoping to catch a glimpse of his work, but he jerked the notebook away.

"Belle! Didn't your mother teach you it's rude to look over someone's shoulder?" He smiled ruefully.

"Didn't *your* mother teach you it's rude to ignore someone when they ask you a question?" She meant to make a joke of it, but hurt infused her voice. How could she not be curious about what he was working on if he sat right beside her, writing as if his life depended on it?

The slightly disgruntled look vanished from his face. "I'm sorry. I didn't mean to ignore you. I just didn't hear you say anything."

Belle opened her mouth, intending to ask how it was possible for him *not* to hear her when she sat only inches away from him, but she thought better of it. Hadn't he always been that way? Half the time he growled when anyone disturbed him, and the other half of the time, he was blithely unaware of what went on around him. That was just George.

Instead, she repeated her question. "What are you writing? Is it a book review or an essay?"

George closed the notebook with a snap and put it on his nightstand. Then he ran a hand through his hair. Why, Arabella wondered, did he seem so flustered?

"Nothing like that. I mean, nothing that I'm writing for a periodical. Just some ideas I wanted to jot down before I forgot. You know how forgetful I can be." This time, his smile put a crinkle in the corners of his eyes. "I suppose I ought to stop writing and get some sleep, unless…?" He arched one eyebrow suggestively, and his gaze slid from Arabella's face to her barely dressed body.

Heat rushed into her face and she averted her eyes. She idly tugged on a strand of her hair as she tried figure out how to explain that although she very much enjoyed lying with George, she needed time to recover from an evening in company. In the end, she fell back on an explanation that, although true, only addressed half the problem.

"I have a headache," she reminded her husband, "so I would like to go straight to sleep tonight."

"As you like. I forgot about your headache." He leaned closer and brushed a kiss against her cheek. "If I read for a little bit longer, will my candle keep you awake?"

"No, of course not," she assured him. A single bedside candle did little to dispel the darkness. "Good night, then." She returned his kiss with one of her own, though she still felt shy making such overtures.

But after she had turned on her side and closed her eyes, the scratch-scratch of pencil on paper resumed. Rather than reading, George had gone back to writing. What *was* he working on, that he had to keep it secret? The question might have kept Arabella awake if it had not been such a long, exhausting day.

Chapter Nineteen

GEORGE'S DAY HAD been just as long and eventful as Belle's, but he could not possibly sleep yet. Not with an idea taunting him, just out of reach. He knew he stood on the verge of something brilliant, but could not quite tell what. He only knew that he needed to explore the idea of Recusants and priest holes. There was a story there, somehow. He *knew* it. He just couldn't quite nail down a workable plot.

He must have stayed up for at least an hour, scribbling down possibilities, only to cross each one off when he realized it wouldn't work. He would probably have kept working for longer if not for the fact that his candle unexpectedly went out.

Oh. He'd forgotten to trim the wick. Had he really been writing for that long? He put down his notebook and pencil and stretched. His hand ached from writing and his eyes burned from lack of sleep, though he had noticed neither irritation until now.

He adjusted his pillow, lay back down, and closed his eyes— but he struggled to sleep. His mind kept sorting through different plot possibilities, trying to figure out how to fit Recusants and priest holes into a social satire about courtship among the aristocracy.

He must have fallen asleep eventually, because late the next morning, Belle shook him awake. "George! You must get up. Your cousin called on us and I have run out of things to say to him. Please don't make me talk to him any longer?"

"Cousin?" George sat up and yawned. He rubbed his face sleepily. The rough stubble reminded him that he'd better shave before he saw anyone. "Wait, did you say my cousin? Which one?" Vincent's parish lay farther south, in Shropshire. So far as George knew, his nearest cousins were Augustus and Benedict, down in Manchester. He could imagine no reason why they would want to visit him, though. He barely knew the relatives on that side of the family.

"I don't remember what his first name was." Belle sounded fretful, and she rubbed her hands together anxiously. "Benjamin, maybe? Bennett? The one we met at your uncle's house in Bath."

"Benedict." *Damn!* George closed his eyes as he silently rallied his spirits. He was not entirely sure that he could face his cousin so soon after waking. Even when George had a good night's sleep, it took considerable time for his mind to start working properly in the morning. Today, after staying up so late jotting down possible story ideas, a mental fog as thick and opaque as a London particular clouded his mind.

"I will be down in a few minutes." He knew it was a rash promise, but what else could he say? *Go away and don't come back!* would have been the most honest response to Benedict's presence, but there were things one simply could not say to one's relatives. "Please have someone bring a cup of tea up to me, though?" He could not face Benedict without his morning cup of tea.

It took more than a few minutes to get himself dressed, shaven, and thoroughly woken up. Mrs. Hastings, bless her heart, sent up a tray with a full pot of hot water, so he could brew his tea as strong as he liked and drink as much as he liked. She also sent a sweet roll slathered with strawberry jam. That went far in helping George find his sea legs, so to speak.

Benedict was probably not happy about being made to wait so long, but George did not particularly mind making his cousin suffer a little. It was his fault for making an unannounced visit to a pair of newlyweds! Most people would have given George and Belle a little time to adjust to matrimony and their new home before showing up unexpectedly. Or showing up at all, really.

When he finally entered the parlor, George did his best to hide his irritation. "Benedict! What a pleasant surprise! What brings you to Pendleford?"

George offered his cousin his hand. For a tense moment, it seemed his cousin might refuse to shake hands. But Benedict finally returned the gesture with a half-hearted shake before returning to his seat.

"I happened to be in the area, and thought I might as well visit you. After all, we are family."

"Indeed we are," George agreed. Family who almost never saw each other, up until that fateful dinner party in Bath. Now George seemed to run into Benedict wherever he went. He did not think that was an improvement. "Here for business, I suppose?" This region of Lancashire had long been a stronghold of the fabric industry, so he ought not be surprised his relatives still in trade might travel through Pendleford.

But Benedict shook his head. "Purely pleasure this time." He smiled perfunctorily. "I am just traveling through on my way north. As you may recall, I am to be married very soon. I thought my bride and I might take a wedding tour in the Lake region, as it is close to home." He paused, then seemed to recall that the Lake District had more than proximity to Manchester to recommend it. "And of course, the area is very charming. Full of scenic sights, and quaint cottages, and, um, poets and such."

"Yes, I believe that's where Mr. Wordsworth and Mr. Coleridge wrote *Lyrical Ballads*." George had, in fact, no very clear idea of where the so-called Lake School poets had lived before the publication of their first book, but the region was certainly associated with their poetry now. "Do you fancy yourself a poet?" He had a difficult time imagining it, but in fairness, George did not know Benedict very well. Perhaps he had hidden depths.

"Oh, goodness, no." Benedict chuckled. "Poetry is more your

line than mine, cousin. But my fiancée, Miss Buxton, is rather partial to poetry. I believe she would enjoy spending a week or two wandering among the, um, moors." The rise at the end of his voice suggested that even he knew that "moors" was not quite the right word.

"There are plenty of charming woods in the area," George suggested. "And rivers, waterfalls, and of course the lakes themselves. They all make for pleasant walks in the morning or evening. It is an excellent place for a wedding tour." He had only visited the Lake District once, but his suggestions felt safe, given that he was merely repeating the standard tourist advice.

"Precisely." Benedict's smile looked no more natural this time than it had before. "Have you any particular locations to recommend?"

"If Miss Buxton is partial to poetry, you could do no better than to take her to Grasmere, in Westmoreland." What George particularly liked about Grasmere was its distance from Pendleford. There would be no reason for Benedict and his bride to stop at Dogwood Cottage again on their way to the lakes, would there? Lord, he hoped not!

"That is exactly what Lucretia said. I mean, Miss Buxton. She would like to see Grasmere." This time, the smile that bloomed across Benedict's face looked genuine.

Interesting. George rapidly readjusted his understanding of the relationship between Benedict and his fiancée. He had assumed that Benedict proposed to Miss Buxton only to secure the inheritance from Uncle William. Benedict might not have the same fond memories of Dogwood Cottage that George had, but he might have been attracted by the financial investments that accompanied the house. Twenty thousand pounds was nothing to sneeze at!

But George knew he had not imagined the fond look that crossed his cousin's face when he talked of Miss Buxton. Benedict must really have an attachment to his fiancée. A faint smile teased at the corners of George's own mouth at this hint that there was more than greed to his cousin.

An unexpected impulse caused George to extend an invitation he'd never expected to offer. "If you like, you and Miss Buxton are welcome to break your journey here. We are a little out of your way, I know, but you would be welcome to our hospitality."

Benedict froze, and some indecipherable emotion swept across his face. It vanished before George could make sense of it.

"We would not wish to inconvenience you," Benedict said, "but I believe Miss Buxton would like to see Dogwood Cottage someday, since she has heard so much about it." He averted his eyes as his cheeks reddened. Probably he had just recalled how recently he and George had been rivals for ownership of the cottage.

"I don't know what your plans are, but would you care to dine with us tonight?" George offered. "Or at least take a little luncheon?"

Benedict's face brightened. "My commitments do not allow me to dine here, but I would be happy to share luncheon with you."

George rang for a maid, then left Benedict alone so that he could find Belle. He looked in every room on the ground floor before he thought to go back upstairs and poke his head into her studio. There he found her at work at her drawing table, using one of her crayons to add color to a landscape she had penciled in earlier that week.

He hovered over her shoulder for a minute, watching her work. Up until now, most of the art Belle had produced since coming to Dogwood Cottage had focused on the garden. She'd sketched groupings of flowers over and over again, and a few of the compositions had satisfied her tastes enough to be redone in color. This picture, however, was not a close-up of a grouping of flowers. It was a full landscape, looking out over the garden gate at the river Pendle, and the focus of the picture was a bird of prey swooping down towards the water.

"Are you going to add a fish?" George blurted out.

Belle flinched. "Oh! I did not notice you were there."

He hurried to apologize. "I ought not have interrupted you." Especially given how much he grumbled any time she interrupted *him* in his writing. "I came up to say that Benedict is going to stay for lunch. I meant to ask if you would join us. But if you are too busy, or do not feel comfortable, I will simply tell him you are out."

Belle rolled her shoulders and shook out her hand. "I could use a spot of luncheon myself," she admitted. "And it is only one guest. I do not mind helping you entertain him."

"Are you sure? I know you are not comfortable with strangers—"

She interrupted him before he could express any more concern. "Your cousin ought not be a stranger here. It is true that I do not know Mr. Benedict Kirkland, but I should like to be on good terms with all your family. As much as possible." She crinkled her nose, as if thinking of the many conflicts that might sow disunity in a large, extended family. "Just let me wash up a bit, and I will join you." She held her right hand up, revealing an assortment of colorful smudges.

"You are as bad with your crayons as I am with my ink," George said cheerfully. "By all means, wash up." He hastily checked his own hands to make sure that there were no ink stains left over from last night's work. He knew it was vain of him, but he did not want to remind Benedict that he, too, worked for his bread.

The lunch went far better than George could have anticipated. Belle seemed in good spirits. She remained as quiet as she usually did when meeting strangers, but she poured tea and handed around sandwiches as gracefully as if she had spent years hosting meals.

A flicker of pride danced in George's heart as he watched Belle play the part of the lady of the house. That was *his* wife! His thoughts turned to pity for his town-dwelling cousin. Benedict would probably never have a charming rural cottage or a wife this beautiful. Poor man!

After lunch, George happily showed Benedict around the house and garden. Though the morning had been sunny and warm, a rainstorm rolled toward the cottage, bringing with it a cool breeze that made walking through the orchard refreshing rather than fatiguing.

Benedict stayed quiet for most of the tour, asking only a few questions about the history of the cottage. George told him what he'd learned about the Finch family, including the fact that Finches were said to have once hidden a Romish priest from the pursuivants. Benedict's eyes widened as George elaborated on his theory that the legend of hidden treasure might have arisen because of the measures taken by the Recusant family.

"Fascinating," Benedict concluded.

"I did not realize that you were interested in history," George admitted. "Is it a hobby of yours?"

His cousin shrugged. "I wouldn't go so far as to call it a hobby, but when one visits a new location, one might as well learn its history." One of his rare genuine smiles brightened his face. "My mother will be proud to hear that I am cultivating my mind. She's always after me to study more."

George nodded, but wisely held his tongue. He'd heard Uncle William grumble that Augustus had gotten all the brains of his family, leaving his twin with "less than a full pint." This seemed unfair, Benedict did not seem at all lack-witted, though he might not be as well-read as the rest of the Kirkland men.

They turned and wandered back up to the house. "Where does that door go?" Benedict pointed at the solid wooden door that opened into the garden.

"It just leads into the main corridor of the house," George explained. "Most people prefer the side door in the kitchen, though I'm not sure why." He gestured in the direction of the kitchen door as they walked slowly around the house. "I suppose that makes it easier to guard the doors, though. We can just let our guard dog sleep in the kitchen at night."

To be sure, they had not yet had a chance to test Bowser's guarding abilities. George had no idea where the puppy had slept last night, for that matter. Maybe Mrs. Hastings had put a blanket down for him in the kitchen, as George suggested. Or maybe someone had taken him out to the barn, as Mrs. Hastings recommended, to avoid any late-night accidents. George supposed he'd better ask about that when he got the chance.

George parted from Benedict in a much better frame of mind than when he woke that morning. He extended his best wishes for the felicity of the new couple, then bade his cousin farewell. Energized by their stroll in the orchard, he sat down to write. For once, he found the right words almost immediately. After months of struggling to put pen to paper, he could finally write.

The problem was, he was writing the wrong story. Since George still had no idea how to fix *Ermintrude*, he began what he thought would probably be a short story about an old house with a secret cupboard, a hidden staircase, and a mysterious box of letters. But two hours later, he looked at what he'd drafted and realized that it was the opening chapters of a much longer work. Somehow, George had accidentally started drafting a new novel.

He stared at the paper as he stretched his cramped hand and rolled his neck. Only now did he notice the minor aches and pains left after sitting hunched over his desk. He would have liked to keep working, but he didn't think his hand could stand any more writing. Pushing himself too far would be a good way to develop rheumatism in his writing hand!

What time was it, anyway? He had no idea how long he'd been writing. He put a hand in his waistcoat pocket, but though he had two clean handkerchiefs today, he did not have his pocket watch. He must've left it upstairs. But his stomach rumbled a suggestion that it must be near dinner time. Certainly, luncheon seemed hours away.

George got to his feet and stretched, then bounded upstairs in such a hurry that he nearly crashed into Belle coming down the stairs.

"You're not dressed for dinner yet?" Her eyes opened wide with surprise.

"Er, no," he admitted. "But it'll only take me a minute."

A line formed between Belle's brows. "I suppose since it is just us, you could dine without changing. There is nothing wrong with your clothes." She studied him intently, and her frown deepened. "Apart from the ink stains on your cuff, I mean."

"Let me at least change my shirt." Swapping out his soiled shirt for a clean one was easy, a matter of minutes. Putting aside all thoughts of his new novel in order to pay attention to the meal proved more challenging.

During the soup course, George wondered if writing from the first-person perspective might be better than using an omniscient narrator. He very nearly forgot to carve the beefsteak because he couldn't decide whether to include a love story in addition to the main plot. And he completely ignored dessert while trying to decide what quirky character traits he could use to distinguish the antagonist from his equally nefarious assistant.

"Is something wrong?" Belle asked.

"Hmm?" He looked up from his empty wineglass. "Why would something be wrong?" So far as he was concerned, something had finally gone *right* for a change! He was writing again. New ideas rushed into his mind, one after another, like a fresh spring welling up in the desert. He had not realized how much he'd thirsted for creative work.

"You seem distracted." Belle spoke softly, and she stared down at her plate, as if she were afraid to criticize him.

"I'm sorry," George said quickly. "I am distracted. I've started working on a new—" He almost said, "a new novel," but he caught himself in time. "A new idea. For an essay, I mean."

"Oh." She lifted her eyes, and her whole face brightened. "What are you writing about?"

"Ah…" George glanced about the room, as if hoping to find the answer hidden somewhere. Hidden? Of course! "Recusant families. You know, since there were so many of them here in Lancashire. I thought I might as well take advantage of our location. I could do some local research." He felt proud of himself for having come up with so plausible an answer on such short notice.

"Oh, interesting!"

They continued to talk, but as soon as he could, George excused himself from the table. He hurried back to the study, dipped his quill in ink, and returned to his writing. He knew from experience that if he did not get all his ideas down now, they might disappear entirely. Best to strike while the iron was hot!

Chapter Twenty

August 1817

ONE WARM SUNDAY morning, George and Arabella attended the morning service at St. Edmund's church, in Pendleford. They did not linger outside the church chatting, as some of the parishioners did, but hurried home. Confinement in the stuffy, crowded church had given Arabella a headache that grew even worse on the walk home. Even with a bonnet shading her face, the sun was too bright today.

By the time the cottage came in sight, her headache had become a hammering beat that made it difficult to think. "I wish we had a carriage," she blurted out. "This walk is rather much in the heat."

"It will be too much in the rain, too," George pointed out. "Perhaps we ought to buy a horse and gig? A gig with a hood, of course, so we can use it rain or shine. What do you think?"

Arabella did not even need to think about the question. "Yes. I would hate to have to walk to town in rain or snow this winter." A gig didn't cost too much, did it? But they might have to hire a groom to look after the horse, and that would be an additional expense. Horses ate feed in the winter, too, she thought. Bran or oats or some such. "Can we afford it?"

George looked down at her and smiled. "Of course! It's an essential. I ought to have thought of it earlier."

But Arabella still worried about the cost. All their income came from money in the Funds: Uncle William's gift and Arabella's dowry. If their spending ate into their principle, they would have even less income in the future. It would be far better to live below their means, so that they could save more. Someday they might have daughters in need of dowries, or sons in need of professions, and they would want reserves to draw upon.

Despite her skepticism, Arabella remained silent. Her head ached too much for her to even attempt arguing with George. It wouldn't hurt to look into the cost of a horse and a gig. Mr. Hastings might be able to advise them. He might know someone who could work as a groom, too.

She rubbed her head, wishing she knew some magic that would make it stop hurting. Her mother used to brew willow bark tea for her, but she did not even know where to get willow bark. Would the apothecary sell it? Maybe she should find out, because she usually had these headaches at least once a month, just before—

She stopped in her tracks and her whole body drooped. These pounding headaches always showed up a day or two before her courses arrived. Well, that answered the question about whether she was with child yet, didn't it? Ugh. Forget the willow bark. She ought to send someone to the apothecary for laudanum. A few drops of laudanum could make the difference between curling up in an agonized ball while her innards cramped or resting peacefully.

Arabella turned to George, intending to ask him if Mrs. Hastings kept laudanum on hand, but George interrupted her.

"What the devil is the dog doing in the garden?"

She looked over the gate, confused. Sure enough, George's bulldog puppy stood on his hind legs, resting his paws on the gate. His tongue lolled out of his mouth and his tail stump wagged with abandon.

"Maybe Mrs. Hastings let him into the garden?" Arabella suggested. She saw nothing out of the ordinary about that. Dogs belonged outside! "Maybe she was afraid he would soil the kitchen floor."

George opened the gate, carefully blocking it so that Bowser could not get out of the garden. "The whole point of a guard dog is to guard," he grumbled. "How can he watch the kitchen when he's outside?"

Arabella restrained the urge to roll her eyes. Instead, she pointed out the obvious. "No one can get into the kitchen without going through the garden. He can guard the house just as well from outside." Moreover, any food that might have been left on the kitchen table or counter would be all the safer for Bowser's absence. She suspected Mrs. Hastings would fear Bowser poaching food more than she would fear a burglar.

"You have a point." George crouched down to greet the puppy, but he cast a sheepish glance in Arabella's direction. "I suppose if he's in the garden, he can protect the whole house and not just the kitchen."

"Precisely." Arabella's lips twitched as she hid a smile. The so-called guard dog was currently zooming around the garden, having been transported to a state of ecstasy by their return. She suspected he would greet any would-be evildoers with similar enthusiastic friendliness. "If you don't mind, I believe I will go inside and get a cool drink."

"Of course, of course." George had already turned away from her so he could take a stick away from the puppy. But the puppy had a different game in mind. Instead of releasing the stick, he backed away with it, pulling George into a tug of war.

This time Arabella did not even try to restrain her smile. She watched her husband playing in the garden with as much as abandon as if he were a pup himself rather than a grown man. Then she headed towards the cottage.

When she got to the door, though, she found it locked. No one answered her knock, either. Strange. She glanced back over her shoulder. "George?"

He was so involved in tug-of-war with Bowser that it took him a moment to look up. "What? Is something wrong?" While he stared at her, Bowser snatched the coveted stick away from George and started running victory laps around the garden.

"The door is locked," she explained.

"Oh, right!" The puzzlement instantly vanished from George's face. "I gave all the staff the morning off, so they could go to church or chapel."

"Chapel?"

"The Hastings worship at the Methodist chapel, not the parish church," he explained. "They'll be back before dinner, and Mrs. Hastings promised to leave a cold luncheon for us. We ought not want for anything."

Arabella nodded. They could surely handle the house by themselves for half a day. She had only one concern. "How are to get back into the house?"

"With the key." George rose to his feet, futilely brushing at the soiled knees of his pantaloons. He reached into his pocket, but frowned when he pulled only a pocket watch and a crumpled handkerchief.

Her heart sank. "Did you lose the key?"

"It must be here somewhere!" He frantically patted all his pockets. Then he froze. "Hellfire! I had the key this morning, but I think I left it on my dressing table."

By now, Arabella's heart had sunk so low it might as well be in the root cellar. Her head ached, sweat crawled maddeningly down her back, and she would have given half her dowry for a glass of cold lemonade. Her hands began to tremble from sheer pain.

"What are we to do?" She spoke more to herself than to George. Then a happy thought hit her. "There's a pump near the kitchen, isn't there? We can at least get a drink of water." There would be shade in the garden, too, she reminded herself. She could cool off a bit. A day lolling about the garden was not at all what she wanted, but it would be better than nothing.

"We can do better than that," George said. "There's a spare key to the back door hanging in the garden shed. I'll go get it."

"Oh, good. I'll meet you at the back door." She scurried around the house, lowering her chin in an attempt to keep the sun out of her eyes. She needed a bonnet that provided better protection from the sun!

But although the kitchen door remained properly locked, the back door was not only unlocked, but also ajar. She touched the handle hesitantly, as if it might bite. Just a moment ago, she had desperately longed to get inside, away from the dust of the road and the August heat. Now a frisson of fear crept down her back, and her mouth went dry.

Was someone else in the house? Someone who shouldn't be there? In normal circumstances, she might have dismissed that idea as paranoia. Given the repeated break-ins the cottage had suffered, though, she could not dismiss the possibility. Instead of hurrying inside, she waited for George to return with the key.

It seemed to take an eternity before he loped up to the door. "Sorry it took me so long. Had trouble finding the right key. None of them are labelled." His eyes widened when they fell on the open door. "I say, did you open it without the key? How'd you manage that?"

Arabella shook her head. Her heart pounded heavily, and the slight tremor in her hands had become a full body tremble. "The door was already open."

"What?" George's jaw dropped.

She repeated herself. "The door was already open when I got here. Someone left it ajar."

He shook his head. "It must have been one of the maids, I don't believe either of the Hastings would forget to lock the door."

"What if it's someone else?" Arabella whispered.

George gave her an odd look. "Who else would be in our house?" Then he stilled, apparently having worked out what she meant. He thought for a moment before coming to a decision. "I will go in first. You stay here until I'm sure there are no intruders inside."

She shook her head. "I am not going to stay out here by myself. What if there is someone outside the house?" She glanced over her shoulder at the garden and the orchard that lay beyond it. She saw no sign of any intruders, but they might be good at hiding. She turned back to George and caught his eye, hoping to convey how strongly she felt about this. "I will go with you."

George looked like he wanted to argue, but he wisely held his tongue. "At least let me go in first," he suggested, "and you can follow a few feet behind me."

"Very well." She was not sure what she ought to do if they really did run into an intruder. Run away?

She twisted the cross on its chain as she watched George moving slowly down the corridor. He cracked open the dining room door and peered in, then shut the door. He glanced back over his shoulder and shook his head. Then he moved across the hallway to the kitchen door. This door swung open at his touch. Someone had left it ajar, just like the door into the garden.

George peered through the open door, and his whole body visibly stiffened. "Damn it all to Hell!"

Arabella's heart skipped a beat. "What happened?" Visions of murder or arson flooded her mind, and she took a cautious step backward, preparing to turn around and run if necessary.

"Someone made a wreck out of the kitchen again," he grumbled. "This time they've gone too far. They knocked over the old walnut dresser!"

"Oh?" She nearly added "Is that all?" She caught herself, though, seeing how much the damage distressed George. He charged into the kitchen before she could ask any clarifying questions, such as "Are you sure the intruders are gone?" or "Is anything broken?" After a moment, Arabella followed him.

She sucked in her breath sharply when she saw the destruction. The heavy wooden dresser that occupied most of one wall had been tipped over—with all its contents still inside. Broken crockery and shards of china littered the kitchen floor.

George stooped to pick up the spout of what used to be a very pretty Wedgwood teapot. "This belonged to my Aunt Helena." He scowled at the broken china in his hand. "She only used it on special occasions, but one year Caro's birthday fell during the middle of our visit, and she let us have tea using this set rather than the nursery set."

"There was a nursery set?" That surprised Arabella. The house didn't even have a nursery! "I thought your uncle had no children?"

George looked back over his shoulder and twisted his mouth into a wry smile. "I believe Aunt Helena bought it when she was first married, under the assumption that they would eventually need it. I suppose she did need it, given that Caro and I came to visit almost every summer. Sometimes Vincent and his sisters were there at the same time." His smile softened into something more genuine. "She loved having children in the house." He shook his head and gently placed the broken fragment on the kitchen table.

Arabella's first thought was that the damage was only a costly inconvenience. She knew a good deal about both bone china and porcelain, and so far as she could tell, none of the broken tableware was particularly valuable. Pretty, yes, but not rare or collectible. She and George could replace the tea set with something even better.

Then she asked herself how she would have reacted if any of her fairy tale figurines had been broken. That Little Bo Peep figure she bought long ago had little value to a collector, but it meant a good deal to Arabella. She would have been distraught if it had gotten chipped, broken, or lost in the move to Dogwood Cottage.

To George, the broken cups and saucers were not mere objects. Pieces of his childhood lay broken in a million pieces all over the kitchen floor. So, instead of telling George that "they are only things," Arabella said, "I am so sorry. Can anything be salvaged?"

"I don't know," he said grimly. "I think we ought to get this dresser upright again so that we can see."

That proved to be beyond their strength, though. The dresser weighed far more than both of them combined. In the end, George conceded that he would need the help of a few strong people to haul the piece of furniture back into position, assuming it could even be salvaged. One of the legs had cracked.

While George examined the damaged dresser, Arabella hunted for promising-looking pieces of china. She found most of the teapot and set those pieces aside in the hope that it could be mended. She knew more than one expert on ceramics who might advise them on that.

Her best discovery was a single teacup that had sustained only a slight chip in the rim. She put that on one of the built-in wooden shelves, feeling relieved that George would at least have one reminder of those long-ago tea parties. She suspected that most of the rest of the broken crockery would end up being discarded.

"I think I'd better have the magistrate in to look at this," George concluded.

"Who is the magistrate?" she wondered aloud. "Mr. Cawley?" He seemed young for the task, but he *was* the principal landowner in the area.

George shrugged. "Maybe. I expect Hastings will know. In any case, we'd better have someone investigate this."

"Because the treasure seekers keep breaking in, you mean?" For that matter, why hadn't anyone tried to investigate the previous break-ins? Maybe this damage could have been prevented.

Her husband surveyed the wreckage again and shook his head. "I don't think this is the work of the treasure seekers. It feels personal. Whoever did this wanted to damage these things. I can think of no reason for that apart from malice."

"But why would anyone feel this malicious towards *us*?" Arabella asked. "What have we done to make anyone so angry?" She shivered as she imagined the malevolence necessary to fuel such senseless destruction.

George met her eyes and frowned thoughtfully. "That is the question, isn't it?" But he could no more explain the vandalism than she could.

Chapter Twenty-One

WHEN MR. AND Mrs. Hastings returned from chapel, they were suitably horrified by the damage.

"Your aunt, God rest her soul, loved that tea set." Mrs. Hastings shook her head as she examined a blue-and-white shard. "She always warned us to take care not to chip the teacups when we washed them. Not to say that we weren't careful with all the china, of course. But Mrs. Kirkland was especially fond of that set."

"Yes, I know." George's heart still ached on Aunt Helena's behalf. It might be just as well that she was not here to see what had happened to her things. "I suppose we'd better get this cleaned up." He stooped down to pick up a broken piece of stoneware, only to cut his hand on the edge. He hissed in pain and fumbled for a handkerchief.

"You just leave the cleanup to us, Mr. Kirkland," Mrs. Hastings suggested. "Peggy and I have swept up many a mess over the years, and we know what we're doing."

Unlike me. George smiled sourly at his now-bleeding hand. That was his writing hand! "I will leave you to it," he promised. He thought he heard Mrs. Hastings utter a sigh of relief once he turned away, but he might have imagined it.

George hurried upstairs to wash and bandage his hand. He meant to ask Belle for help, but she must have fallen asleep the moment she lay down for a nap. Not wanting to wake her, he did his best to bandage his hand by himself. Cleaning the cut wasn't difficult, but tying a clean handkerchief around his hand was a challenge, to say the least.

By the time he had finished, the kitchen had been thoroughly cleaned. Hastings called over a neighboring farmer to help him restore the dresser to an upright position, but the neighbor pointed out that the parish constable might wish to take a look at the scene before they did so.

"Damnation," Geroge grumbled. "We should have sent for the constable before we cleaned up the broken pottery."

"I doubt it'll make much difference," Hastings opined. "If the constable hasn't caught the burglars before, he's not likely to do so now, is he?"

George suspected Hastings had the right of it, but he nevertheless sent for the constable. Then, knowing it would probably take some time to find that individual, he went back upstairs to check on Belle. He found her still slumbering. For some reason, she had stripped down to her shift, and she lay above the covers rather than under them. The walk home from church really must have overheated her.

He stared at his wife for a moment, struck again by her beauty. The fact that so lovely a woman had chosen to marry him—a man so disorganized that he could lose a book seconds after he'd had it in hand, and so absent-minded that he couldn't even remember what he was doing halfway through a task—both awed and perplexed him.

When George leaned over to brush a strand of hair away from Belle's face, she shifted position, rustling the counterpane beneath her. Then she smiled in her sleep. An answering smile unfurled across his face. He briefly considered waking her up so he could suggest a quick afternoon tumble. By now, she'd gotten past most of her timidity in the bedroom, and the broad daylight pouring in around the edges of the curtains would not have deterred her from responding passionately to such an invitation.

The knowledge that Belle probably needed her rest stayed George's hand, but aside from that, lust only made up a small part of his rising tide of ardor. This rush of feeling felt more like fondness, or affection, or—the hand stroking Belle's golden hair stilled.

Or love. He could not have fallen in love with his wife, could he? How very unoriginal! He did not want the story of his life to be so cliché.

The corners of his mouth quirked up as George realized what nonsense that was. His life did not need to mirror the plot of one of his novels. Dramatic love affairs made for good storytelling, but quiet, domestic affection was far more comfortable. And why shouldn't he fall in love with Belle? In his marriage vows, he had *promised* to love her.

He kissed his fingertips, then brushed the kiss against Belle's lips. Then he headed back down to the study, hoping to get a little writing in before the constable arrived. By the time the constable finally showed up, George was so deep into the current chapter that Hastings had to pound on the study door to get his attention.

Returning to awareness of his surroundings felt like coming up from a deep, dark, silent cave into the brightness and noise of regular life. George shook his head, rubbed his eyes, and yawned. How long had he been at work, anyway? He had no idea, but he'd covered several pages with his sloppy script.

It was a pity he had to stop writing now, because he knew exactly what needed to happen next, down to the next line of dialogue! Surely it wouldn't hurt if he wrote down that line. He knew from experience that failing to capture a phrase when it occurred to him often meant losing it for good.

"Mr. Kirkland? Mr. Johnson's here. The constable you sent for?"

"Be right there," he yelled back. But he did not stop writing until he reached the end of the paragraph. There! At least that was one less line for him to forget.

When he finally opened the door, Hastings looked disgruntled. "Constable won't appreciate waiting," the manservant grumbled.

George cringed. "I imagine not. I'd best hurry." He scurried downstairs before Hastings could scold him further. George did not mind Mrs. Hastings ordering him around. She had known him when he was a child. In his mind, that gave her the right to treat him familiarly. But her husband did not have that excuse!

In any case, Mr. Johnson did not seem particularly upset by George's delay. George found the constable crouching on the floor next to the fallen dresser, peering underneath it as Mrs. Hastings explained what had happened.

"And I told Hastings, I don't know how much longer I can stand to live in a house that attracts so many criminals, no matter how good the wages are!" She turned her head, caught sight of George, and immediately amended her complaint. "Not that we blame you, lad. This has been going on for months!"

No wonder Uncle William had been in a hurry to give away the cottage! George shook his head. Perhaps he had done his uncle a favor in taking this responsibility off his hands.

"Is there nothing that can be done about the break-ins?" George asked the constable. "I thought putting bolts on the kitchen door would keep intruders out."

"Aye, they might've done, if the back door had been bolted too." The constable lowered his eyes respectfully, avoiding any hint of confrontation.

George nevertheless clearly heard the critical note in Mr. Johnson's voice. A flush burned along his cheekbones. "We had better make sure all the doors are secure, then." He ought to have thought of that himself! Since the vandals had always entered through the kitchen door in the past, he'd assumed securing that door would be adequate. In hindsight, even George had to admit he'd been quite foolish.

Before the constable could offer any more suggestions, Bowser nudged George's hand, looking for attention. George glanced down at the pup and smiled ruefully. "And why didn't you protect the kitchen, hmm?"

Bowser, apparently not recognizing his failures, cocked his head and wagged his tail stump.

"Mayhap he'll be more useful when he's older," Mrs. Hastings suggested. "He's only a baby himself." She slipped what looked suspiciously like a biscuit to the dog. Bowser's tail stump wagged harder. "Or, if he doesn't guard well, perhaps he'll be good at catching rats and mice. We could use a good rat catcher about the house!"

George startled a little. "Are there rats? I've not seen one." He hated rats! Nasty, bitey things! He knew a boy at school who had died after being bitten by a rat.

Mrs. Hastings snorted. "You don't have to see a rat or a mouse to know it's there. They leave signs."

"Aye, but I shouldn't think a bulldog would be any good at catching rats," Mr. Johnson warned. "You need a terrier for rat catching. Farmer Wright raises the best ratters in this parish," he informed George.

"I will keep that in mind." George spoke politely, though he couldn't help but notice how far the conversation had wandered from the original subject. He was more concerned with vandalism than with vermin just now. "Is there anything more you can tell us, Mr. Johnson?"

The constable scratched his head and frowned. "'Fraid not. But call me right away next time. Don't wait till after you've tidied up the scene of the crime!"

Mr. Johnson's reproachful gaze made George feel about five years old. "Yes, sir." He only realized how ridiculous it was for him to address the local constable as "sir" once the words had already left his mouth. But perhaps it was not a mistake. Mr. Johnson stood up taller and the frown on his face eased.

"We'll get to the bottom of this," he promised.

A thousand objections strove to break out through George's firmly closed lips, but he contained the hasty words, contenting himself with a polite nod.

As soon as the door closed behind Mr. Johnson, the three men—George, Hastings, and Hasting's friend from a nearby farm—worked together to lift the dresser back up. When they'd scooted it back into place against the wall, George dusted off his hands and stepped back to take a good look. The old oak dresser had been dented in a few places, and a crack ran through part of one leg, but it stood solidly on all four feet, prepared to weather another half-century of use. Too bad the same could not be said for the porcelain and stoneware that once graced its shelves!

George sighed and wondered once again how he could possibly have an enemy so bent on senseless destruction. He hoped adding bolts to the back door would protect the house from further assault, but he no longer had much confidence about that. They probably hadn't seen the last of the mysterious vandal.

Chapter Twenty-Two

A FEW DAYS later, Arabella stood outside in the shade of a dogwood tree, hurrying to catch the glint of afternoon light off the river before the sun sank any further toward the horizon. She was nearly finished with the crayon landscape of the river. She'd sketched this view in pencil many times, but this was the first time she had tried to color it. Mixing all the different shades of green and river brown challenged her more than the simple crayon illustrations of flowers she'd been working on for the last two weeks.

The landscape required all the more focus as she intended to frame it and send it to George's Uncle William as a thank-you gift, along with a picture of the cottage itself, which she had not yet begun. If William Kirkland loved Dogwood Cottage as much as George claimed, he might appreciate a memento of the house. There were, of course, many pastoral scenes to delight the eyes in the country around Bath, but their beauty was quite different from the charm of the cottage, its garden, and the placid river.

She had just put down her crayon when she spied an open carriage rolling sedately down the road. When it drew nearer, she recognized it as the Cawley vehicle, and waved cheerfully at its occupants. She expected them to wave back as their horses trotted past the cottage. Instead, the carriage stopped right at the garden gate.

Mr. Cawley must intend to speak with her, Arabella assumed. Well, she had spoken to him after church, as well as having dined with him, so he ought not intimidate her. She drew a deep breath and left her art behind as she approached the carriage.

"Good afternoon, Mr. Cawley. Lovely day for a drive, isn't it?" She had expected to see him accompanied by either his wife or perhaps his elderly aunt. Instead, two young boys occupied the facing seat of the carriage. Both had freckled faces and hair as pale as dandelion fluff, but one was a little taller than the other. Otherwise, Arabella would have wondered how people distinguished them from each other.

Mr. Cawley did not smile back immediately. First, he glared at the two boys, who lowered their eyes shamefacedly. Then he looked back at Arabella, one corner of his mouth twisted up in a crooked smile. "Good afternoon, Mrs. Kirkland. My boys have something they'd like to say to your husband. Is he home?"

"Yes, of course! He's working in the study." Arabella frowned, wondering why her words made the two boys look even less happy. "Won't you please come in?"

They followed her inside. She led them down the short hall to the study before she remembered that George would not want to receive visitors there. If he did not like Arabella stepping foot inside his study, he would certainly not want the Cawley children poking about.

"Let me show you to the parlor," she suggested, "then I will fetch George. I mean, Mr. Kirkland." Her face flushed as she realized how badly she was bungling the usual forms of politeness. "Would you care for any refreshments?"

The two boys looked up hopefully, their eyes wide. But Mr. Cawley shook his head. "No, thank you. The boys do not deserve a reward." The children hung their heads, staring guiltily down at their shoes.

What on earth had they *done*? Arabella wondered as she scurried down the hall. She tapped on the door to the study and began counting as she waited for George to respond. When she got all the way down from ten, she knocked again, more loudly. When George answered, the heavy door muffled his words so much it took Arabella a moment to work out what he'd said.

"I'm busy right now! Can't it wait?"

It was not a particularly encouraging response, but Arabella opened the door anyway. "George, I'm very sorry to disturb you, but you have guests waiting to see you."

Her husband sat hunched over the desk. He'd taken his topcoat off and tossed it onto a chair, then wisely rolled up his sleeves. As a result, his shirtsleeves were blessedly free of ink stains, though the same could not be said of his hands.

George put down his pen, straightened his back, and ran a hand through his already-rumpled hair. "Don't tell me it's my cousin Benedict again!"

Arabella giggled at the sight of his mussed hair. "No, not Benedict! It's Mr. Cawley and two boys. His children, I think." She could not remember how many children the Cawleys had, but she knew they had more than one.

"Really?" George blinked, then stretched, and rose to his feet. He started to walk out the room in his shirtsleeves.

"Don't forget your topcoat." Arabella spoke hesitantly, worried she might be overstepping. She wasn't at all used to being in a position to correct anyone else. For most of her life, she'd been the one at the receiving end of a scolding.

But George grinned at her, turned on his heel, and grabbed his coat. She waited in the doorway while he rolled down his cuffs and shrugged the coat on.

"Are all the layers women have to wear as annoying as the ones men wear?" He grimaced at the ink on his hands, then buttoned the topcoat. "Because I get very tired of having to wear a coat in August."

She wrinkled her nose. "Sometimes the stays are rather annoying. I don't like the way the whalebone feels, even with a shift underneath." She spoke in a whisper, not wanting anyone else to hear her discussing women's underthings with a man. Not even if she was speaking to her husband, who had seen her without such articles of clothing. "And in hot weather, my shift always sticks to my skin. I hate that." She shivered as she remembered how miserable she'd been walking home from church Sunday afternoon.

George finished buttoning the coat, then lifted his chin to meet her gaze. "Is that why you sometimes take your clothes off when you nap? I thought perhaps the stays were too tight."

She shook her head. "Properly fitting stays don't hurt, but when I get overheated, I can't stand having so many layers. That's why I sometimes strip down to my shift in private." She eyed his snug-fitting wool jacket. "I suppose men probably have it worse in the summer," she admitted.

"At least the fashion now is for loose dresses," Arabella continued. "My mother showed me one of her old dresses from decades ago, with a narrow waist and panniers on the hips. I can't imagine walking around with that!" Or, for that matter, walking in the high heeled shoes that had been popular in Mama's youth. Arabella much preferred flat-soled slippers or comfortable half boots.

George reached up and tugged playfully on one of the ringlets hanging on the side of her head. "You would look smashing even in full court dress," he informed her. "Or in a flour sack."

Not knowing how to respond to such a compliment, Arabella bashfully lowered her eyes—but a shy smile teased at the corners of her mouth.

Her smile faltered when she saw the way the two Cawley boys cringed in their chairs when the Kirklands entered the parlor. The children only rose to their feet after their father pointedly cleared his throat.

"How do y'do, Mr. Cawley?" George asked. "These must be your boys?"

Mr. Cawley nodded grimly. "This is Stephen"—the taller of the two executed a clumsy bow—"and Owen." The younger one bobbed his head. "I've brought them here because they have a confession to make."

"A confession?" George frowned as he took a seat. "Have they been scrimping apples in the orchard? I wouldn't have thought the apples were ripe yet. Not that they'd be worth stealing even if they were ripe. The cherries are much better."

Arabella put a hand to her mouth to hide her grin. Surely children stealing cherries from the orchard was no better than scrimping apples? Especially as Mrs. Hastings seemed to know an endless number of dishes that utilized fresh cherries. Arabella enjoyed trying to predict in what form cherries would next appear on the dinner table. So far, her predictions had been consistently wrong.

"We have our own apple orchard!" the elder boy retorted. "And the apples aren't ripe yet, anyway."

"I always found the ones in my uncle's orchard too sour, to be honest," George confessed.

"They may have improved since you were a child," Mr. Cawley suggested. "Your Hastings is quite good at gardening. I believe he improved the drainage in the orchards here. Or so my gardener tells me." He shrugged, as if denying any knowledge of gardening. "But no, that is not why we are here today." He looked at the boys and raised his eyebrows.

"We broke into the house looking for treasure!" the oldest boy blurted out. "And we damaged the wall."

"And the floor," the younger boy added.

"*You* did that?" George's mouth gaped wide for a moment. "Did you knock over the big dresser in the kitchen last Sunday? I shouldn't have thought the two of you were strong enough for that."

"Oh no!" the smaller boy exclaimed. "We didn't touch the furniture. Just the wall. And the floor the time before that." He cringed.

"What my brother means to say," the older boy clarified, "is that last spring, we tried to dig up the paving stones to see if there was a cellar under the kitchen floor. But we didn't find anything, so we thought there must be a hidden room behind the kitchen wall. On our second visit, we tried poking through the wall with an awl, looking for the hollow space. But that was weeks ago, and we never touched the dresser, sir!"

George rested his forehead on his hand, as if it pained him. "There is no hidden room in this house! If there were, my sister and I would have found it years ago."

"Precisely what I said!" Mr. Cawley shook his head and directed a look of pure reproach at his children. "But even if there *were* a hidden room, that would not justify breaking into someone else's house and damaging the floor or the walls. Trespassing and vandalism are both against the law. Mr. Kirkland would be within his rights to turn you over to the magistrate!"

The boys' eyes widened as they nervously turned their attention from their father to the householder whose property they had damaged.

George made a sound suspiciously like a smothered laugh. He hastily cleared his throat. "I don't think we need go that far." He spoke to the two children in much the same tone he might have used after the puppy left a puddle on the kitchen floor. "But you should *never* break into someone else's house."

"We didn't break in!" the younger boy protested. "We had a key to the kitchen door!"

Both Mr. Cawley and George stared blankly at the boys for a moment. Mr. Cawley recovered from the surprise more quickly. "How on earth did you get that?"

"From Aunt Tilly," the older boy explained. "Mrs. Kirkland gave her a copy of the key a long time ago. They were friends."

"I see." George's impassive face gave away nothing of what he might be thinking. His voice remained calm and gentle, though. "I think you had better return that key, boys."

"Yes, sir." The older boy dug around in his pocket, pulling out a handful of marbles, the remains of a peppermint stick, and, finally, a large metal key. He handed this to George and returned the other paraphernalia to his pocket.

"Thank you very much, Master Cawley." The corner of George's mouth twitched, and Arabella guessed he was more amused than annoyed. "I hope this is a lesson to you not to trespass on other people's property. Not even if you think there's a hidden treasure. I assure you, this house has no hidden rooms!"

"Yes, it does!" the elder boy protested. "There's a secret room under the stairs."

"There is?" Arabella's eyes widened as she looked towards George for confirmation. He had never mentioned a secret room under the stairs. On the contrary, he insisted there were no secrets about the house, and no hidden treasure.

George merely chuckled. "Do you mean the storage closet under the stairs? There's nothing there but old odds and ends."

The boy lifted his chin, looking stubborn. "No, I mean the hole underneath the floor inside that closet. Haven't you ever seen that?"

George's mouth gaped for a second. Then he shook his head, disbelief written all over his face. "That can't be. I searched this house for secret rooms every summer from the time I put on short pants until I turned fifteen or sixteen. There *couldn't* be a room I didn't know about!"

"It's more like a hole than a room," the boy explained. "Let me show you."

Arabella turned to Mr. Cawley. "*Is* there some kind of hole beneath the closet? A root cellar, perhaps?"

Their neighbor shook his head. He looked just as baffled as George. "I've never heard of any kind of cellar under the stairs. But then, I've never lived here, either."

"It *is* there!" the younger Cawley boy piped up. "We found it when we were exploring last winter."

Mr. Cawley frowned. "You should not have been exploring in someone else's house! How many times did you break in?" The boys hung their heads again, looking supremely guilty.

"Never mind that," George interjected. "I want to see this hole, or cellar, or whatever it is. Can you show me?"

"Oh, yes!" The older boy rose to his feet with alacrity. He was probably relieved to be met with curiosity rather than condemnation. "Follow me!"

They all followed him out of the parlor to the front hall. Mr. Cawley looked confused, but George looked just as excited as the boys themselves. Arabella struggled to hide her smile. She did not want George to know how much he amused her. He was rather like an overgrown child himself.

But she followed the others anyway. If there were some sort of secret room in their house, she wanted to see it, too.

Chapter Twenty-Three

COULD THERE BE some sort of storage space under the closet? The idea wasn't completely implausible, but George could not imagine such a thing existing without his knowing about it. Not unless Aunt Helena and Uncle William had deliberately concealed the space. Which, he had to admit, was possible. Aunt Helena hadn't liked it when any of the children explored the attics. She might have felt the same way about this cellar. Assuming it existed, that is.

Stephen Cawley led them all straight to the closet under the stairs. Then he tugged at a large basket containing the laundry line and an assortment of wooden clothespins.

"It's under here," he explained.

George stepped up to give him a hand. Together, they moved the basket out from under the stairs. Then everyone looked at the newly exposed patch of flooring. There was absolutely nothing special about it. It was just a wooden floor.

Although, now that he thought about it, wasn't it a little odd that the floor in the closet was made of wood? Stone pavers covered the floor in the entranceway, just like the kitchen. But then again, there was probably wood under the carpet in the corridor. George could not be sure, since he had never seen the corridor without the carpet.

Mr. Cawley stated the obvious. "There's no trapdoor here,

Stephen. What are you talking about?"

"Yes, there is!" Stephen insisted. "The latch is hidden." He knelt down and ran his fingers along the floor until he found what looked like a knot in the grain. He pushed on it, and suddenly a small section of the floor popped up.

"Good Lord!" Cawley breathed. "There is a trap door! Why didn't Aunt Tilly tell me about it?"

"She says you never sat still long enough to hear the whole story," the younger Cawley boy explained.

Belle, who stood on her tiptoes to peer over George's shoulder, clapped a hand over her mouth to smother a giggle. George caught her eye and grinned, and her shoulders shook with silent laughter.

"This is precisely why one should always be respectful to elders," George told his neighbor. "You never know what secrets they might be hiding."

"Apparently." Cawley continued to study the open trapdoor. "So, what's inside this cellar?"

"Nothing!" Graham Cawley punctuated his answer with a rude sound. "It's empty. No treasure."

"Unless the treasure is hidden," his older brother qualified. "We didn't really look around, we didn't have a candle."

George straightened up. "That's what we need! A candle! I'll go grab one from my nightstand."

To his surprise, Belle stopped him. "I have a better idea." She spoke softly, but without hesitation or stammering. George hoped that meant she was growing more comfortable around their new neighbors. "I will go and ask Hastings for a lantern," she continued. "There must be one around here somewhere. That will be easier than trying to carry an open flame."

"Excellent point," George agreed. He meant to fetch a lantern himself, but just then the youngest Cawley child tumbled into the hole head-first. In the subsequent chaos, he entirely forgot about the need for a light.

Mr. Cawley cautiously lowered himself into the dark pit. A

sudden yelp indicated that he'd hit his head on something, but the string of hushed profanity that followed suggested he hadn't been seriously injured.

"All right down there?" George called anxiously. He desperately wanted to climb down the hole, too, but he had no idea how big the space was. He would probably just get in the way.

"Right enough," Cawley answered. "The ceiling here is rather low, though. Not enough room for a man to stand up. I mean, a tall man," he qualified.

George grinned. "I might fit, since I'm not as tall as you." Maybe for once there'd be an advantage to being of middling height.

"Maybe. There's not much room down here though," Cawley warned. "Kirkland, if I lift my son up to the trapdoor, can you help pull him out?"

"Of course!" It was done in a trice. Young Master Graham seemed no worse for his experience, apart from the new layer of dirt all over his clothes. George dug out one of his ubiquitous handkerchiefs and helped dust the child off. Mr. Cawley remained in the cellar, making noises that sounded as if he were tapping on the walls.

It really wasn't fair that Cawley got to explore the secret cellar first, given that this was George's house! George very nearly blurted out, "My turn to jump through the trapdoor!" Fortunately, he realized just in time how childish that would sound.

Even more fortunately, Belle arrived bearing the requested lantern. The candle inside burned steadily, without wavering.

Hastings followed behind her. "I thought perhaps you might need help, sir," he explained to George. But the way he eagerly peered at the trapdoor suggested that curiosity motivated him at least as much as helpfulness did.

"We've got a lantern if you want it, Cawley," George called into the pit. "Or I can join you down there to look about."

Cawley poked his head up through the open trapdoor.

"You're welcome to have a turn in here, but I predict that there won't be much to see. As far as I can tell, it's just a little earthen room." He hauled himself out of the cellar and dusted himself off. "There is a ladder built into one wall, though. You don't have to drop straight down into it."

"That's a relief." Though in fact it disappointed George a little. Somehow, a ladder made the hidden space less mysterious, more mundane. It really was nothing more than a forgotten root cellar.

Still, he clambered down the ladder eagerly, carefully holding the lantern in one hand. He didn't have to climb far, because the empty space beneath was less than six feet deep. No wonder Cawley had hit his head on the thick wooden ceiling! Even George could not stand fully upright in the space.

"What do you see?" Belle peered down through the trapdoor. "Are there shelves or bins for vegetables?"

"Nothing like that," George said. "Place seems to be empty! Wait, there's a jar or something in the corner."

"Oh, right, I nearly tripped over that," Cawley said. "What is it?"

George picked up the object and turned it over in his hand, puzzled. "It looks like a chamber pot?" He had expected to find a stoneware crock of the sort used to store preserves. But though he turned the pot around, studying it from every angle, it looked like nothing but a chamber pot.

"How strange," Belle said. "Why would anyone put a chamber pot in a cellar?"

George stilled, and his heart began beating more quickly. "Maybe this isn't a root cellar," he suggested, remembering the men's conversation about the cottage at Cawley's dinner party. "Maybe it really *is* a priest hole."

"Those were usually in manor houses and castles, weren't they?" Cawley argued. "I wouldn't expect to find one in a farmhouse occupied by yeomen. I imagine one had to be wealthy to afford a priest hole."

"But you said the Finches were Papists," George reminded him. "Recusants. Is it really so unlikely that a house of this size might contain a priest hole?" There were villas in Richmond smaller than Dogwood Cottage, after all.

"I suppose it's possible." Cawley still sounded doubtful. "But if there were a priest hole in the cottage, you would think I'd know!" A distinct note of vexation crept into his voice. "Why would Grandmother have told Aunt Tilly about this room but not me?"

"Maybe it's a secret passed down among the women of the family." Belle's soft voice unexpectedly broke into the conversation. Everyone turned to stare at her, and her face flushed. "I suppose that sounds silly. But sometimes women will trust other women with. . . well, knowledge, or information, that they wouldn't confide to a man."

Cawley drew his brows down over his eyes. "Women certainly do have their mysteries," he agreed, "but I wouldn't have thought hiding a Jesuit was a feminine secret!"

"Maybe the women of the family were more devout," George speculated. "I mean, maybe they were the ones who kept the old faith alive in the family. Children often follow the religion of their mothers, don't they?" He had no idea where he'd heard that, but it seemed reasonable.

"That does make sense," Cawley granted. "But I still think that, as the current head of the family, I ought to have been told! It isn't as if the secret poses any kind of danger to the rest of the family now. It's not illegal for priests to say Mass in England anymore!"

"I don't know how to explain it, Cawley. Should we speculate that maybe your grandmother didn't like you that much?" George grinned at the older man, hoping he would not take offense.

Fortunately, Cawley responded with a short bark of laughter. "That might very well be the case. I suppose she always was closer to Aunt Tilly than to my father. Can you hand that thing up?" He reached his arm down so George could pass the chamber pot to him.

George handed it over, glad to be rid of it. It would be easier to climb out of the cellar if he had both hands free. And so far as he could tell, there was nothing but earthen walls and support beams to be seen in the pit. No shelves, no potato bins, nothing that suggested the space had been used for storage anytime in the last century. Implausible as it sounded, George was increasingly convinced that they'd really discovered a priest hole.

Everyone crowded around Cawley, staring at the plain earthenware pot he held. It had single large handle and no ornamentation.

"Is that treasure?" the younger Cawley boy asked eagerly.

Cawley laughed again. "No, this is a potty," he informed his son. "Like what you might use in the nursery instead of going downstairs to use the water closet."

"Oh." The boy's face fell. "I thought there would be treasure. Gold and silver, Aunt Tilly said."

Cawley sighed. "I suppose I'd better have a talk with Aunt Tilly. There maybe are other things she didn't tell me."

George drew a deep breath, trying to decide whether he could reasonably invite himself into that conversation. On the one hand, this was Cawley family business, and he had no connection to the Cawley family. On the other hand, Dogwood Cottage most certainly *was* his business now. He tried to catch Belle's eye to see what she thought, but she was busy examining the stoneware crock.

She lifted her head at last. "Someone who studied stoneware might be able to date this. I mean, at least to a specific century. Don't you think?"

"I have absolutely no idea, ma'am," Cawley said. "You may be right, but I wouldn't know how to find an expert on chamber pots." The curl of his lip suggested he didn't take the suggestion very seriously.

"I might know someone," Belle said. "The problem is, how to

get the pot all the way to London without damaging it?"

"Oh, you mean your antiquarian acquaintance? That elderly chap who collects crockery?" George hadn't made the connection between Belle's collection of ceramic figurines and the plain, homely pot in her hand. But she most certainly did have acquaintances who knew all about the history of ceramics in England. "That's a smashing idea!"

"You know an antiquarian who collects pottery?" Cawley sounded surprised. After all, he knew nothing about Belle's hobbies and collections.

"Yes. Most of the people I know are interested in porcelain and bone china—the work of Meisner and Wedgwood. But I also know a few people who collect Staffordshire pottery. I will write to one of them and see if he can advise us." She nodded decisively. "This must technically belong to your family, Mr. Cawley, since none of the Kirklands seemed to know about this cellar. But if you don't mind, I'd like to keep it until I hear back from Mr. Hodges."

Cawley held his hands up, palms outward, declining any interest in the pot. "You may keep it forever so far as I'm concerned! We don't know for certain that it ever belonged to the Finches. And I doubt an ancient chamber pot is at all valuable, no matter what my aunt says about treasure." He smiled ruefully.

"It might have historic value," Belle suggested. "But only to an antiquarian, I suppose." She glanced at George. "If you don't mind, I'd like to take this to my studio and make a drawing of it. That may be more helpful to Mr. Hodges than a mere verbal description."

"Of course! You will have to tell us when you hear back from him." George studied the trapdoor again. "I suppose there is nothing more we can do to figure out if this really is a priest hole."

"I will talk to my aunt," Cawley promised. "Her memory isn't quite what it used to be, but her mind is still clear." He turned to Belle and cleared his throat. "Perhaps you would like to drop in for tea Tuesday next? My wife is at home then, and Aunt Tilly joins her when her health allows. You might have a chance to speak to her then."

Belle bit her lip nervously and hesitated before nodding. "I shall try to do that."

George wondered if Cawley noticed the way Belle avoided committing herself to the morning call. "Trying" to pay a call left her an out if she had one of her bad headaches, or became caught up in her art. That was better than George's habit of committing to plans and then completely forgetting about them. He ought to learn from her!

They all went their separate ways after that. The Cawleys went home, Belle took the chamber pot up to her studio to sketch it, and George returned to his study, hoping he could pick up the thread of the plot where he'd left off. But all he could think about was the possible priest hole and the chamber pot inside it.

He paced back and forth for a good ten minutes, wondering how he might incorporate the days' discovery in this manuscript. It wouldn't do to mention a chamber pot. There were some things ladies simply wouldn't read about. But there could be something else found in a priest hole, surely. Something related to priestcraft.

What did Romish priests use to say Mass? Never having attended a Roman Mass, George had no clear idea, but he thought they used ornate cups and plates. His father would know more. George sat down to write a long-overdue letter to his father. It took all his powers of creativity to ask questions about liturgical objects without revealing that he wanted the information for a novel. His father would never support George writing that! But he might be interested in the discovery of the cellar. George whistled as he became absorbed in his correspondence.

Fortunately, writing out the letter seemed to reopen the floodgates of his creativity. He knew what needed to happen next! He set the letter aside and resumed work on his manuscript. When it came time for dinner, he asked for a tray so he could eat while he worked. Belle surely wouldn't mind dining alone for once. She was probably just as involved in her art, anyway.

When he asked to have his dinner sent to the study, the maid-servant gave him a doubtful look, and opened her mouth as if to protest. Then she closed her mouth, bobbed her head, and went to do as requested. If George wondered at all about her hesitation, the question was soon forgotten as he continued to write.

❧

Chapter Twenty-Four

B ELLE SENT HER letter off to Mr. Hodges, the pottery collector, and then did her best to wait patiently despite her many questions about the hidden cellar. She continued working on her crayon pictures of the cottage and the river, until at last even she had to admit that both landscapes were as good as she could make them. She glazed the art with her usual isinglass mixture, then packed them to ship to Bath.

George might very well want to send some sort of note to his uncle, she thought. Best to ask him before she sent off her package. When she peeped into his study, though, she found it empty. Nor did he seem to be writing in the garden today.

Arabella popped into the kitchen to ask if anyone knew about George's whereabouts. He was rather bad at letting her know when and where he was bound when he left the house, but sometimes he told Mrs. Hastings so she would know whether to expect him for meals.

"I believe he went for a ramble along the river, ma'am," Mrs. Hastings said. "He said something about needing to think, though I can't imagine what that has to do with walking. Rather eccentric, isn't he?"

"Eccentric?" Arabella cocked her head to one side, puzzled by the word. George seemed perfectly normal to her.

"Meaning no offense, ma'am," Mrs. Hastings quickly added.

"He's a very pleasant gentleman to work for, generous and respectful. But he does have that habit of taking his meals in the study, and he doesn't like anyone to come in and clean. Says he can't stand other people in his room. The place has become a mess, if you don't mind my saying so."

Arabella frowned. She could not deny that George kept his workroom in a perpetual state of disorder. The last time she glanced inside, she'd seen a clutter of teacups and saucers, as well as papers scattered all over the floor. Probably fragments of food as well, given what he'd previously told her about his talent for getting crumbs everywhere.

"Would you say it's becoming a problem?" she asked. If George never returned his teacups to the scullery, they would eventually run out of clean cups.

Mrs. Hastings sighed and glanced over her shoulder as if checking to make sure there was no one else in earshot. "The fact of the matter is, Peggy says she saw a mouse scurrying out of the study this morning. And I've seen signs that there might be mice in the house. Mice do leave evidence behind, if you know what I mean."

"Oh dear." Arabella wrinkled her nose. "We can't have that."

"No, indeed not, Mrs. Kirkland." Mrs. Hastings nervously pleated her apron in her hands as she waited for Arabella to respond.

Am I supposed to say something? As the awkward moment dragged on, Arabella swallowed to moisten her mouth. She reached for her necklace, intending to play with it. But she had forgotten to put it on this morning. Unable to soothe herself by fidgeting with something, she instead clasped her hands tightly together.

"I will talk to Mr. Kirkland about keeping the room in a tidier state." She had doubts about whether George could be tidy even if his life depended on it, but she kept that skepticism to herself. Then a happy thought struck her. "In the meantime, I can at least carry all the dirty dishes out of there."

Mrs. Hastings relaxed. "That would be a help, ma'am." She bobbed her head and turned back to the kitchen.

Arabella drew a deep breath. If George had gone for a walk, this might be the perfect time to pick up all the dirty dishes left in the study. She wouldn't have to worry about interrupting his writing or getting in his way. And he could hardly complain about her tidying up after him, could he?

She hurried to the study, where she found a bigger mess than she'd remembered. No matter! It only meant taking two or three trips to get all the dirty plates, cups, and utensils back to the scullery.

On the last sweep through the room, she found only a single cup resting on a bookshelf and a dessert plate half-buried beneath a pile of papers. She lifted up the papers so she could pull out the plate, then hesitated as an unexpected word caught her eye. Was George writing an article about Recusants? Interesting. She could not help but read on, though George's handwriting was even less legible than usual.

It took several pages before she admitted to herself that what she was reading was neither an informative essay nor a book review, but a story, complete with dialogue as well as narration. When did George start writing fiction? He wrote descriptions quite well, she thought critically, but some of the dialogue seemed off. She reached for a pen, intending to jot down a brief comment about the stilted wording, but remembered just in time that George would not appreciate her marking up his manuscript.

Unfortunately, that was when George returned. He walked through the door to find her still holding a stack of papers in one hand. He froze, his mouth gaping.

Arabella put down the pen. "I was just tidying up a bit," she explained.

George interrupted her. "Are you reading my manuscript? Without asking?" His anguished voice made it sound like a personal attack.

She cringed and put down the papers. "I didn't mean to!"

There was, she reminded herself, no reason for her hands to sweat or her heart to pound more quickly. This was a simple misunderstanding.

"But what are you even doing in here?" He shook his head. The gesture seemed to unlock his frozen muscles, and he strode towards the desk to pick up the manuscript she'd been reading. "I thought you knew better than to poke around in my study, Belle! I would never rummage around in your art studio, would I? What made you think you had a right to look through my private papers?"

Arabella's hands began to tremble. She felt like a child reprimanded by her governess. Any minute now, she expected to be sent off to her room without any supper. Or worse. *But George would never hit me.* She was not a child who could be switched with a hickory stick for every infraction. He might be angry, but perhaps he had reason to be.

"Well?" He crossed his arms in front of his chest and scowled more fiercely than ever. "Aren't you going to answer me, Arabella? What have you got to say for yourself?"

He did not yell, but his sharp tongue hurt nearly as much as a childhood caning. Maybe more. Was there anything more painful than the disapproval of a loved one? And he had called her *Arabella*, rather than using his usual nickname for her. No matter how other people might address her, she was always *Belle* to George. The last time she could remember hearing her full name on his lips had been during their wedding ceremony.

She stared down at her shoes. Her husband stood before her, staring for a long painful moment, while she longed to crawl under the desk and hide from his wrath. Better yet, she wished she could explain herself. But she could not speak. She could only shake her head and blink her eyes rapidly.

George sighed. "I ought not yell at you," he said more quietly. "Forgive me for losing my temper. I just wish you accorded me the same respect I show you. I think you had better go now, Belle. If you linger here, I'm afraid I will say things I don't mean."

He glanced away, but the tense set of his jaw hinted at his anger.

"Yes," Arabella rasped. "I am sorry. Very sorry." She scurried from the room, eager to put distance between them. He needed time to calm down, and she needed time to collect her tumultuous emotions.

On the way to her bedchamber, Arabella took the stairs so quickly that she nearly slipped. When she reached the refuge of her studio, she flung herself into a comfortingly worn armchair and covered her face with her hands.

But she did not cry. Though her eyes still stung with unshed tears, she did not break down into the embarrassing fit of weeping she half-expected. She supposed she ought to feel proud of that self-control. But pride was the farthest thing from her mind. She sat hunched in the chair, holding her head, until she had regained some semblance of calm.

Then she reached for her sketchbook and a pencil and began to draw. This was no quick, rough sketch, but a painstaking process of mapping out lines and shadows, angles and planes. Gradually, the drawing took form. Drawing from memory, she depicted George's desk, cluttered with papers, books, discarded quill pens, and an empty saucer.

Arabella began drawing with the intent of working through her unsettled feelings, but the act of creating did more than soothe her. As she stared at the simple sketch, her fears and regrets gradually faded. The finished picture seemed inexpressibly dear to her. A smile slowly unfurled across her face. Who would ever have guessed that she might be charmed by George's habitual disorganization?

George could no more help being messy than Arabella could help being shy, so scolding him for his habits would be worse than useless. She knew this from experience, as her parents' lectures about her retiring behavior had never done anything except make her more nervous. Not only had she worried about what other people would think of her manners, but she'd had to worry about whether her own family would disapprove of her social interactions.

But it *was* a pity that George did not want anyone else entering his study. Arabella would have been perfectly happy to help him keep the place free of dirty dishes, muffin crumbs, and mice. Maybe if she promised never to read the work he left out, he wouldn't mind her cleaning up from time to time.

Arabella sighed, stretched her cramped hand, and rose to her feet. Her rumbling stomach suggested it would be time for dinner soon. But she needed to find George before she dressed for dinner. She did not want to sit down to an uncomfortable meal. Better to resolve their quarrel first! She fortified herself with a deep breath and headed downstairs.

George did not answer when she lightly tapped at the study door. Perhaps he was not ready to talk yet. She returned to her chambers to dress, trying not to take his silence personally. He would probably come up to dress soon, too. They would speak then. She could explain about the mouse problem, and together they would find a solution that kept his study vermin-free, without disturbing his writing.

His writing, though! Why hadn't George told her he was writing a novel? He must have known she would want to read it! She could not help feeling hurt that he'd kept so large a secret from her. Didn't he trust her?

Arabella stared at the mirror's reflection of her frown, wondering why her husband wouldn't want to share his work with her. She speculated that he didn't want her to see it in its raw state. She certainly understood that. A sketch at the beginning looked very little like the finished project. She would not want anyone to judge her art based on the first lines she put down on paper. For all she knew, writing might work the same way.

And after all, it wasn't as if George had wronged Arabella in any way. He had not lied to her, merely refrained from telling her what he composed during those long hours locked in his study. It was well within his rights to keep such a secret. It wasn't as if their wedding vows had included a promise to discuss their creative work with each other. Arabella had no real grounds for feeling hurt or disappointed over the exclusion.

She took a book down to the parlor and tried to read while she waited for George. They were not particularly formal about their meals, but on days when they did not come downstairs together, they generally met each other in the parlor to wait. He would be here any minute.

Shortly after that, Peggy shyly poked her head into the parlor to announce that dinner was ready.

"I will wait for Mr. Kirkland, Peggy," Arabella said. "I'm sure he won't be long."

But the minutes continued to tick past, and she heard neither the sound of George's feet on the hallway nor the drone of his not-particularly-tuneful humming. She got up and tapped at the study door, but once again, there was no answer. This time, she cautiously opened the door and peered inside.

Arabella's heart sank as she studied the unoccupied room. Something about the state of the room bothered her, but she wasn't sure what. She reached up to twist one a curl around her finger as she scanned the room, trying to figure out what was missing. Finally, she realized that the problem lay with his desk. Or rather, the problem lay with what should have been on the desk but wasn't.

Normally, George left his workroom looking as if he had gotten up in the middle of writing a sentence and meant to come back shortly. But not today. Though his handsome brass inkstand still stood in its usual place next to the pounce-box, the desk's surface had been cleared of papers. All of George's writing had been put away And George was nowhere to be seen.

Where *was* he?

Chapter Twenty-Five

FOR THE FIRST half mile of his walk, George savagely kicked a stone along the road. The poor stone had done nothing to vex him, but something ought to suffer for the betrayal he'd experienced. Admittedly, "betrayal" seemed like too strong of a word, but he could think of it no other way.

George was not angry about Belle entering the study to clean up after him. If anything, that left him with the familiar sickness of shame in the pit of his stomach. She shouldn't have had to come in there to pick up his dirty dishes, he ought to have put them away after using them. He knew that.

In his younger years, his mother had frequently scolded him for leaving the writing table in his room such a mess. In London, his charwoman had grumbled about his habit of leaving crumbs and dirty spoons everywhere. So, he should have realized his messiness might inconvenience other people here at the Cottage. He would have to come up with some better system.

Unfortunately, knowing he needed to clean up after himself had never helped him change his behavior in the past. His messiness, like his procrastination, seemed to be a habit he could not correct, no matter how ashamed he might feel about it.

The longer George spent reviewing his life, the more his spirits sank. God, he really was a failure, wasn't he? What was it Priscilla had called him at the end of their *affaire*? Ah, a "feckless good-for-naught." He could hardly forget those words.

Maybe Priscilla had the right of it. Missing the deadline on that essay about Mesmer had cost George the opportunity to write any further articles for *The Current Review*. There were editors of other journals who might still be willing to work with him, but none of those journals had circulations anywhere nearly as high as *The Current Review*. None of them paid as well, either.

As for Peabody & Sherman—well, George had not even told Mr. Sherman that he'd given up working on *Ermintrude, or the Lady in the Tower*. His current project was shaping up to be much stronger, but the novel about Recusants was nothing like his previous work. What if Mr. Sherman didn't want it? Then George would have to find a new publisher, that's what! Who knew whether a different editor would even be able to read his messy handwriting?

By the time he reached Pendleford, George had gone from being angry at Belle for poking her nose into his work to despising himself for making such a mess of things. Or, rather, for being such a mess himself. Nothing he did ever turned out right. He could not turn an essay in on time, he could not write a novel that would sell, and he could not even clean up after himself. Even Charlie was better at tidying up the nursery than George was at keeping his study in order. Belle must be regretting marrying such a good-for naught.

It did not, at that moment, occur to him to wonder whether Belle considered him worthless, or thought him at all childish. He knew perfectly well that she'd been hurt by his snapping at her in the study. Clever and talented though she might be, there were some ways in which Belle seemed as fragile as the porcelain she collected. She ought never have married a blundering boar like George, and the sooner she realized—

"I say, Kirkland, what are you doing in town?"

George lifted his head and looked about, startled out of his self-recriminations. He'd been so abstracted, it took him a moment to place the young man who stood before him, carrying a heavy-looking black satchel.

Not a satchel, but a doctor's kit. This was the young surgeon he'd met at the dinner party a couple of weeks back. George had seen him only briefly at church since then, but what little he'd seen had confirmed his impression that Arkwright was a man worth knowing. He seemed nearly as good natured as Cawley, and maybe a bit cleverer.

"Good afternoon, Arkwright. I just wanted a good long walk today. Helps me think, you know." George shrugged his shoulders, feeling sheepish. He knew perfectly well that other people did not need to walk back and forth to get their minds moving, and he had no idea why he needed so much movement.

"You picked rather a foul day for a stroll," Arkwright pointed out.

"Did I?" Wasn't it a fair day? The sun had been shining this morning, and—"Oh!" The moment he peered up at the sky, George saw what Arkwright meant. Ominous black clouds had covered the late-afternoon sun. He took a deep breath and caught the tell-tale scent that heralded a thunderstorm.

Worse yet, a heavy rain drop plopped down right at George's feet, leaving a dark spot on the dusty road. "Da—I mean, dash it all, you're right. And I didn't think to bring an umbrella." He was lucky to have remembered his hat.

"Bad luck," Arkwright said sympathetically. "But I've just seen my last patient, and my throat is dry as a bone. Why don't you come have a pint with me at the Dove and Rose?"

"My wife will be expecting me home for dinner." But before George could make his apologies, the heavens opened up. The light spattering of rain turned into a steady downpour. "On second thought, a drink might be nice."

Arkwright chuckled and led him to a good-sized inn further down the main street. Not a big posting inn, the place seemed to serve primarily as a pub, with a few rooms for travelers. George supposed there probably weren't many travelers who came through Pendleford, as it did not lie on a toll road.

"Mr. Arkwright, good to see you," the publican called. "The usual for you?" He looked at George with undisguised curiosity.

"Yes, Robertson," Arkwright said, "and a pint for Mr. Kirkland, too, if you please."

"Coming right up!"

Arkwright led the way to a booth near the hearth. "We are lucky to grab so good a seat," he noted. "The place gets crowded in bad weather, because anyone who can stop to get in out of the rain, does."

"I didn't expect to see it so busy," George admitted. "Is it the only pub in town?"

"No, just the best. Mrs. Robertson used to cook at a great house near Preston, and the fare here is better than at most inns."

George could see for himself that the public room was relatively clean, though the floor was growing damp from the flow of people coming in out of the rain. It being summer, no fire burned on the hearth, and the scent of fresh air suggested someone had opened a window recently. Compared to the smoky, fetid dining rooms at many public houses, this one was quite comfortable.

A young woman brought them heavy pint glasses. "Be you Mr. Kirkland?" she asked George.

"Yes, I am he." George sat up straighter, feeling self-conscious. As a new resident in a middling-sized market town, he often found himself under observation. People naturally wanted to know about him. Particularly, they wanted to know how to persuade him to spend money in the local shops.

"Was that your brother who visited here last week?" the barmaid asked.

"What? No, I haven't any brother." Much to his father's dismay. The Reverend Mr. Kirkland had hoped for a like-minded son to follow in his clerical footsteps. Instead, he only had a slovenly ne'er-do-well addicted to scribbling.

"I see. Only I thought he said his name Kirkland, too."

George frowned, trying to remember when Benedict had visited the cottage. "One of my Kirkland cousins visited Pendleford in July, but that would've been a couple of weeks back. Could you be thinking of him?"

"Nay, that was another gentleman," she insisted. "The one in July was taller than you, and his hair was sandy brown. But the fellow who was here Saturday last was shorter and his hair were straw-colored. He had blue eyes, too, I think. Or were they green?" She frowned.

"You don't say!" The only Kirkland George knew with blue eyes and straw-colored hair was his cousin Augustus. But there were certainly other men by the name of Kirkland in England. Maybe the straw-haired young man came from the Cheshire branch of the family. Or maybe he wasn't related at all, and his visit was pure coincidence.

"I'm afraid I don't know the gentleman's given name, sir," the serving girl said. "He said he was here to visit a friend, and he only stayed the one night. Left Sunday afternoon in rather a hurry."

George tightened his grip on the handle of his pint glass. "Sunday, you say," he repeated. "Curious. We didn't see him at all. Perhaps he wasn't one of my cousins." He forced a smile to his face. "Thank you for the information, miss."

After she left to serve other customers, he stared down into his pint pot, lost in thought.

"Something wrong?" Arkwright suggested.

"Don't know." George looked up and grinned crookedly. "Seems a little odd if my cousin came through last Saturday and didn't stop to visit with us. He must've been in a hurry."

Or, George silently added, Augustus deliberately visited Dogwood Cottage while all its residents were at church or chapel, leaving the house ripe for trespassing and vandalism. Until now, it hadn't occurred to him to suspect his cousins, he'd had no reason to think they were in the area. But if Augustus had been in Pendleford Sunday morning, he suddenly moved to the top of the list of suspects.

Well, in all honesty, he was one of the *only* suspects on

George's list. Assuming the Cawley boys told the truth when they denied having knocked over the dresser (which they weren't strong enough to move) George couldn't name anyone else who might have wanted to investigate the kitchen. Most of the local people knew about the legends, but how many of them would be desperate enough to break into the house? A local burglar couldn't be ruled out, but George didn't have the faintest clue where to begin searching for such a person.

Augustus and Benedict certainly had motive to break into the cottage. More than one motive, in fact. At that dinner party in Bath, Augustus had been very interested in the story of the treasure. Having failed to secure the cottage or Uncle William's money himself, he might very well hope to find the mythical treasure as a consolation prize.

Alternatively, one or both of the brothers might feel vindictive about George having beaten them in the race to win the cottage. Some people would be perfectly willing to break in and smash Aunt Helena's china just to get revenge. George did not know his cousins well enough to rule out that possibility.

"Is something wrong, Kirkland?"

Arkwright's concern yanked George out of his flight of fancy and down to earth. He lifted his head and looked around the bar room. Outside, the rain fell more heavily than ever. Inside, the room had gotten louder and more crowded as people sought shelter from the downpour.

"Nothing's wrong, exactly," George said slowly. "At least not right now. I hope." But who knew whether the burglar would strike again? If Augustus or Benedict had knocked over the dresser, would they consider that sufficient revenge, or would they try again?

"Well, if it's a medical problem, I'm here to help you. Can't help if it has anything to do with farming, though."

That brought a grin to George's face. "Nothing to do with health or agriculture." He hesitated for a moment, considering how much he could tell a stranger. "It's rather a curious problem," he said slowly, "and it began with a story about treasure."

George ending up telling Arkwright everything, though not necessarily in a clear, coherent order. He hadn't intended to say anything about Uncle William's ridiculous marriage competition, but he found it impossible to explain his suspicions about Augustus and Benedict without talking about that.

Arkwright's jaw dropped at that part of the story. "Do you mean to tell me you married your wife only to get the cottage?"

A flush burned George's cheeks. "We were already friends! It wasn't as if I ran off and married the first stranger I met." Though, now that he thought about it, that would make a good premise for a novel! "Er, one moment, please." He pulled out his notebook and quickly down scribbled the idea.

When he looked up, Arkwright raised his brows, and George's embarrassment grew to epic proportions. "Sorry, I just wanted to jot down an idea before I forgot it. I'm a little absent-minded, you know." *Little* wasn't quite accurate, but he would rather not explain just how absent-minded he really was. "Where was I?"

"You were explaining how you won your grandfather's race, or whatever it was," Arkwright said. "And now you think your cousins might be trying to steal the treasure?"

George sighed. "It sounds very silly when you put it like that. But some people obviously believe there's a treasure at Dogwood Cottage. And I know my cousin Augustus is greedy, so. . ." He shrugged, unable to think of any more evidence to support his theory.

Arkwright nodded. "It makes sense. Have you talked to the constable about your suspicions?"

George furrowed his brow and drained the last sip of his ale. "Problem is, I don't really have any evidence. And it's not as if the constable at Pendleford is going to travel all the way to Manchester to interview my cousins on the off chance they might have committed a crime."

"And it's not as if they would admit the truth if you asked them about it," Arkwright said. "What if you wrote to your uncle? Wouldn't he be concerned?"

George turned that idea over in his mind, trying to see it from every angle. "You know, that is what I should do. Thanks!" His cousins would want to stay on Uncle William's good side, since there were still thousands of pounds to be inherited when he died.

He sat up straight and subtly rolled his neck around, feeling some of his tension dissipate. He felt better now that he knew what to do next—as long as he didn't forget. He pulled out the notebook and his pencil to make sure he recorded Arkwright's suggestion. An otherwise miserable afternoon looked a bit more promising now.

When he glanced out the window, though, his face fell. "It's still raining, isn't it?" The rain had let up, becoming a drizzle rather than a downpour, but he would still get thoroughly soaked on the walk home.

"Why don't you dine at our house," Arkwright suggested, "and I'll drive you home in my gig afterwards?"

"That is very kind of you, but my wife will worry about me if I don't come home for dinner." Especially since they'd quarreled before George stalked out of the house. But he didn't plan to tell Arkwright *that* part of the story!

"She'll realize you took shelter from the storm, won't she?" Arkwright argued. "I doubt she'll expect you to make good time in this weather. Most people stay off the road in the rain, if they can. There's always a chance the river will overrun its banks if the rain is heavy enough."

That convinced George. He really didn't want to walk through mud and rain without an umbrella. His boots would be ruined! Well, except that they were already in terrible shape as it was. But they would be even *more* ruined. And Belle would understand his tardiness once he explained about the possibility of the river overflowing. She might be angry with him after the way he'd spoken to her, but she would not want him to drown in a flood.

At least, he hoped not.

Chapter Twenty-Six

G EORGE DID NOT come home. Dinner time came and went, and the food grew cold while Arabella waited for her husband, but he did not return. Eventually, Mrs. Hastings coaxed her into eating a little chicken and some fruit. She did not have the appetite for more than a few bites.

"No need to worry, my dear. Mr. Kirkland is keeping himself safe and dry in one of the pubs," Mrs. Hastings assured her. "No one likes walking River Road during a rainstorm. I expect you'll see him tonight or tomorrow morning, whenever the rain stops."

Arabella tried to clear the lump from her throat. "I am sure you're right." She smiled, but her smile wavered so much, she let it fall. Mrs. Hastings must not have been fooled, she patted Arabella's hand gently.

After giving up her fruitless attempt to eat, Arabella took her embroidery into the parlor, sat in her favorite armchair, and tried to bury her worries in needlework. She had long since finished embroidering monograms on handkerchiefs. Now she was embroidering a set of bibs for Caroline Gray's baby. Caroline's most recent letter happily reported that she had already felt the baby moving. Having quickened, Caroline was more optimistic about the outcome of the pregnancy.

I ought to tell George about that! After the wedding, Caroline had announced that she would address all her letters to Arabella now, because Arabella answered her letters in a timely manner rather than leaving them to languish in a pile of unread correspondence, as George seemed to do.

Arabella liked to read Caroline's letters out loud to George at breakfast, though he sometimes had trouble paying attention. But he would want to know about his sister's improving condition. He did not talk about Caroline's pregnancy often, but she knew he'd been worried about it. Everyone who knew Caroline worried, since she'd come so close to dying during her miscarriage two years ago.

George tarried so long that night, Arabella had time to finish embroidering the last of the bibs. Since she had no idea what the Grays would name their baby, she could not add a full monogram. Instead, she stitched a fanciful "G" for Gray, accompanied by a fluffy lamb.

How could she keep herself occupied now? Arabella doubted reading would distract her from her cares the way art did. Maybe she could make another blanket? She could embroider lambs in the corners, to match the bibs. Better yet, she could put lambs in two of the corners, and ducklings in the others. In order to do that, she would have to plan out the pattern, and her sketchpad and pencils were all upstairs.

Arabella left the parlor, taking her candle with her. She had almost reached the top of the stairs when the sound of the front door swinging open made her whirl around so quickly, she nearly fell. She frantically caught hold of the banister, but dropped her candle, plunging the steep staircase into a late summer twilight.

"George?" For one painful second, she wondered if it could be someone else. The burglar, maybe? Or someone come bearing news of a terrible accident? Or—

"I didn't mean to startle you! Are you all right?" George galloped up the stairs. He slipped an arm around her waist to keep her from falling.

Arabella kept one hand on the banister, just in case. "I'm fine. Are *you* all right? I expected you home hours ago."

"Right as a trivet," he assured her. "The rain kept me in town for a few hours, that's all. Mr. Arkwright offered to drive me home in his gig, but I had to wait until after his dinner."

"Oh. That makes sense." Mrs. Hastings had been right all along. George hadn't been staying away because he was angry with Arabella, or because he had gotten into some kind of trouble. Only the weather was to blame.

She sighed and leaned in closer so she could rest her head on George's shoulder. She hadn't realized how tense she'd become until she felt her body slowly relax against George. George must have felt a shift, too, as he embraced her more tightly.

"I need not have worried after all," she murmured.

"Did you think I'd been swept away by the river?"

There was a note in George's voice she didn't quite recognize. Amusement? But it sounded too warm to be mockery.

"You can laugh all you want, but yes, I was concerned! It would break my heart if something were to happen to you." She blinked, surprised by her own vehemence. Where had *that* come from? Would it really break her heart to lose George?

Yes, she supposed, it would.

"I am glad to hear that, I am rather fond of you too, you know." George's breath stirred a loose strand of her hair.

But his words did not go far enough to suit Arabella. "I am not just fond of you!" She wanted to be precise about her feelings, to leave no possibility of misunderstandings. "I *love* you. You are my husband and I love you and I was afraid I'd ruined everything because I pried into your personal papers and you were not going to come back and—"

George mercifully interrupted her babbling. "Belle, of course I meant to come back! You are my wife, and I love you, too." He tipped her chin up so he could press a soft kiss against her lips.

Arabella's eyes widened. When he said "love," did he mean friendly affection, which she already knew he felt, or the sort of love poets wrote sonnets about? Before she could ask for clarification, he kissed her more deeply. Somehow, that felt like answer enough.

She closed her eyes and kissed him back, nibbling on his lower lip until he opened his mouth for her. He tasted of sweet after-dinner port, and she would've liked to blame her sudden giddiness on that, but she knew perfectly well that the effervescent happiness bubbling up from her heart had nothing to do with wine and everything to do with being loved by George.

Well, some of it might be less the result of his affection and more the result of the way his body pressed up against hers. He was cold and wet from the rain, so embracing him ought to have chilled her, but it had the opposite effect. Heat flushed throughout her body, pooling in a few particular places.

But Arabella stopped her husband when he began to fumble with the closure at the back of her dress. "Not *here*," she whispered raggedly. "Anyone could see." *Or hear.* George seemed to like hearing her voice her pleasure, but she would die of mortification if anyone else heard.

"Upstairs, then?" He jerked his chin in the direction of their bedchamber.

"Yes." She hated having to release him in order to finish climbing the stairs, but it took only a few steps down the corridor to reach their bedchamber. Once the door closed behind them, she did not have to worry about anything but loving her husband.

Arabella had imagined that after George got home, they would sit down and have a long conversation about missing silverware, biscuit crumbs, and mice. She hoped they could find a compromise that allowed George the privacy to work interrupted without turning his study into either a literal or figurative rat's nest.

As it happened, they had very little verbal conversation that evening. George had been tired out from walking all over creation and Arabella had been exhausted from worrying, so they fell asleep in each other's arms after exchanging only a few words—though there had been a good deal of physical communication.

The next morning, after breakfast, Arabella steeled herself to begin a discussion about the mess in the study. But George surprised her by inviting her into the room.

"You had something to say to me?" She stood near the door, looking around at the disarray. Some of George's books were lined up on shelves, but others were simply stacked in piles wherever a clear space could be found. He needed more bookshelves. Fortunately, the study had unused wall space. If they added in a new bookcase, maybe—

"I wanted to come clean about what I've been writing this summer," George said.

"Oh!" That was not at all what she had expected to talk about.

"Why don't you sit down?" He moved a stack of papers off the chair near his desk and gestured for Arabella to take a seat.

She settled down, sitting up straight, as her old governess would have wanted. She clasped her hands on her lap and steadily met George's eyes. To her surprise, he chuckled.

"You look like you are about to face a firing party. Relax. I am not going to bite you—unless you want me too, of course."

Her face flushed and she dropped her eyes. There was, in fact, a faint bite mark on her neck that she'd had to cover up with a shawl. Fortunately, the day was cool and cloudy, so the outfit did not feel uncomfortably warm, but Mrs. Hasting had still given the shawl a puzzled look this morning.

Arabella cleared her throat and tried not to worry about whether the whole household knew how enthusiastically she had been tumbled last night. "So, you want to talk about your writing?"

"Yes." George still held the stack of papers that had been sitting on the armchair. Now he handed it to her. "This is the novel on which I've been working. But it's not the first one I've written."

"It's not?" Her eyes widened. She'd assumed that writing novels was a new occupation for George. So far as she knew, his publications were confined to essays and book reviews.

"It's not." George smiled wryly. "I've been writing novels for a couple of years now. I started back when I still clerked for Mr. Horner."

"A couple of *years*?" she squeaked. "How did you keep it secret? *Why* did you keep it secret?"

"I write novels under a nom de plume, Belle." He drew a deep breath and held it for a moment. "My pen name is Alec MacPherson."

Arabella frowned. Why did that name sound so familiar? She rummaged around in the back of her memory, trying to recall where she'd heard it before.

George saved her the effort. "I wrote that book you disliked so much, *Rosalind, or the Lady in the Forest*."

She clapped a hand to her mouth, shocked. "Oh no!"

He chuckled ruefully. "Oh yes! You've no idea how crushed I felt when you told me everything wrong with it."

Arabella closed her eyes and shook her head, ashamed of her own critical words. "I would never have said that if I'd known—"

"I know, I know!" George sounded embarrassed. "That's not the point, anyway. My point is, I've had two novels published already, and I'm working on a third. Or at least I was supposed to be. I mean, I was supposed to be working on a different third novel, not the one I'm working on now, but I couldn't get anywhere with it, so—"

She opened her eyes and interrupted him before he could get even more hopelessly tangled up in his explanation. "But why didn't you tell me? Does your sister know?" It wasn't at all like Caroline to keep a secret like that from Arabella!

He shook his head. "No one knows. You know my father, Belle. He thinks novels are a waste of time at best and a source of corruption at worst. I can't let anyone in the family know I write them."

"Yes, I see," she said gently. She had forgotten about Mr. Kirkland's opinion of novels, though she had certainly heard him pontificate on the subject. "But you could have told me. I *like* novels!"

George hung his head. "I know, I know! I shouldn't have tried to keep it a secret from you. I suppose I thought it would be fun to surprise you when my third book came out. . ." He shrugged dismissively. "I don't know what I thought. Maybe I was afraid you wouldn't like my writing. And you didn't!" He whispered the last sentence, and Arabella's heart ached for him.

"I am so sorry," she repeated. "But you know, I am very proud of you for publishing a novel at all."

He lifted his head and looked her in the face. "You are?"

"Of course I am! Anyone would be proud!" Anyone except his father, that is, she silently amended. Probably best not to dwell on that, though. "So many people think they can write, but how many of them ever finish a novel, let alone publish it?"

She herself had tried to write a chivalrous romance in blank verse about knights and fair maidens, back when she was fourteen or fifteen and convinced she would someday meet a hero on a white horse. Her romance had never been finished, her ear for rhythm—so necessary for managing the meter of a poem in iambic pentameter—was not nearly as well developed as her eye for color.

"I might have been wrong about *Rosalind*, anyway," she added. "I only read a few chapters of it, after all. Perhaps if I'd finished it, I would have a different opinion." And she most certainly would have finished it if she'd known George had written it!

"No, I suspect you were right about it." He sounded glum again. "Neither of my novels sold very well. I have high hopes for the one I'm writing now, but it's quite a different style from the other two, and I don't know what my editor will think of it."

"I see." She knew little about the process of publishing a book, but she could see how worried George was about this. "What is the new book about?"

George's face lit up. He leaned forward in his chair as he

began to explain his newest book, which seemed to be based on the legends about Dogwood Cottage. Arabella could not quite follow the plot—indeed, she was not sure even George knew where the plot was going—but she gathered that the story would contain a murder, a skeleton in the closet, and possibly a mad monk.

George seemed a little doubtful about the last point, because, as he explained, "I don't know anything about monasteries."

"So you're writing a Gothic novel?" Arabella concluded. It did sound very different from *Rosalind*.

"Yes, but not a Gothic novel set in France or Italy or Spain," he explained. "A Gothic novel set right here in the north of England. And why not? There've been witch trials on Pendle Hill, and priest hunters looking for Jesuits, and water mills, and who knows what else?"

"Water mills?" She could not for the life of her see what mills had to do with witchcraft or recusancy.

"Well, never mind that. But you see the potential, don't you? All I have to do is finish writing it!" He paused and scanned the room. "But it's causing problems for the household, isn't it? My messiness?" His warm brown eyes looked at her pleadingly.

Arabella held his gaze and nodded. "It *is* causing problems," she agreed, seeing no reason to sugarcoat the truth. George dropped his eyes, looking as guilty as Bowser did after chewing up one of Arabella's pencils. "But," Arabella continued, "I am sure we can find a solution to the problem if we work together."

George stared at her as a doubtful line formed between his brows. "You think so?"

"Yes. I am certain." If the confidence with which she spoke owed more to Arabella's acting ability than to her real opinion in the matter, well, that was something George didn't need to know. They would figure out a way to make this work. "You were always good at getting us into trouble when we were children," she reminded him, "but I had a talent for getting us out, didn't I?"

A grin lightened George's face. "So you were! You were always better at solving problems than me. I'm sure we'll think of something."

"To start with," Arabella said, "you are going to have to let a maid in here sometimes, so the place isn't littered with crumbs."

His face fell. "I hate it when people move my things about. I have enough trouble finding my things even if I'm the only one moving them." He looked down at the surface of his desk, already cluttered again.

She nodded. "I know. So let's think about where we can put everything." She rose to her feet and turned around slowly, studying the room. "When everything has a place, it will be easier to find what you need."

George continued to look skeptical about this, but he listened as Arabella suggested some changes to the room. Maybe this was going to work after all.

And if it didn't, well, they could get a cat to keep down the mice. Arabella preferred cats over dogs, anyway.

Chapter Twenty-Seven

GEORGE COULD ONLY conclude that when Belle looked at a room, she saw it very differently than he did. She dizzied him with her suggestions for shelves, racks, and boxes. And she horrified him with the gentle suggestion that he would benefit from a different desk.

"I don't see how that would help!" Besides, he'd been using this desk since he was a schoolboy.

"You need a desk with lots of pigeon-holes," she insisted, "so you have places near at hand to put your papers."

He shook his head. He did not believe any quantity of pigeon-holes would cure his disorganization. But he did not protest. He might as well let Belle rearrange the room to her heart's content. Then he could happily clutter it up again.

In the meantime, he kept writing. He did not yet have a title for his novel, so when he referred to it, he simply called it *Secrets*. But he did take the important step of writing to Mr. Sherman to explain that he had abandoned *Ermintrude*.

"I do not think my style is best suited for a comedy of manners," he wrote. "I am working on something more in the line of a historical romance. I understand this manuscript may not suit Peabody & Sherman. If you do not wish to see it when it is finished, simply let me know."

He aimed to sound nonchalant, as if it did not matter in the slightest whether Mr. Sherman wanted to see *Secrets*. In truth, it mattered very much. George had made such rapid progress on the novel that he would likely finish in a matter of weeks. If he needed to find a different publisher, he would like to know sooner rather than later.

On a warm Monday afternoon in late August, Hastings returned from an errand in Pendleford with two letters for George. One was addressed in his father's familiar handwriting: bold, decisive, and slightly sloppy (much like George's handwriting, in fact). The other was written in Mr. Sherman's neat professional hand.

George opened the letter from his publisher first. It was short, direct, and it took a weight off his mind. Mr. Sherman agreed that George's previous novels had not done as well as he'd hoped. He would be happy to look at George's new work whenever it was ready, as there were still many readers longing for tales of abbeys, castles, and family secrets.

So, there was a chance for his new story. That was all George needed. He felt certain that this novel would be the one to sell, the one that would make "Alec MacPherson" a name as famous as Sir Walter Scott or Horace Walpole. To be sure, he'd thought the same thing of his previous novels, but this time would be different!

The other letter took him by surprise. His father had sent two sheets of paper, crossed so as to fit as many words as possible. George had to move closer to the window to read some of the lines.

In his last letter home, George had asked his father about the objects Roman Catholics used to say Mass, particularly after the passage of the Popish Recusants Act of 1605. As he'd expected, his father had books on the subject. He sent George verbose descriptions of chalices that could be taken apart to hid from priest hunters, golden plates, and portable altars. *How could an altar be portable?* George shook his head and read on.

Mr. Kirkland was indeed interested in the strange hidden

cellar discovered beneath the stairs. His letter went on to discuss a man named Nicholas Owen, who built priest holes until he was arrested and executed in the wake of the Gunpowder Plot. Rather more to the point, the senior Mr. Kirkland described the location and design of various priest holes.

"Some houses contained more than one hiding place," the letter concluded. "I recommend looking carefully inside all closets and behind shelves and paneling, especially in rooms with particularly thick walls."

George frowned over this advice. They'd already searched this house so many times! After so many years of treasure hunting, there couldn't be anything new to be discovered at Dogwood Cottage. Except for the strange hole in the cellar, that is. If something like that could be hidden from the house's owners for decades, who knew what else could be in the cottage?

Until now, George had dismissed all the rumors of treasure as purely legendary. After all, the same people who claimed there was treasure hidden in the kitchen at Dogwood Cottage also claimed the house was haunted. In all his visits to the cottage, George had never seen or heard anything more frightening than a branch scraping against the window or a moth fluttering above a candle flame. He'd assumed the tale of hidden treasure was just as fanciful as the story of the wailing ghost who supposedly haunted the attic.

But his father seemed to take the possibility of a second hiding place very seriously. George read over the paragraph about priest holes, then went to look for Belle. He would be guided by her reaction. If she thought it worth their while to search the house for hidden spaces one more time, he would set aside his doubts and turn priest hunter himself.

It took him awhile to find Belle, as she had chosen to work in the garden rather than in her studio today. Rather than drawing or coloring, she was working on embroidery.

"Is that another baby blanket?" How many blankets could one baby need? Caro's new baby would be absolutely spoiled!

Belle looked up and smiled, squinting her eyes against the afternoon light. "No, this is a tablecloth for our house." She held it up so he could see the design of roses and briars along the border. "I thought this would be good for dinner parties."

George sat next to her on the garden bench. "Would you like to host dinner parties?" He tried to keep his voice neutral, rather than revealing how surprised he felt.

"Not exactly." She wrinkled her brow and thought a moment. "But we could have Mr. and Mrs. Arkwright to dine. And maybe Mr. and Mrs. Cawley. But no more than that. No large parties."

"What about the vicar and his wife?" George suggested. It couldn't hurt to be on Mr. Richardson's good side. The local clergy tended to have a good deal of influence in small towns.

To his surprise, Belle shook her head. "Not the Richardsons, I think. Not unless we must. I don't think Mrs. Richardson and I see eye to eye on. . . things."

Before George could ask for clarification about what "things" Belle and Mrs. Richardson disagreed on, she changed the subject. "Is that a letter from your father?" She gestured to the folded papers in his hand. "I hope nothing is wrong at Norton Combe."

"Oh, no. He just had a lot to say about priest holes and chalices." He did his best to briefly summarize everything his father had packed into two full pages.

"That reminds me," Belle said. "I got a reply from Mr. Hodges yesterday, but I don't think I ever told you about it." When George looked at her blankly, she clarified, "He's the pottery collector in London. I wrote to him about that pot we found below the closet."

"Oh, the chamber pot!" George had entirely forgotten Belle's intention to consult some with an expert on pottery. "What did Mr. What's-his-name have to say, then?"

"Mr. *Hodges*"—she emphasized the name with a glare— "agreed it was a chamber pot, but he said that without seeing it in person, he couldn't date it. It could have been from the sixteenth or seventeenth century, or it could have been more recent."

"Not particularly helpful," George concluded. He supposed it had been too much to hope for that the pot could be definitively proven as a relic from the years when the penal laws were strictly applied.

Belle shrugged. "We would probably need an antiquarian to personally investigate both the cellar and the pot to determine if it really could have been a priest hole. And I doubt this discovery is important enough to bring an expert in. But it's interesting to *know* that some houses had more than one priest hole. Didn't most of the treasure hunters here look in the kitchen?"

"Yes. That's where the treasure was supposed to be." Though, now that he thought about it, George could not even remember who had told him that. It didn't seem like the kind of thing Aunt Helena would have said. On the contrary, she always discouraged the children's interest in legends about the house. He must have heard it from one of the servants.

"Could there really be a second room there?" Belle asked. "How could it possibly be hidden so well that no one found it all this time?"

George unfolded the letter in his hand. "According to my father, priest holes could be anywhere. Under stairs, like the one we found. In attics or between floors. Hidden behind paneling or shelves."

"Shelves," Belle mused. "There are built-in shelves in the kitchen. Did anyone ever look behind them?"

"Not that I know of," George admitted. "But of course there were people who searched the cottage for hidden treasure long before I was born. They probably examined all the shelves." He caught Belle's eye and frowned. "Do you think it would be worth looking again?"

She responded with an uncharacteristically mischievous smile. "We might as well take a look at the shelves and walls again. What could it hurt?"

"If we learned anything from the Cawley boys, it's that looking for hiding places inside walls can hurt plenty!" George retorted. He did not know how much it had cost to repair the damage the children did to the kitchen wall, but he knew it had been a royal pain to the staff.

"I promise not to break anything." Belle folded up the tablecloth she'd been embroidering and tucked it into a large, heavy-looking basket. George took the basket out of her hands without being asked, leaving her free to carry only her sewing basket.

Their timing was all wrong, a fact George realized only after he'd already marched into the kitchen, calling a halt to all the work. He'd forgotten dinner preparations would already be underway at this hour.

"Can I help you, Mr. Kirkland?" Mrs. Hastings's words were polite, but her stare looked downright hostile. The fact that she stood at the kitchen table, her hand deep inside a plump duck, might have accounted for her antagonism. It was clearly the wrong time to visit the kitchen.

"We wanted to take a look at the kitchen, but we can do that after dinner, right?" George caught Belle's eye and she nodded her assent.

They backed out of the kitchen as unobtrusively as possible. As soon as the door closed behind them, Belle began to giggle. She put a hand over her mouth to stifle her laughter.

"We didn't think that through very carefully, did we?" George said.

She wrinkled her nose. "We did not. We ought to wait until the dishes have been washed and put away before we step foot in the kitchen again."

Unfortunately, neither of them realized just how long it took to clean up after dinner. By the time the kitchen had been put to rights, twilight had fallen. The usually bright kitchen looked surprisingly gloomy with the fire banked and the windows full of blue-gray gloaming.

"Maybe we should wait until tomorrow?" George suggested. "It's not terribly dark yet, but it might be better to wait for the best light."

"There's usually a lull in the kitchen after breakfast," Belle told him. "If we wait until then, we should be able to search the kitchen in full daylight without getting in Mrs. Hastings's way."

So, they once more reluctantly set aside their plan to search the kitchen. George told himself it didn't really matter, because he was convinced they wouldn't find anything. As Uncle William had always said, if there were treasure in the cottage, it would have been found by now! The house had withstood assaults by destructive burglars, adventurous children, and other treasure hunters. Its secrets must have all been discovered long ago.

True, no one in the Kirkland family had known about the hiding place under the stairs, but that was an out-of-the-way space, never used for anything but storage. The kitchen, on the other hand, had been in constant use for as long as the house existed. George couldn't imagine how anything could remain hidden in such a heavily trafficked room.

Even so, he went to bed determined to search the kitchen as soon as he could do so without disturbing the kitchen staff. After a hasty breakfast of one roll and three cups of strong tea, he sat down in his study to while away the time by writing. He meant only to finish drafting the chapter he'd been working on yesterday, but once he got to the end, he let the momentum carry him into the next chapter.

George had so completely lost track of time that when Belle hesitantly rapped at the study door, he knocked over the half-empty cup of tea sitting on his desk. "Blast!" He scrambled to sop up the mess before it ruined his manuscript. At least he had a handkerchief in his pocket this time!

"George?" Belle called. "The kitchen is free if you want to explore it with me. Or should I just search on my own?"

"What?" He pulled out his pocket watch and saw, rather to his surprise, that it was already afternoon. Where had the morning gone? "Be there in a minute!" He moved the stack of paper to a safer place and took the teacup with him, thinking he might as well return it to the scullery.

By the time he deposited the cup next to the sink, Belle had already begun studying the shelves built into the interior wall opposite the cookstove and the bread oven.

"Found anything?"

"Not exactly." She took a step closer and removed a platter from the bottom shelf. "But doesn't it seem like these shelves should be deeper? The walls between the downstairs rooms are quite thick. There would have been much more room for storage if they'd just dug a little deeper."

"Maybe there are support beams in the way," George suggested, not that he knew anything about construction. But he could see what she meant. The scullery had built-in shelves, too, but those were much deeper. It was strange that this set of shelves was so shallow. It seemed especially strange once he wandered across the room to examine the shelves near the oven. They extended much further into the wall.

He returned to Belle's side, thinking the shelves deserved a closer look. "We should probably move all this crockery out of the way before we damage it." Mrs. Hastings would not thank them for breaking any more of the crockery.

"Yes, let's put these things on the table."

Belle pulled off a pair of small jars, George reached for the biggest platter, and together, they quickly cleared the shelves. After they'd removed everything, George wondered whether Mrs. Hastings would be upset if they put things back in the wrong places. But it was entirely too late to do anything about it. He hadn't bothered to pay attention to what went where.

He turned back to the wall and ran a finger along one of the narrow wooden shelves. The entire set of shelves seemed firmly attached to the wall. If there were any secret levers or latches here, they were well hidden.

"Is the back solid? Could there be space behind that?" Belle leaned closer, crowding him.

George sidestepped to get out of her way. As he moved, his

hand slid along the wooden back of the shelf unit. Very much to his surprise, he felt the surface shift. The left side of the wooden backing swung inward by half an inch. George's eyes widened and his heart pounded more quickly as he stared at the thin, dark crack now visible between the back of the shelves and the frame.

Belle gasped. "Could that be a door? Does it open inward?" She paused for a moment, then more practically suggested, "Or maybe the back just came loose."

"Could be a false back." George pushed harder, and the thin black line expanded. The wooden backing swung inward, revealing a dark, empty space behind the shelves. "Well damn! There really is another priest hole!" For one bittersweet moment, he wished Aunt Helena were still alive so he could prove to her that there was truth behind the legends after all.

"I doubt there's any treasure, though." Belle leaned close again, peering into the darkness.

"We need a candle," George said. What they really needed was a dark lantern, but he doubted there was one about the house. He pulled a candle off the nearest wall sconce and lit it from the still-burning cookfire.

Holding the candle up to light the empty space, he peered between the shelves. Had this space really been used to hide people? If so, how? There would be just barely enough room for a man to sit, or stand if he were short, but not to lie down. George could not imagine spending hours in such a cramped space, let alone days.

"Is there something on the floor?" Belle asked. "At the very back?"

George squatted down and extended the candle into the space as far as his arm could reach. This close, he could clearly see what had caught Belle's attention: a small wooden chest wrapped with metal bands.

"Well, what d'you know," he breathed. "It's a treasure chest!"

Chapter Twenty-Eight

A RABELLA RELEASED THE breath she'd been holding. There really was a treasure? No, she corrected herself, they could not assume that. They had no idea what the box contained. For all they knew, it might be stuffed with legal documents made meaningless by their age.

"I'll hold the candle for you if you want to get it out," she offered to George. He handed the candlestick back to her, then crawled halfway into the narrow space so he could gingerly lift out the wooden chest. He just barely fit in the gap between the floor and the bottom shelf.

He handed the chest to her. She blew out her candle and set it aside so she could lift the box with both hands, though was not as heavy as she had expected. She set it on the table. George stood by her side, examining it with her.

In its construction, the chest resembled a wooden traveling trunk, but on a miniature scale. Arabella tried to open it, but it was locked. She sighed. They ought to have known it wouldn't be easy to open!

"I doubt anyone knows where the key is," she said glumly.

"Probably not," George agreed, "but I also doubt the lock is very complex. It might not be hard to pick it."

She looked askance at him. "Do you know to pick a lock?" It seemed an unlikely talent for the son of a country vicar.

He grinned back at her. "No, but I'm sure we can find someone who can do it. Maybe Hastings will know who to recommend."

Arabella shook her head, but a smile teased at the corners of her mouth. She knew very little of Hastings's background. Theoretically, he might very well be an expert cracksman who had decided to turn gardener. But if he had a criminal past, he wouldn't want to admit it to his employers.

Before George could go in search of the manservant, the door to the kitchen swung open and Mrs. Hastings bustled in. "There you are! Are you done messing with my kitchen?" She rested her hands on her hips and frowned at the jars, platters, and bowls stacked on the table. Then her eyes widened. "Where on earth did that box come from?"

"From behind a secret door!" George indicated the gaping hole in the wall with a dramatic gesture.

Mrs. Hastings's jaw dropped. "Well, I never! Do you mean to say there's been a treasure chest here all along? Won't your uncle be surprised!"

"Yes, I'll have to write to him after we get this box open," George agreed.

Unexpectedly, Mrs. Hastings smiled. "Oh, you won't have to write to him. You can tell him yourself before you open the box."

George wrinkled his brow. "What do you mean?"

Arabella, watching the sly humor on the housekeeper's face, made a guess. "Is Mr. Kirkland here in Lancashire?" she asked. "In Pendleford, even?"

Mrs. Hastings's smile grew. "Yes. Not to put too fine a point on it, he's sitting in the parlor waiting for you. And he brought one of your cousins with him."

Arabella caught George's eye and raised her eyebrows. This did not seem like good news. They wouldn't want Augustus or Benedict to know about the treasure. Or would they? If the treasure had been discovered at last, there would no longer be any reason for treasure hunters to tear up the kitchen. The cottage would finally be left in peace.

"He's here? We've got to tell him about our discovery!"

Arabella followed him a little more sedately. After the surprising discovery in the kitchen, she needed a moment to get her chaotic thoughts in some sort of order. She lingered a moment outside the parlor door, taking a deep breath before she entered the room.

Thus, she missed William Kirkland's greeting. By the time she stepped into the room, George was already shaking his uncle's hand. She watched as he pointedly ignored the outstretched hand of the golden-haired young man standing next to Uncle William.

George glanced over his shoulder at Arabelle. "Ah, here's Mrs. Kirkland now. Belle, this is my cousin Augustus. I don't think you've met him, have you?"

"No, I don't believe so." She could see the resemblance between him and Benedict, though Augustus's hair was lighter and more yellow than his brother's.

Augustus bowed slightly. "Good afternoon, Mrs. Kirkland. It is a pleasure to meet you." His smile faltered when he glanced at George.

"Good afternoon, Mr. Kirkland. And Mr. Augustus Kirkland." The smile on Arabella's face was genuine. She was excited to tell William Kirkland of their discovery. "What brings the two of you to Dogwood Cottage?"

Uncle William cleared his voice. "My nephew here has a confession to make."

"A confession?" she repeated. Her smile fell.

"Yes." Uncle William gave Augustus a pointed look. "Perhaps we should sit down for this?"

Augustus gulped. "A good idea."

Arabella sat next to George on the sofa. The warmth of his body by her side felt reassuring. Instead of clasping her hands together nervously, she took George's hand. He squeezed it affectionately and smiled at her, though his smile dropped away when he turned to face his cousin.

"This confession wouldn't, by any chance, have to do with breaking into the house and ruining Aunt Helena's favorite tea set, would it?"

Augustus stared down at the toes of his boots, effectively answering the question without words. "We didn't mean to break the tea set. We were just trying to move the dresser away from the wall and... we lost control of it." He lifted his chin and looked at them earnestly. "We honestly didn't mean to break anything."

"But you *did* mean to trespass," George retorted. "This is my house. Our house. You had no right to be poking about in the kitchen while everyone was away."

His cousin dropped his eyes again. "Yes, we did trespass. We weren't here to steal anything, though. Just looking for the treasure."

George and Arabella exchanged a long look. Arabella couldn't guess what her husband was thinking, but she wondered if the moment for revealing their discovery had arrived.

George turned back to Augustus. "Who's we? Did Benedict help you?"

"Only because I begged him to help!" Augustus quickly clarified. "Benedict didn't want to break into the cottage at all. He said it wasn't right to do that to one of our relatives. I think he only came along to try to keep me out of trouble. When the big dresser toppled over, he insisted we needed to leave before we damaged anything else."

Good for him. Arabella only wished Benedict had had the gumption to refuse to help his brother at all. On his own, Augustus wouldn't have been able to tip over the dresser.

"That is why I did not force Benedict to accompany us," Uncle William explained. "I believe he really did try to dissuade his brother from this foolhardy plan. And Benedict was the one who came clean to me." He glared at Augustus again. "Augustus here lied when I asked him if he knew anything about the most recent break-in."

"For which I am very sorry!" Augustus exclaimed. "I fully realize that what I did was wrong. And I will never do it again." He sighed and ran a nervous hand through his golden hair. "It was all quite pointless, anyway, since there is no treasure."

George snorted. When he glanced at Arabella out of the corner of his eye, she smiled at him. The timing of this visit seemed downright providential. What would Augustus say when he learned how close he had actually been to the hiding place in the kitchen wall?

"About that," George said. "There's something we have to show you. Won't you both come to the kitchen with me?"

"To the kitchen?" Uncle William repeated. "Did those foolish boys damage something else?"

George's grin broadened. "No, nothing like that. It's just that Belle and I found something interesting in the kitchen today. I really think you ought to take a look."

"If you tell me there really is a treasure and you found it just today, I will eat my hat," Augustus announced.

Arabella tried to hide her giggle, but she wasn't entirely successful. Both the visitors stared at her, clearly confused by her reaction.

"I think you should see for yourself," George insisted.

To say that Uncle William and Augustus were taken aback by the sight of the tiny space hidden behind the shelves would be an understatement. Augustus made a sound like a muffled groan and covered his face in dismay. Arabella wondered if he were castigating himself for failing to discover the door behind the shelves.

Uncle William was dumbfounded. His jaw dropped, and he quickly sat down on the nearest stool, as if his legs could no longer support him. "Do you mean to say there really is a treasure, and no one found it? People have been looking for treasure here for centuries!"

"We don't know what's in the box," Arabella qualified. "It might be full of rubbish rather than any sort of treasure. We haven't been able to open it, because it's locked."

"I don't suppose you have the key, do you?" George asked his uncle.

Uncle William shook his head. He rose from his chair, drew nearer to the box and reverently picked it up. He turned it slowly around, looking at it from every angle. Then he gently tugged on the lid. It remained stubbornly shut.

"The key is probably long gone. We may need to call a locksmith if we wish to open it without damaging the lock."

To Arabella's surprise, Augustus cleared his throat. Everyone turned to look at him. His face flushed a light pink, but he boldly met their eyes.

"I've had a little experience with locks," he said. "If you like, I could try opening it."

"Why on earth would you know how to pick a lock?" George demanded. "Do you often break into other people's houses!"

Augustus's face turned a brighter shade of red. "No! It was only the once! I practiced on locks just in case." He sighed. "I understand that after what I did, you may not want me touching that box. I just thought I might be able to help, that's all."

Arabella looked to see George's reaction. Shifting emotions crossed his face, but she could not interpret his expression. Finally, he nodded.

"Very well, you can try to unlock it. But please do your best not to damage anything. Anything *else*, I mean." George reinforced his warning with a grim scowl.

"Of course." Augustus spoke in a soothing voice as he approached the box. "Do you happen to have something very small and very sharp? Like a straight pin, or a hair pin?" He addressed the question to Arabella.

"Oh, yes." She drew a hairpin out of her chignon, causing several strands of hair to fall loose. She suspected her coiffure looked the worse for it, but that could not be helped. She handed the hairpin to Augustus.

They all watched with bated breath as Augustus used the

hairpin to explore the lock. Very much to her surprise, the lock eventually clicked open. Uncle William drew in his breath sharply. George gasped. Augustus put down the hairpin and smiled proudly. He reached out to open the lid, but George pulled the box away from him.

"Uncle William should get to open it," George suggested.

Augustus nodded, and George slid the box across the table to his uncle. Uncle William stared at it for so long that Arabella assumed he meant to ask someone else to open it. Then he cautiously lifted the lid. All that could be seen was a layer of some rich black cloth covering the contents of the chest.

Arabella lightly touched the covering. "Velvet," she murmured. Velvet was often used to protect jewelry. Maybe this really was some kind of treasure!

"Well, let's see what's under it!" George slowly drew the covering away. Then his eyes widened.

"It *is* treasure," Augustus whispered. "That's gold, isn't it?"

No one answered him, probably because they were all too busy staring at the objects that had been hidden under velvet. The chest contained a very small cup, a shallow round dish, and a wooden crucifix with a silver corpus. The cup and plate appeared to be made of gold, but they were plainly constructed, with no illustrations or engravings. Not quite the ornate, bejeweled objects Arabella might have expected.

"I believe that's a chalice." George pointed to the small gold cup. "Which means this is probably a patten?" Doubt turned it into a question. "They're used for saying Mass."

"It really is a priest hole, then." Arabella longed to touch the objects, but she kept her hands away, fearing she would besmirch them.

"I wonder how much they're worth," Augustus mused.

Arabella stared at him, surprised he was still concerned with the monetary value of their find. If George had correctly identified the objects, they were sacred. To the right people, they might hold a value beyond the worth of their materials.

"I wonder who they belonged to," Uncle William mused. "They must have been hidden for a good two hundred years, so whoever owned them will be long dead, but—"

"This house originally belonged to the Finch family, didn't it?" George reminded his uncle. "And the Finches used to be Roman Catholics. The last of the Finches live up at Waterbury Lodge. I believe the chest should be returned to them."

"Yes," Arabella agreed. "That seems like the best solution. Maybe Mr. Cawley's aunt will know what to do with these things." She could not remember the elderly woman's given name, but she still retained an impression of her gentle voice and quiet good humor.

"Really? You finally found the treasure, and you're going to give it away?" Incredulity dripped from Augustus's voice. He shook his head in disbelief. "I don't understand you at all."

"Things are never as valuable as people," Uncle William said gently. "Maybe you are too young to understand that yet."

"Yes, we should cultivate good relationships with our neighbors," Arabella said. Returning this chest to the Cawley family could only help foster the friendship developing between George and Mr. Cawley. Keeping the treasure to themselves, on the other hand, might anger the Finch descendants, assuming they ever heard of it.

"I don't think that's what Uncle William meant, Belle."

George's tone of voice surprised Arabella. Why, she wondered, did he sound so solemn?

He continued before she could ask any questions. "If you ask me, our lives together are more important than any treasure, no matter how historically important." He smiled, reached across the table, and brushed a loose strand of hair away from Arabella's face. "You are my treasure, Belle."

Arabella's face burned with embarrassment. She studiously avoided meeting the eyes of either of the visitors. If they were shocked or amused by George's very public affection, she did not want to see it.

"Exactly!" Uncle William's enthusiastic response brought Arabella's attention back to him. His often-scowling face was now wreathed in smiles. "That is precisely the lesson I wanted you boys to learn. A house and a fortune are not as important as a family." His smile fell when he looked at Augustus. "Apparently it takes some of you longer to learn than others."

Augustus gulped. "I see." But the confusion on his face suggested he did not really understand.

Arabella understood, though. She caught George's eye, and he smiled at her. The corners of her mouth kicked up in a returning smile. Uncle William had taken rather unusual measures to drive home the desired moral, but she and George had both learned something.

"Do you intend to give all your nephews houses and fortunes to make them fall in love?" George asked his uncle.

Uncle William's smile was replaced by his customary scowl. "That is my concern, young man, not yours."

Fall in love? Was that what had happened to them? Yes, she supposed it was! Arabella drew a deep breath as a sweet bubble of happiness welled up in her heart.

"Now that we've got that settled, what would you all say to a cup of tea and a slice of Mrs. Hastings's seedcake?" She would not—or could not—remind George how much she loved him. Not now, with their guests listening to every word. Some feelings were best kept for private moments. But she could *show* him her feelings by playing the role of mistress of Dogwood Cottage to the best of her ability. Judging by the warmth in his eyes, he seemed to understand.

Epilogue

September 1817

THE END. GEORGE scrawled the words with a flourish. Though, on closer inspection, the flourish looked more like an illegible blot. What did that matter, though? He was done with *Midnight Secrets*! He glanced over to the small secretary desk in the corner, where Belle painstakingly copied his handwriting into something legible. He no longer had to worry about whether Mr. Sherman could read his chicken scratch writing. Plus, Belle had a good memory, so she noticed if he accidentally changed a character's given name or hair color over the course of the manuscript.

"How is it shaping up?" he asked anxiously. His wife was a tougher critique than half the reviewers in London. If *she* thought the novel was any good, he could be confident about it. And he knew she would never lie to him about his writing. If it were bad, she would let him know.

She looked up at him and smiled wryly. "It's just as good as the last time you asked that. The last time this afternoon, I mean." She crinkled her nose, turning her crooked grin into a mischievous one. "There are some parts that I suspect your editor will want you to condense, but apart from that, it's the best of your writing I've seen."

The tense lines in George's face relaxed into a relieved grin. "I'm glad to hear that. I hope my readers agree."

She opened her mouth, then paused, a question in her eyes.

"What is it?" he asked warily.

"Have you decided what you'll tell your father?" she asked. "If you really do publish this under your own name, it will be impossible to keep him from knowing."

George nodded. "I know. Believe me, I've thought about it." No matter how many times he went over the pros and the cons, he always came back to the fact that this novel was so markedly different from his earlier ones that it did not make sense to publish it under the name "Alec MacPherson." Readers of the earlier books would merely be confused by his departure from his previous style.

And if he had to choose a new name under which to write, why not use his own? Or rather, part of it. He intended to sign the book "G.W. Kirkland." He did not actually have a middle name, but he had chosen "W" to honor Uncle William. It seemed fitting, since the fortune Uncle William had signed over to George was what gave him the time to write this novel.

"My plan is to tell my father in person rather than writing to him," he explained. "I'll sit down and talk to him about it when we visit at Christmas. All the eggnog will put him in the right frame of mind for the news."

"Maybe our other news will keep him from dwelling too much on his disappointment." Belle spoke in a whisper, though there was no one nearby to overhear. A faint blush rose on her cheeks.

"Are you even going to be able to tell people?" George teased. "Or will you expect me to break the news? Because I don't think the pregnancy will be visible yet." He might have been wrong about that, though, since he knew very little about childbearing. He supposed he had some studying to do in the months ahead.

She shrugged. "Maybe not. I plan to tell my mother and let

her tell everyone else, so I won't have to keep repeating the news myself. But you can tell your parents. Tell them right after you tell your father you're a novelist. Then he can't scold you."

"Brilliant," George said. Then he went back to work. He did not pause for a break until someone put a plate down on the desk some hours later. "Hmm? What's this?" He looked up and rubbed his eyes. Too late, he realized he'd had ink on his hand. He'd probably just spread it all over his face.

"Mr. Hastings says the golden apples are ripe," Belle explained. "He wanted you to try one."

George scrunched up his face in disgust. "The apples from this orchard were always sour."

"That's probably because you were eating baking apples," she said patiently. "They're supposed to be tart! And Hastings says the orchard wasn't properly maintained when you were a child. These are from trees Hastings planted himself, a few years ago. They aren't the sour apples you remember! I already tried one, and it was good. You ought to give them a chance."

He picked up the apple and sniffed it cautiously. At least it smelled good. That boded well, didn't it? "If you're wrong, you will owe me," he warned, deliberately not specifying what she would owe him.

Belle rolled her eyes at him. "You'd think by now you would trust my judgment!"

"About writing, yes," he granted. "But about the apples at Dogwood Cottage? I'm not so sure. I've had too many bad experiences in the past, you know!"

But he supposed he owed it to Hastings to try one of the apples, given how much labor the gardener put into the orchard. Truth be told, even the sour green apples tasted fine when baked in one of Mrs. Hasting's desserts.

George closed his eyes and took a tiny test bite. And wouldn't you know? It really *was* sweet!

The End

About the Author

Anne Rollins is the pen name of an English professor who lives in Northern California with her family, too many cats, and an enormous collection of books. She has spent untold hours of her life rereading Georgette Heyer novels, and hopes that someday people will compulsively reread her novels, too!

Join me at the following:
annerollins.com
facebook.com/profile.php?id=100094523334798
instagram.com/annerollins23
threads.net/@annerollins23